IMPOSSIBLE MONSTERS

IMPOSSIBLE MONSTERS

Edited by Kasey Lansdale

SUBTERRANEAN PRESS 2013

Impossible Monsters

Individual story copyrights on page 205.

First Edition

ISBN

978-1-59606-505-5

Subterranean Press

PO Box 190106

Burton, MI 48519

www.subterraneanpress.com

Table of Contents

Introduction

KASEY LANSDALE

Like so many of you, I grew up watching every monster film made by Universal Studios, with an affinity for Dracula. This was long before anyone would dare call a vampire sparkly, or want to. Before special effects dominated the screen, what kept me wanting more was the simplicity of the monsters themselves and the very real fear I was struck with when watching them. There was something within each of them that made you think, "you know, this *could* happen..."

Oftentimes people will say, "I don't know how you watch those," or "I don't like to be scared." For me, there are things that I see every day in the real world far scarier than any Frankenstein's Monster or Invisible Man, who when you get right down to it are just like the rest of us, just want to be accepted for who they are.

I could list dozens of flicks and stories about Monsters, show you the similarities and continue telling you why I love them, but that's not why you have this book. You have it because something within the unknown speaks to you. You enjoy the rush of adrenaline that courses through you as a creature pursues its next victim. Will they make it? Would you if you were in the same position? The blood splatter left on the walls, the unexplained disappearances, how can all these things go unnoticed? For you, they don't, and it gives you a sense of contentment like nothing else. Me too.

It was that early love that inspired me to seek out some of my favorite writers to be involved in this collection. In *Impossible Monsters*, there are creatures never before seen, or those that take a classic monster and step them up a spine-tingling notch. They are stranger, wilder, fiercer than just your average, everyday, closet-lurking beast. I am honored by the people who chose to be in the lineup and hope these stories bring you back to those early fears of childhood, nostalgic for the days when all you needed was a cross, a silver bullet, or some wits about you.

I would be remiss not to mention my appreciation of David J. Schow for the title of this anthology. So to you, of course my father, and all the wonderful writers/friends involved: thank you for your *Impossible Monsters*.

Kasey Lansdale is a published author of short stories and articles.
She is also known for her career in music as a vocalist and songwriter.

www.kaseylansdale.com

Blue Amber

DAVID J. SCHOW

When Senior Patrol Agent Rixson first spotted the shed human skin draped over the barbed wire fence, she thought it was an item of discarded clothing. Then she saw it had empty arms, legs, fingers, an empty mouth-hole stretched oval in a silent scream, and vacant Hallowe'en-mask eyesockets. Carrion birds had already picked it over. Presently it was covered with ants. It stank.

If you had asked her, before, what her single worst experience working for the Border Patrol had been, Carrie Rixson might have related the story of how she and her partner Cash Dunhill had happened upon a hijacked U-Haul box trailer full of dead Mexicans eighteen feet shy of the Sonora side of Buster Lippert's pony ranch. Something had gone wrong, and the coyotes—the wetback enablers, not the scavengers—had left their clients locked in the box, abandoned, under 101-degree heat for over three days. The Cochise County Coroner concluded that the occupants had died at least two days prior to that. The smell was enough to make even the vultures doubtful. The victims had deliquesced into an undifferentiated mass of meat that had broiled in convection heat that topped 400 degrees, about the same as you'd use to bake a frozen pizza.

That had been bad, but the flyblown husk on the fence seemed somehow worse.

"Should I call it in?" said Dunhill, sweating in the pilot seat of their Bronco. He was a deputy and answerable to Carrie, but neither of them were high enough in the grade chain to warrant collar insignia.

"As what?" Carrie shouted back, from the fence. She was already snapping digital photographs.

Dunhill unsaddled and ambled over for a look-see. No need to hurry, not in this heat. "I think this falls out of the purview of 'accidental death,'" he said. "Unless this ole boy was running away so fast he jumped the bobwire and it shucked off his hide."

"That happened once," said his partner. "Dude in New Jersey. Hefty guy, running away from the cops, tried to jump an iron railing and got his chin caught on the metal spike up top. Tore his head clean off. It was still stuck on the end of the spike. I saw it on the internet."

Cash and Carrie had been the target of department punsters ever since their first pair-up assignment. She was older, 37 to his 29 years. They had never been romantically inclined, although they teased each other a lot. Cash's high school sweetie had divorced him in a legal battle only slightly less acrimonious than the firebombing of Dresden, and Carrie had been about to marry her 10-year live-in life partner—Thomas "Truck" Fitzgerald, a former Pima County sheriff turned Jeep customizer—when he up and died of cancer that took him away in six weeks flat. Neither Cash nor Carrie was in the market for loving just now, although they both suffered the pangs in their own different ways.

"Oh, don't *touch* it, for christsake," Cash told her.

"I'm thinking cartel guys," she said as her hand stopped short of making actual fleshy contact. "This is the sort of shit they do. Skin your enemies. Cut off their heads, stuff their balls into their mouths, dismember them and leave the pieces in a public place with the name of the cliqua written in blood."

"You see that on the internet, too?" Cash dug out a toothpick. He was battling mightily to stop smoking.

"Nahh," she said. "I usually only look at lesbian porn. Girl-on-girl, slurpy-burpy." The way Cash usually rose to the bait when she egged him on was reliably amusing, under normal circumstances.

She used a dried stick of ironwood to lift one of the flaps. "Definitely not a scuba suit or a mannequin. There used to be a person wearing this, and not so long ago." The shadow side of the castoff skin was dotted with oily moisture, as though it was still perspiring.

"Whose property is this?" Cash was looking around for landmarks.

"This is outside Puzzi Ranch. I guess it might be Thayer McMillan's fence."

Cash and Carrie's daily grind was to patrol the strip of International Highway (both a description of the actual road and its real name) between Douglas, Arizona and Naco Highway. Naco—the town—straddled the U.S.-Mexico border and had always been a sizzling hot spot for violations of all sorts. In the dead-ass stretches of high desert separating the two towns, there was just too goddamned much open space for something not to go wrong.

"Secure Fence Act, my ass," said Cash, for about the zillionth time. His views on a wetback-proof fence were abundantly known. "I'll call base; see if we can get a number for McMillan." He popped an energy drink from the Bronco's cooler and blew down half the can in one gulp.

"Gross," said Carrie. "That candy-flavored salt water is bad for you." The logo on the can shrieked *Kamikaze*! "'Divine wind.' 'Empty wind' is more like it."

Then Cash would say...

"May the wind at your back never be your own."

They were okay, as partners. When the meatwagon arrived over an hour later, Billy Szwakop, the coroner's assistant, scowled at them as though he was the butt of yet another in an endless series of corpse gags. It wasn't even really a dead body, he said. It was just the skin part. For all they knew, no murder had been committed.

"Yeah, he's probably still walking around, all wound up in duct tape to keep from leaking," Cash said. Billy's gentle disentanglement of the...item...had revealed it to be male.

It had also revealed a broad split from sternum to crotch, not an incision. After it was bagged, Billy added, "I don't think this was a Mex, either."

Carrie got interested. "What makes you say that?"

"Most Mexicans are Catholic, and most Catholic males are circumcised."

"Ugh," said Carrie. "Too much information."

From the concealment of a broad, shaded thicket of skunkbush and screwbean mesquite, bulbous indigo eyes watched them, then died.

The zigzag access road to the McMillan compound was dead on the eastern property edge, about half a mile back from where Carrie Rixson had spotted the thing on the fence. It paralleled several secure horse corrals before it widened into a gated archway featuring a wrought iron double M (itself a zigzag) up top. The building cluster was organized around a broad donut of paved road—big barn, smaller barn, main house, guest house, and a generator-driven industrial icehouse side-by-side with a smaller smokehouse. Further north, in the rear, would be a long, narrow greenhouse with solar panels. Thayer McMillan had made part of his pile breeding Quarter Horses and Appaloosas. In residence were several trainers and wranglers, in addition to a cook, a housekeeper, and an on-call executive personal assistant. Two of the eight McMillan children still lived at home—Lester, the heir apparent to King Daddy's throne, and his younger sister Desiree, a recent divorcee with two children of her own, both under 10 years old. Thayer, the patriarch, was on his fourth wife, a brassy Houston fireball named Celandine, 25 years his junior, or about Desiree's age. Call it fortyish.

There was also, it was rumored, security staff.

It was further rumored that McMillan was pouring concrete to the north of the greenhouse for a private helicopter landing pad.

There were many other rumors about the McMillans, mostly of the sort slathered about by jealous inferiors, but the one about the chopper pad piqued Cash Dunhill's interest. That close to the border? Cash had always wanted an excuse to investigate further.

The light green Bronco kicked up a tailwind of grit as it barreled along the access road. Half a mile in, there was a red pickup truck parked on the shoulder. One of those showoffy, urban cowboy rigs with a mega-cab, a Hemi V-8 and double rear tires. Nobody inside or close by. The clearcoat was covered in dust.

Cash checked it out. "The keys are inside," he said. It was as though someone had pulled over for a piss and just sank into the earth before he or she could zip up.

"Nobody on the home line," said Carrie, snapping her cellphone shut. "Just voice mail."

"No horses, either," said Cash. He could see the corrals from where they'd stopped. "Not a single one."

"It's midday; maybe they're cooling off in the barn." No doubt the barn was air conditioned.

"Guess we guessed wrong about the security, too," he said, a bit distantly, the way he did when he was trying to puzzle out evidence. "Nobody on us yet, nobody at the gate."

"Maybe they upgraded," said Carrie. "Cameras and lasers instead of people."

"Maybe." You could score useful points by agreeing with your partner on things that did not matter. They rumbled over the cowcatcher rails at the gate, within sight of the Cliff May architectural masterpiece that was the main house—a classic of the modernist California Ranch style that blended hacienda elements with the Western aesthetic of building "out" instead of "up." There was a lot of woodgrain and natural stone. The bold, elongated A-frame of the roof line allowed sunlight to heat the huge pool.

"How many bedrooms, you figure?" said Cash.

"Five," said Carrie. "No, six, and probably at least one bathroom for each. Japanese soaking tubs, I bet. I love those."

A large blob of brown was piled near the gate to the northernmost corral.

"What the hell is that?"

"Horsehide."

"No, it isn't," said Cash, stopping the vehicle again. "Horse."

Hollow, split and empty, just like the thing they had found on the barbed wire fence.

Carrie already had her weapon out. "There's a dog over there. But a whole dog, not just skin." She moved closer to verify. There were spent shotgun cartridges strewn around a dead Rottweiler near the front walkway. "We'd better—"

"Call this in, now!" Partners often completed each others' sentences.

Cash was advised that available law enforcement, this far out, was on a triage basis and they would be required to wait at the scene.

"Cash, look at this."

Carrie indicated a smear of blackish fragments in the dirt, like ash or charcoal. "I stepped on it. But look, here's another one."

It was a dried-up bug. There were several of them in the yard. "Looks like a cicada," said Cash. "Or one of them cockroaches; you know they get three inches long around here."

"But it isn't. Look."

She stabbed it with a Bic pen and held it aloft for inspection. It sounded crispy, desiccated. What resembled an opaque, thornlike stinger protruded from one end, its razor-sharp edge contoured to flare and avoid contact with the body.

"This isn't right," she said. "It can't be. This is mutated or something. Or a hybrid. No bilateral symmetry."

"I don't understand a thing you just said."

"Bilateral," Carrie said. "Identical on both sides. We're all base two—two eyes, two arms, two legs. Ants have six legs. Spiders have eight, and eight eyes. One side of the body is a mirror of the other. But not this. Nothing I know of is based on three."

Cash, prepared to blow her off, grew more interested. "Maybe it's missing a leg."

"From where?" She turned the thing over in the waning sunlight. "There's no obvious wound."

"Maybe that stinger thing is really a leg? Or a tail?"

"Yeah, and maybe it's a dick," she said, disliking patronization.

"Leave it for the plastic bag boys," said Cash. "Just don't touch the sharp thing, okay?"

"No way."

"You suppose maybe a swarm of these locusty things flew in and ate everybody from the inside out?"

"Then why aren't there dead ones inside the..." Carrie sputtered out, groping for the right word. "Carcasses? That much fine dining, there should be a couple thousand of them around."

Cash knocked loudly and rang the bell while Carrie thumbed the latch on a door handle that probably cost three weeks of her pay. "It's open," she said.

"Probable cause?"

"You've gotta be shitting me, Cash."

Then Cash would say…

"I wouldn't shit you, darlin, you're my favorite turd."

But he, too, had his weapon limbered up, a Ruger GP100 double-action revolver in .357 Mag. Carrie packed a full-sized Smith & Wesson M&P-40 that held sixteen rounds with one in the pipe—cartridges that Cash knew to be semi-wadcutters.

Feeling increasingly absurd, they both called into the acoustically vacant recesses of the house. The coolers were on full-blast.

"Jesus," she said. "It must be below fifty degrees in here."

"Like the frozen food aisle at the supermarket." They covered each other excellently. Goosebumps speckled their sun-licked flesh.

Cash shook his head. Think of the utility bill.

"Well, room by room, I guess," he said, uncertainly.

The showplace central room was large and vaulted, with a grape-stake ceiling and a fireplace large enough to roast a Smart Car. Very open. All other rooms were peripheral.

The deeper they ventured, the more tenantless the house seemed. Neither one of them called out any more—that was just instinctive, the old telepathy of partners sharing a silent warning.

Carrie checked the behemoth Sub-Zero Pro fridge for sealed bottled water, just for hydration's sake. Do it when you can. Several more of the bugs, chilled and lifeless, were on the top shelf near an open half gallon of milk.

Keeping her voice low, Carrie said, "I'm thinking disease, Cash; what are you thinking?"

Cash nodded. "Something insect-borne, something special. That means government spooks and security. But not here; the goddamned door was open." He gratefully plugged water down his throat. It was so cold it gave him a migraine spike.

"Either that or a really pissed-off butcher with some kind of vendetta. But I don't see any blood anywhere. How about we just back off?"

"Crime scene," said Cash. "We've got to stay."

"What's the crime?"

"We really oughta leave this for larger minds," he said, full up with doubt.

"Don't you chicken out on me, Cash Dunhill. It's not seemly."

"Something is going on; we're just not smart enough to figure it ou—"

She held up her free hand to cut him off. "Hold."

A noise; they both heard it. A soft noise. A soft, shuffling, sliding noise.

Something was moving toward them in the hallway.

///

"Mommy," said the thing.

It appeared at a fast glance to be a little girl in bluejeans and a bright yellow Taylor Swift T-shirt (logoed *You Are the Best Thing That's Ever Been Mine*), lurching along as though drugged, in a pair of blocky K-Swiss Tubes. Her bronze-colored hair was lank and damp.

"Holy shit," whispered Carrie.

The voice was all wrong. That "Mommy" had come out as a froggy, guttural croak. The front of the T-shirt was soaked, as though she had vomited. She looked past the two officers, not at them. Half her face seemed to be melting off. The whole left side was slack and drooping, elongating her eye and hanging her jaw crookedly down.

"Mommy make samwich peen butter gahh."

Thick yellow mucus was cascading out of her nose.

Carrie moved to kneel, arms out. "Honey...?"

"Don't touch her, for godsake!"

"Found it," the girl said, voice hitching with phlegm.

"Found what, sweetie?" Carrie was keeping her distance.

"Pretty," said the girl. She opened her hand. One of the bugs was there. Crouching at the abrupt light, tripod legs tensing. It was alive.

"Oh my god," Carrie said as the bug sprang across the three feet between them like a grasshopper, hit her in the face, and sank its wicked-looking barb into her cheek. In the light, Cash swore he could see fluid drain from the translucent stinger.

Cash shouted and charged, kicking sidelong to lay out the kid, swatting with his hand to dispose of the attacking bug. It hit the floor with its legs up, dead already, like the ones they'd found in the yard.

"Stupid, *stupid*!" Carrie had landed on her ass.

"Lemme see that. Quick, now."

"Squeeze it. Cut it if you have to!" Her cheek was swelling and darkening already. Her right eye was going crimson.

Cash put his thumbs together to try to evacuate the poison—if that's what it was—from the entry wound, but no dice. A tiny dot of bluish wetness welled up at the puncture, but nothing was coming out. He almost tried to suck it, using snakebite protocol.

"Don't put your *mouth* on it, Cash, for fuck's sake!" Carrie was sweeping her arms around, preparatory to trying to stand again, but her movements went thick and wide.

"Astringent," Cash said. "Disinfectant." There had to be something in the kitchen or a nearby bathroom. In a glass-doored liquor cabinet he found some 120-proof Stolichnaya vodka. Stashed behind it was a crumpled soft pack of Camel Lights with two bent cigarettes inside, which he stashed in his uniform blouse's flap pocket. Two wouldn't kill him.

He dashed vodka over Carrie's wound. "I can't even feel it," she said. "It should burn."

The kid was standing back up.

"Bike," she said. Her eyes were looking two different directions. The skin on one arm seemed skewed, as though her hand was mounted backward on the bone. With the other hand, the girl pawed at her face and caught hold of her slack, hanging lower lip. She pulled it downward and it began to peel away. The buttery flesh on her neck split and began to slough. Her yellow shirt absorbed more discharge, from within.

For that single second, Cash and Carrie were transfixed in mute witness.

The little girl's face flopped around her neck like a rubber cowl. In its place was a knob of pale meat resembling a clenched fist, with two bulging button eyes, shiny, featureless orbs that were not black, but a very deep indigo.

Together, Cash and Carrie opened fire.

Their slugs hoisted and dumped the thing, which had begun to walk toward them again. It fell back into the corridor in a broken jackstraw sprawl.

"It was starting to tear off the skin," Carrie said, distantly. Its raised arm lingered, clenching a handful of wadded-up neck. Then it toppled over and hit the marble floor tiles with a juicy slaughterhouse *smack*.

Whatever was leaking out of the bullet holes looked like plain water. Faintly bluish.

"Come on," urged Cash. "To hell with this. We've got to get you out of here, pronto."

"Good idea," said Carrie. Her voice was going furry and opiate, as from a severe allergic reaction. Congestion, histamine levels redlining.

He lifted her bodily, not thinking of all the times he'd wanted to brush her boobs, her butt, just playfully.

Then Cash would say…

"Hang on, darlin, you and me are traveling." Warily he observed the pewter light in the windows. Twilight had already fallen. Sundown came fast in the desert.

Just get to the vehicle, he thought. *Just burn ass outta here.*

But the Bronco, sitting in the front turnaround, had already been dumped on its side, partially spiderwebbing the windshield.

And two more things of full-grown human size were waiting for them, with their bulging, dark, ratlike eyes.

///

They had shucked their human envelopes and stood on either side of the upended Bronco. Like UFO "grays," but lumpier and mottled. Two arms with pincer hands. Two legs. Bilateral symmetry. No facial features except the convex eyes, deep blue, no pupils or irises. They looked spindly. But they had turned the Bronco over.

Cash had to place Carrie on the ground in order to execute a speed reload. If he shot them center mass, they only flinched. Headshots put them down more definitively.

"Shotgun," said Carrie from the ground. "Truck. Keys. Run."

Then Cash would say…

"I'm not leaving you!"

"Don't be an idiot," she said. She managed to prop herself on one elbow to dump the Smith's clip and refresh. "Get the shotgun. Run as fast as you can to the truck and bring it back. I'm not going anywhagh…"

She coughed viscously.

"You sure?" Weapon up, Cash was scanning the perimeter nervously. *Go. Stay. Go. Stay.*

"Go," Carrie said. "I'm a big girl."

Cash wasted several more seconds trying to upright the Bronco by himself. No go. The adrenalin surge of legendary vehicular rescues had failed him. He retrieved the Mossberg pump from the cabin mount (he never locked it unless he was handing over the vehicle; in his worldview, speedy readiness outranked rules). The veins in his head were livid and throbbing. Thirty yards distant was the structure that shaded the big freezer unit and the smokehouse.

The freezer. The cold house. Sunset. These monsters did not like the light or the heat. They coffined up in the daytime. Now it was nighttime.

The bugs stung you, injected you. These things grew inside you, then peeled you off like a chrysalis. When they did, there wasn't any *you* left. You had become nutrient and a medium for gestation.

Their purpose or motive could be hashed out later by others, people with degrees and ordnance and expensive backup. Right now, Carrie was stung and waning. Who knew what her timetable was, or whether the effect could be neutralized? In the movies, monsters who upset the status quo were always defeated by something ordinary and obvious, usually discovered by accident—seawater, dog whistles, paprika, Slim Whitman music. In movies, the salvational curative was always set up in the first act as a throwaway, sure to encore later with deeper meaning.

In movies, you found a cure, gave the victim a pill or an injection, and they were instantly okay. A miracle, wrap it up, the end, roll credits.

Cash ran faster, his bootheels thudding on the roadway, the sound reminding him of a shopping cart with a bum wheel, the kind he always seemed to draw at the market. How did the wheels get those bumps, anyway?

With proper warmup and training, track sprinters could do eight hundred meters in three minutes. That was without a gunbelt and equipment, without cowboy boots or Cash's lamentable diet. Without panic or terror. What a laugh, if he ran himself right into a heart attack.

Then they'd find his body and use him as an incubator.

Then Carrie would say...

Man up. Don't be afraid. Solve the problem. Work fast and sure.

But he was afraid. Normally fear got shoved behind revulsion or duty. Fear was tamped down and tucked away. Cash did not want to go back. He wanted to show this place his ass and taillights, never to return.

Carrie would have come for him, so he forced himself to stay on track. To do the manly thing, the brave-and-true thing. He did not wish to look bad in her eyes.

Gunshots echoed behind him. Five, six, seven rounds.

"Dammit to hell!" He spit the toothpick from his already arid mouth.

The red Ram pickup was twenty yards away, chrome bumpers glinting.

Cash roared the truck through the archway, cutting hard left to skid clear of where he had left Carrie. The dual rear wheels churned a broad curtain of dust.

Carrie was not to be seen in the yard or near the porch. Two more of the bipedal things were spreadeagled in the dirt, missing most of their heads, forming big, wet puddles around themselves. Carrie's .40 was there on the ground, too. The action was not locked back; it still had rounds in it.

Cash was sure that if he wanted trouble, he'd find it in the big freezer. The creatures he had seen were pallid, like cadavers; featurelessly smooth, like a reptile's clammy underbelly; undoubtedly alien or aberrant, which suggested a moist toxicity as incomprehensible as a biowar germ. The smart thing to do was *leave.*

The right thing to do was rescue Carrie, if she could still be saved.

Reverse out the strangeness—that's what Cash's thinking mind told him to do. Put yourself in their place. Somehow, some way, they come to consciousness on McMillan's ranch. Maybe they had no idea where they were. Perhaps they lacked the facility to process sounds or smells. Maybe their vision was into the infrared spectrum, like a rattler's. Anyway, they hit the ground (or came up out of the ground, if they didn't fall from outer space or burst out of radioactive pods) and commence reproducing, to strengthen their numbers or gain some kind of immediate survival foothold. They discover that for the most part, they cannot walk around in the daytime because it's too hot, too bright. They wander around and maybe incur a few casualties in their experiential curve. They're like men on the moon, seeking a shelter with oxygen and environment. Perhaps they were transitional beings in the process of adaptation, evolving to live in new circumstances.

Illegal aliens, Cash thought with a sting of irony.

Edging up on the icehouse door was one of the hardest things Cash had ever done. There might not be any ceiling to this madness, but there might be a floor, and that bedrock had to be composed of Cash's own resolve. This could not be about anything, right now, except retrieving his partner. All the rest, the theories, the what-ifs and mad speculation, had to be left for later. And yes, the fear, too. All Cash needed to know was that bullets seemed to put the creatures down just dandy.

The icehouse door was latched by a large silver handle. It made a complicated clockwork sound when Cash cranked it, as though he was breaching an immense safe. Cold air and condensation ghosted out around the insulating gaskets.

Nobody home.

He could not find a lightswitch and so brought up his baton flashlight. There was something in here, but it wasn't a cadre of shufflers waiting to eat his face or a line of frozen beef sides to mock his fear.

The object looked like a big, broken section of latticework, laced with frost, propped against the stainless steel wall. About five-by-five, it was obviously a segment of something larger, something elsewhere, or perhaps the sole piece worth salvage. When Cash tilted his head to one side he saw that it resembled a big honeycomb, with rows of orderly, stop-sign-shaped pockets. Each octagonal chamber held one of the bugs, suspended like prehistoric scorpions in amber, although this medium was a pliable, transparent blue gel the consistency of modeling clay. It gave when Cash pressed it with the tip of his ballpoint pen, then sprang back.

Twenty or thirty of the little compartments were empty.

Peek: There were—head count—sixteen creatures outside now, cutting him off from the truck. They had hidden themselves, and waited for him to enter the freezer. The empty area between Cash and his opponents hinted that they had gotten the idea to keep their distance.

They were learning.

Best tally, he could clear twelve with the shotgun and the Ruger before he had to reload, if he did not miss once. He still had little idea of how fast they could move when motivated. He could hang tight and wait for dawn, a fat ten or eleven hours...but not in the freezer. They might not even disperse at dawn. They might wait until noon, when it got hotter.

Beyond fear was exhaustion. How long could Cash keep his eyes open and guard up?

Longer, he realized, than he could go without taking a dump. His last visit to the throne had been over twenty hours ago, and his bowels were threatening to burst like a sausage casing in a centrifuge. Great.

He could surrender. But not yet.

He could spy on them and pick a moment. They might dither around trying to form a plan of attack, or an ambush, or a diversion. Not yet.

He checked the door again. They hadn't moved. He tried to squeeze his ass cheeks to interrupt the inevitable. *Go or no go?* He did not laugh at his own folly, because if he started, he might not be able to stop, and when authorities locked him in a padded cell, he'd still be laughing.

Utterly humiliated, he moved to the back corner of the freezer, dropped his pants and tried to move his bowels as fast as possible. The tang of his own refrigerated shit brought him about as low as he'd ever felt, and rendered him infantile.

The pack with the two cigarettes rustled in his pocket, beckoning his attention. He craved a smoke, just to purchase a smoke's worth of time. Brilliantly, he lacked the means to light up.

"Emerge. Cash emerge now."

It was a voice from outside. It sounded like a very bad imitation of Carrie's voice, clotted and syrupy.

Cash hurried his pants on and buckled up so he could refill his hands with guns.

All right, full disclosure: Cash had always wanted to see Carrie's breasts. But not this way.

She was naked, striding through the group, her flesh disorganized and baggy. Her face was melting right off her skull. Cash saw her breasts. They hung offsides due to the V-neck rip in the center of her chest. The skin that had drooped along her arms accordioned at the wrists the same way as a paper wrapper mashed down from a drinking straw. She reached up with elephantine hands to grab at the tear in her chest. The tissue rended apart, gone fishy and rotten, as the mouthless being stepped out of the incubation envelope that used to be Cash's partner. Its knot of throat bulged as it mimicked speech via some unguessable mechanism.

"Cash. Emerge."

It had been less than an hour since Carrie had been stung.

When Cash came out, shotgun-first, the entire group moved forward several emboldened steps. He shot one, then another, and they dropped. In the nightmare slow-motion of a fever dream, he saw the one that had issued from Carrie pick up her Smith from the ground. One tendril of the clawlike pincer wrapped the butt while the other sought the trigger. It leveled the pistol at Cash and fired.

The slug went high and wide.

It's not her, not any more...

That hesitation almost killed him. As he brought the Mossberg to bear, a second shot flew in true and punched him in the upper left chest, spoiling his aim. A hot rivet of pain fried his nerves. He grimaced, corrected his muzzle, and cut loose. The thing that had peeled off Carrie's body lost half of its knoblike head and spun down in a shower of gluey mulch, dropping the pistol, slide open.

While the rest rushed him.

Cash side-stepped to the smokehouse, dealing out the remaining rounds from the shotgun and getting one more hit, one miss, and one wing-strike that blew away a pincer at the elbow.

It was at least ninety degrees inside the smokehouse. The air was ripe with cured pork. There was an interior crank handle that could be barricaded if he could find something to wedge under it.

Carrie had favored light loads for diminished recoil. As a result, the semi-wadcutter had lodged in Cash's breast and failed to exit. Dense blood, not completely oxygenated, was already blotting his shirt. Heart blood.

The creature had picked up Carrie's gun, fired once, corrected, and hit him on the second shot. They were learning. Now they would know the purpose of any other firearms loitering around, say, inside the house, if...

Cash remembered the spent shotgun shells in the yard. Someone else had tried earlier, and failed. Someone had shot their own dog, the Rottie, to keep it from changing, too.

Cash hoped they would not come into the smokehouse due to the heat. They might waste time deciding what to do, but wouldn't breeze on in. Not yet. He should have just bolted. Run for the hills and made it someone else's problem. Now he was cornered, low on ammo, and in need of medical attention. But if he ran, he still had no idea of how fast they could pursue him.

Or maybe Cash could wait until they adapted more, or learned enough to come in after him, at which time he still had the option of putting a slug into his own head.

But not yet.

Thudding and thumping, next door. They were inside the icehouse.

They could imprint off horses, dogs, people, anything. Until Cash was all that was left to use.

Outside there came a sputtering noise, like a motor missing cylinder strokes. The generator for the icehouse had been chugging away for the better part of a day or two without being refueled. It was running out of gas. Cash knew the sound. The icehouse would thaw and the stored bugs would melt free. Would the smokehouse cool off as the freezer warmed up?

Buttoning up for hours was no longer an option. Cash had scant cognizance of the passage of time. He did not wear a wristwatch. Almost nobody did, any more; everybody had mobile devices. Cash's own cell was still in the door pocket of the Bronco.

Not yet.

////

Cash used his fist to hammer a pork shank under the door handle, because the creatures outside had come to test it. Right outside the smokehouse door, they were less than a foot away from his face.

Shooting through the door would get Cash nothing except ricochets and a less secure door. Maybe, if he could get to the roof...

The smokehouse was a wood frame veneered in sheet metal. There was a white oak curing barrel that could be flipped to provide a step-up. Every time Cash tried to correct his balance to bulldog his way through the ceiling, his wounded shoulder blew new spikes of pain all the way down to his feet and the bullet hole began to pump fresh. His life was dribbling out.

Obscured from view was a tiny skylight, probably for ventilation. It was difficult to see since the ceiling had browned to a uniform pattern. Too small for his body, but there. He had to bang the corroded hasp back with the grip of his Ruger.

Yeah, don't attract any attention to yourself with the noise.

The hinges squeaked as he pushed against the hatch with the heel of his good hand. His entire right side was going numb and his vision was getting spotty. Shock was setting in. He could just get his head through the hole if he was willing to sacrifice an ear. Outstanding; his last tetanus shot had been years ago. Amoebic infections from tainted meat were the worst.

Soon he would not be able to trust the evidence of his own senses. He would hallucinate, grow dopey, pass out.

Cash had to clamber down to find a plastic crate for more elevation, then repeat his unsteady ascent. He could just get his head through the hatch. The ceiling was as solid as a carpenter's warranty, no rusty nails to auger loose, firm framing or your money back.

Cash could see the pickup truck. There were no creatures in sight except the ones he'd terminated. They were knocked down in their own mud, near the hideous skin-pile that used to be Senior Patrol Agent Carrie Rixson.

To the left, clear; to the right, ditto. The view to the rear was harder since Cash had to peer through the interstice between the hatch and the roof, but it looked okay behind him, too.

This calm could not hold. They had retreated to regroup, find weapons, or make more. Cash could belay his fear and move now, or try to clench and await what came next, as he grew more helpless by the second. The tension was far worse than trying not to shit. You couldn't win. Your own biology would doom you.

He nearly fell on his face getting down from the clumsy barrel-and-crate arrangement. He nearly started weeping when the chunk of pork stuck under the door handle refused to wiggle loose. But in three more heartbeats, the door was open and he was moving as fast as he could manage for the truck, hoping his adversaries had not become savvy enough to take the keys.

They were gone from the yard.

"I'm sorry," he said to Carrie's remains. She deserved better. "God, am I sorry."

That did not slow him down, though. The pickup's cab door was still open. The keys were still in the ignition. And Cash was alone in the turnaround.

"You fuckers!" he shouted hoarsely. "I'm coming back! I'm coming back for all of you! I'm gonna kill every single one of you!"

No response. Locked into the cab, windows up, Cash unbuckled his gunbelt to get at his trouser belt, which he unthreaded to bind his own wadded-up T-shirt tight against the oozing bullet ditch in his shoulder. The Ram truck fired up positively on the first try. Not like in the movies, where the vehicle won't start while the monsters close in. The seatbelt alarm pinged annoyingly.

Cash laid the pedal down and thundered over the cow-catcher at the archway, highbeams up to max. The fuel stood at half a tank. He did not allow himself to breathe until he rocketed back onto the International Highway. Now it was safe to crack the windows and blow the AC on high.

He remembered the cigarettes in his pocket, dug one out, and lipped it. A little nicotine would be better than nothing at all. But the truck did not have a dashboard lighter. Few of them did, anymore.

The black tarp in the pickup bed, unsecured, blew free just in time for Cash to glimpse the big section of blue amber honeycomb, his cargo, before his dulled eyesight focused on the bug that had been left for him inside the cab. It tensed to spring, just out of swatting reach. That's what the monsters had been up to in the icehouse—setting a trap and backing off, to let Cash ambush himself.

The big Ram truck swerved off the road and stopped. It would sit for a while, metal pinging as it cooled, the AC still blasting. Then, eventually, it would resume its journey into the city.

Click-Clack the Rattlebag

NEIL GAIMAN

"Before you take me up to bed, will you tell me a story?"

"Do you actually need me to take you up to bed?" I asked the boy.

He thought for a moment. Then, with intense seriousness, "Yes, actually I think you do. It's because of, I've finished my homework, and so it's my bedtime, and I am a bit scared. Not very scared. Just a bit. But it is a very big house, and lots of times the lights don't work and it's a sort of dark."

I reached over and tousled his hair.

"I can understand that," I said. "It is a very big old house." He nodded. We were in the kitchen, where it was light and warm. I put down my magazine on the kitchen table. "What kind of story would you like me to tell you?"

"Well," he said, thoughtfully. "I don't think it should be too scary, because then when I go up to bed, I will just be thinking about monsters the whole time. But if it isn't just a *little* bit scary then I won't be interested. And you make up scary stories, don't you? I know she says that's what you do."

"She exaggerates. I write stories, yes. Nothing that's been published, yet, though. And I write lots of different kinds of stories."

"But you *do* write scary stories?"

"Yes."

The boy looked up at me from the shadows by the door, where he was waiting. "Do you know any stories about Click-clack the Rattlebag?"

"I don't think so."

"Those are the best sorts of stories."

"Do they tell them at your school?"

He shrugged. "Sometimes."

"What's a Click-clack the Rattlebag story?"

He was a precocious child, and was unimpressed by his sister's boyfriend's ignorance. You could see it on his face. "Everybody knows them."

"I don't," I said, trying not to smile.

He looked at me as if he was trying to decide whether or not I was pulling his leg. He said, "I think maybe you should take me up to my bedroom, and then you can tell me a story before I go to sleep, but a very not-scary story because I'll be up in my bedroom then, and it's actually a bit dark up there, too."

I said, "Shall I leave a note for your sister, telling her where we are?"

"You can. But you'll hear when they get back. The front door is very slammy."

We walked out of the warm and cosy kitchen into the hallway of the big house, where it was chilly and draughty and dark. I flicked the light-switch, but nothing happened.

"The bulb's gone," the boy said. "That always happens."

Our eyes adjusted to the shadows. The moon was almost full, and blue-white moonlight shone in through the high windows on the staircase, down into the hall. "We'll be all right," I said.

"Yes," said the boy, soberly. "I am very glad you're here." He seemed less precocious now. His hand found mine, and he held onto my fingers comfortably, trustingly, as if he'd known me all his life. I felt responsible and adult. I did not know if the feeling I had for his sister, who was my girlfriend, was love, not yet, but I liked that the child treated me as one of the family. I felt like his big brother, and I stood taller, and if there was something unsettling about the empty house I would not have admitted it for worlds.

The stairs creaked beneath the threadbare stair-carpet.

"Click-clacks," said the boy, "are the best monsters ever."

"Are they from television?"

"I don't think so. I don't think any people know where they come from. Mostly they come from the dark."

"Good place for a monster to come."

"Yes."

We walked along the upper corridor in the shadows, walking from patch of moonlight to patch of moonlight. It really was a big house. I wished I had a flashlight.

"They come from the dark," said the boy, holding onto my hand. "I think probably they're made of dark. And they come in when you don't pay attention. That's when they come in. And then they take you back to their...not nests. What's a word that's like nests, but not?"

"House?"

"No. It's not a house."

"Lair?"

He was silent. Then, "I think that's the word, yes. Lair." He squeezed my hand.

He stopped talking.

"Right. So they take the people who don't pay attention back to their lair. And what do they do then, your monsters? Do they suck all the blood out of you, like vampires?"

He snorted. "Vampires don't suck all the blood out of you. They only drink a little bit. Just to keep them going, and, you know, flying around. Click-clacks are much scarier than vampires."

"I'm not scared of vampires," I told him.

"Me neither. I'm not scared of vampires either. Do you want to know what Click-clacks do? They drink you," said the boy.

"Like a Coke?"

"Coke is very bad for you," said the boy. "If you put a tooth in Coke, in the morning, it will be dissolved into nothing. That's how bad Coke is for you and why you must always clean your teeth, every night."

I'd heard the Coke story as a boy, and had been told, as an adult, that it wasn't true, but was certain that a lie which promoted dental hygiene was a good lie, and I let it pass.

"Click-clacks drink you," said the boy. "First they bite you, and then you go all *ishy* inside, and all your meat and all your brains and everything except your bones and your skin turns into a wet, milk-shakey stuff and then the Click-clack sucks it out through the holes where your eyes used to be."

"That's disgusting," I told him. "Did you make it up?"

We'd reached the last flight of stairs, all the way in to the big house.

"No."

"I can't believe you kids make up stuff like that."

"You didn't ask me about the rattlebag," he said.

"Right. What's the rattlebag?"

"Well," he said, sagely, soberly, a small voice from the darkness beside me, "once you're just bones and skin, they hang you up on a hook, and you rattle in the wind."

"So what do these Click-clacks look like?" Even as I asked him, I wished I could take the question back, and leave it unasked. I thought: *Huge spidery creatures. Like the one in the shower this morning.* I'm afraid of spiders.

I was relieved when the boy said, "They look like what you aren't expecting. What you aren't paying attention to."

We were climbing wooden steps now. I held on to the railing on my left, held his hand with my right, as he walked beside me. It smelled like dust and old wood, that high in the house. The boy's tread was certain, though, even though the moonlight was scarce.

"Do you know what story you're going to tell me, to put me to bed?" he asked. "It doesn't actually have to be scary."

"Not really."

"Maybe you could tell me about this evening. Tell me what you did?"

"That won't make much of a story for you. My girlfriend just moved in to a new place on the edge of town. She inherited it from an aunt or someone. It's very big and very old. I'm going to spend my first night with her, tonight, so I've been waiting for an hour or so for her and her housemates to come back with the wine and an Indian takeaway."

"See?" said the boy. There was that precocious amusement again. But all kids can be insufferable sometimes, when they think they know something you don't. It's probably good for them. "You know all that. But you don't think. You just let your brain fill in the gaps."

He pushed open the door to the attic room. It was perfectly dark, now, but the opening door disturbed the air, and I heard things rattle gently, like dry bones in thin bags, in the slight wind. Click. Clack. Click. Clack. Like that.

I would have pulled away, then, if I could, but small, firm fingers pulled me forward, unrelentingly, into the dark.

Cavity Creeps

CODY GOODFELLOW

Storage space #369 was four feet deep and eight feet wide, with a narrow, two-by-six appendix of useless "bonus space" they couldn't subdivide into another unit. It was just enough room to fit a modest human life and the body that had lived it. Filled to a height of eight feet with all of his records, books, sheet music and old instruments, there was just enough bonus space for Oscar Gurewich to sit in his favorite chair, and listen to his phonograph.

This is your home, now. Don't cry, for God's sake. At least you have one...and all your precious, heavy possessions.

He was taking an awful chance. The old hi-fi was plugged into an extension cord that ran out under his rolldown door and along the corridor to the service closet, which he'd propped open with a strip of duct tape. But he had paid for this space with money he'd earned. He didn't accept charity, but he'd be damned if he'd suffer in silence. And yet so long as no one tripped over his cable, he was outwardly as silent as the dead. He almost felt as if he was stealing something.

Oscar detested the headphones, but he couldn't risk being discovered. He had never knowingly broken a law or even a rule, and he really had no other choice, nowhere else to go. The world had taken everything else from him, and if he sold his things, who would want them? He would still be penniless, homeless and too old to start over, and without his music and memories, he would be less than an animal.

To dwell upon his circumstances, to honestly examine his fortunes and scheme upon any reversal, was pointless self-flagellation. The balm of Brahms' *4th Symphony* soothed his nerves like no empty words ever could. In its elegiac opening tones, he found serenity, the sense that it was all part of someone's greater plan, but the flow soon turned stormy and defiant, making his heart race and his jaw clench.

He was on an unhealthy romantic jag tonight, having worn a hole in the Moldau and his whole Mahler catalog. Berlioz, Grieg, Saint-Saens and Tchaikovsky lay out of their yellowed onionskin sleeves, the brittle, heavy disks more like pressed anthracite than flimsy postwar vinyl. His dithering fingers fumbled the *Moonlight Sonata* out of the milk crate at his knee, but replaced it. He was not strong enough, tonight.

When had the world lost its taste for such beauty? One could plot the "progress" in all human endeavors over the last century against the decline of music, from insipid jazz standards to the fecal sturm and drang of modern pop music, and observe an unmistakable correlation...but which was the symptom, and which the cause?

Perhaps, he reflected morosely, the end had begun with the recording of music itself. When playing music ceased to be a magical skill to conjure fleeting melodies out of tyrannical silence, and instead became a lot of common heat and noise that came out of a can, it lost its magic, its potent ability to speak to the soul...or perhaps men had sold or lost their souls first...

When Brahms himself submitted to record one of his Hungarian dances for Thomas Edison in 1889, perhaps he had seen the terrible changes the new invention would wreak. Almost buried beneath surface noise like a swarm of vicious rats, the master's muted piano work had the resigned air of a formal surrender.

As the *4th* tossed and turned like a dreamer lost in troubled sleep, he laid down the photo album he'd been leafing through and patted himself down for a tissue. The desiccated clippings swelled with the droplets of his tears. Discolored memories of his years with the San Diego Symphony and as a DJ at a flurry of short-lived classical FM stations, and his last vacation in Vienna, with Elaine. They didn't come to life with the infusion of fluid. They only got wet.

Suddenly, he jerked upright and snatched the headphones off his head. Though his hearing was not what it once was and the music was turned very loud, he'd heard something intrude on his reverie, a rough pounding that spoiled the perfect counterpoint of the music. The sound didn't repeat itself, but he felt somehow guilty for retiring into the embrace of his headphones.

He knew he was not alone in trying to live in the storage spaces. He'd seen others who hopped the fence just before the office locked up, who snuck into their spaces and bolted themselves in with cut padlocks, and some vulgar idiots who left soda cups and beer bottles refilled with urine in the outside lot. Such shameful circumstances did not make men eager to bond, but in the still of the night, you could hear the sounds of men weeping, raging or ranting into imaginary telephones. The steel ducts that connected the four hundred spaces with the indifferent air conditioner distilled the chorus of raw emotions into a bland, murky tone poem of despair; Ligeti's *Lux Aeterna* for condemned choir. A monotonous clicking of some loose vent or faulty thermostat regulator often sounded for hours on end when the heaters blew their rank breath of combusted dust throughout the storage complex, providing a sort of robotic rhythm section. Sometimes, he thought he heard babies crying. It was enough to drive a man to opera.

Oscar was grateful for the headphones, then. When he looked around at the stacks of heavy, antiquated LP's in their crumbling folios alongside Elaine's corny old rhumba records and Les Baxter and Dave Brubeck 45's and the battered instrument cases, he felt like much more than a broken music teacher. He felt as he supposed those young people in their Brobdingnagian monster trucks and paramilitary SUV's must feel, breezing along in implacable bubbles of creature comfort and blathering into cell phones with one half-lidded, heavily medicated eye on the ebb and flow of likewise disengaged traffic. More and more of them were marked with a bumper sticker from a local megachurch on the tinted rear window. *NOTW*, they defiantly proclaimed, with the T as a cross that looked more like a sword. *Not Of This World*. Back when someone had explained it to him, it'd seemed like the infantile height of modern stupidity, but now he wholeheartedly empathized. However high or low, hard or soft, the things of this world were an unbearable burden, and the longing to be free of them was not such a bad thing to feel.

He still had his possessions, his passions and his illusions. He had an air mattress, a gallon of fresh water to drink and clean himself, and a serviceable chamber pot. Eat your heart out, Sardanopolus. You *can* take it with you.

This was only temporary, to be sure. He still taught private lessons at Benoit Music on Ventura, though they were barely enough to cover the storage space. He could try out again for the Los Angeles Symphony. Maybe this time, they'd deign to let him be an usher.

It had nearly killed him, lugging all this old junk into this tiny box of sheet metal, cinderblock and naked concrete, when the bank threw him out of the house on Vesper Street that he'd bought with Elaine eighteen years ago. He'd had to make his final trip with a stolen shopping cart, because they'd repossessed the camper.

When he walked from the storage space on Sepulveda to the library on Moorpark in the morning, he passed it sitting in the repo yard, the green GMC with the Roll-Along shell they'd bought when she was laid off from teaching at the middle school. That was what she'd wanted, to be footloose and fancy-free for the rest of their days, but her heart wasn't up to it, and took her away before they could hit the road. Soon, the camper would be auctioned off, and someday, all of this crap would fall to some scavenger who would no doubt groan at the dismal prospect of selling it all on eBay. More and more spaces were turned out, of late, once the renter couldn't be found. It was a wonder they hadn't found more of the renters packed away with the junk they couldn't pawn or part with, the best parts of them divided up long ago by the banks and the rats.

Enough. He didn't come here to wallow in self-pity. When he closed his eyes, he could almost dissolve into the music, and rise above it all in a way that made him think death wouldn't be so bad, if it was like this. If Elaine was there, and music.

The last bombastic stabs of the *4th* subsided into the fireside crackle of needle on looping groove. Saint-Saens next. *Carnival Of The Animals* was a juvenile parade of frivolity, but it was one of her favorites.

He dropped the record when he heard the sound again, damn it. Fists rapping on sheet metal.

His heart turned a backflip in his chest. He'd been found out. Too late to make any difference, he switched off his battery-powered camp lantern and tamped out the ember in his meerschaum pipe. What the hell was he thinking, smoking in here? Maybe if he just played dead, they'd move on. He was hardly worth the trouble, and they had to know he had nowhere else to go.

A warbling tremolo of wordless fear came through the wall, and someone banged again with their open hand. The sound wasn't coming from outside his door, but from the wall at his back.

Someone in the next space.

He'd resided in the storage space for almost two weeks now, and he'd never seen his next-door neighbor, nor had he any reason to suspect he had one. Tugging the headphones off, Oscar struggled to sound courteous. "Yes, what can I do for you?"

"Help me, please, can you help me?" Through the wall, he couldn't tell the man's age or background. The voice sounded bleary from sleep or drink or both, but there was a sour chord of hysteria in his tone that shivered the corrugated tin between them. "My light's gone out, it's dark and they're—I think they're... eating me..."

Oh dear, this didn't sound promising. Maybe the poor fellow was having night terrors, or had committed the mortal sin of the modern age, and gone off his meds. But no man is an island, Oscar reminded himself, not even at the Xtra Space Hotel.

Scooting his chair away from the wall, he knocked over a stack of records in the dark. They skidded and cracked under his stocking feet. He cursed under his breath, an old habit from the days of Elaine's swear jar. He switched on the camp lamp and winced to survey the damage. The Mahler was a loss. Still, he tried to be civil. "Are you in distress? I don't have a phone—"

"I need light! My batteries are dead, or—gone, I don't know, but they, they come when it's dark. I blocked my vent...you know about that, right? But I can hear them, I think they're already in here with me, please—"

Was he talking about rats? Oscar had never seen one on the premises, though there were poison bait stations everywhere. "I don't have any extra batteries, and just the one lamp... why don't you open your door?"

The lights in the corridors were on motion triggers, and would switch on in fifty-yard stretches of the cavernous arterial corridor outside. A security guard was on duty in the front office and occasionally watched the video monitors, but he was studying for the LAPD exam—probably not for the first time—when he was awake at all. Surely a harsh blast of fluorescent light would wake him out of his nightmare, and Oscar Gurewich could mind his own business again.

The man on the other side snapped, "What the fuck do you think I am, new? I can't do that, I tried, but it's locked! Creeps locked me in! Fucking creeps..."

Well, that tore it. Oscar turned away from the wall, gingerly replaced his chair and picked up his headphones. Big, clunky old full enclosure Technics studio cans, he wouldn't have heard artillery or a Roman orgy in the next space, during his previous two selections, *Marche Slave* and Holst's *The Planets*. He wondered how long his neighbor had been making a drunken spectacle of himself. For surely that was all it was...

What would Elaine tell him, right now? He didn't need to ask his memory to replay her catalog of lectures. He didn't owe this stranger anything, but he owed it to himself not to have to look at a coward in the mirror every morning.

He grabbed the nylon rope leash and tugged his door open. It rolled jerkily up into its housing, but refused to budge beyond waist-height. Oscar ducked and stepped into the hall. The fluorescent lights flickered and came on, so cold he expected to see his breath, so bright that his shadow between his feet was a bottomless hole in the floor.

He looked up and down the corridor, but of course there was nothing moving, nothing alive. His extension cord snaked past five doors to vanish into the service closet. As bright as they were, the lights cast discrete cones of sterile illumination on the floor. The dark crowded around it, ate it up.

Oscar hesitated before he went to #368. He could be dangerous, he could be sleepwalking or on drugs...

Just you go and do nothing, then, and see what that gets you.

Thanks, Elaine. He went to the door, and bent over the lock. The light in here was funny, his deep black shadow made the familiar door look like the dark side of the moon. He instantly regretted touching it. The lock was covered in some kind of rubbery slime, a septic blackish gunk like what grows inside a garbage disposal in a widower's house. He clamped his lips tight to keep from vomiting, but he took hold of the lock and tugged.

It was one of the cheap padlocks everybody bought from the front office, but it wasn't cut with bolt cutters, like the ones everybody rigged over their unlatched doors, to fool the security. It fooled no one, Oscar was sure, but it let the management deny that they were a cut-rate flophouse. If the night watch wasn't practicing his sleeper hold on a CPR dummy in the office, he might just get caught, before things got out of hand.

Maybe it was security playing a game with them, or one of their faceless neighbors, because someone sure as Chopin put the filthy padlock on the door to seal him in.

Creeps, the man had said, with a particular whine of primal terror. *Fucking creeps...*

He looked over his shoulder. Nothing moved. No one lay poised to pounce on him. Then he heard a sound that made him jump back and clutch his chest. That clicking that he heard from the ductwork, that faint but persistent sound that he'd written off as a failing component in the climate control system...he heard it now, but it was not a faint, faded sound. It came from just the other side of the door, which shook, just a little, as he backed up against the opposite wall. It sounded like scissors opening and snapping shut.

"It's okay, I'm sorry, I'm okay...just go away, okay?" The man who'd begged him for light now sounded like he was counting backwards on the operating table. "Just...go..."

Nothing he could say could answer that, but nothing, now, could make him obey. Briskly, Oscar jogged down the hall to the closet. As the lights passed by overhead, his shadow grew long and stretched out behind him, then shrank until it puddled at his feet to seep out ahead of him, as if it took three days to reach the closet and throw open the door.

Dark inside, but he found the switch. He'd got the key from Mustafa, the daytime office manager, and he was pretty sure the grim Yemeni fellow knew what was going on. But Oscar was no bumbling Watergate burglar. He taped up the strikeplate so no one who didn't pull on the door would know it wasn't locked.

Shelves stocked with Waxie floor cleanser, Goo Gone, and industrial strength graffiti remover, next to a bonfire pile of mops, push brooms, and a bucket on wheels. He almost despaired of finding them before his eyes picked the bulky yellow rubber grips out of the mess. The ungainly weight of the bolt cutters almost tugged him off his feet. He slipped sideways in his sweaty Argyle socks, but checked himself against the doorframe with one shoulder as he charged out into the hall.

Almost immediately, he sensed something behind him. The dim orange glow of his camp lamp was like the ember of a dying campfire in a coalmine. He kept running and all he could hear was his own labored breathing, like shovels full of wet sand hitting a brick wall. He ran harder, lurching and listing with the bolt cutters in the crook of his left arm. He risked a fleeting glance over his shoulder as he ran, and saw a flash of black and yellow teeth at his back, before the lights went out.

Still running, he whipped around and for a moment, the sixty-one year old music teacher galloped backwards like a first-string NFL receiver wielding Excalibur, lashing blindly out at the gurgling darkness.

Once he swung them, the bulky steel shears took over his momentum. It was like swinging two solid baseball bats one-handed. The carbon-steel teeth caught something that checked their wild trajectory and made the blackness shriek like dry ice on metal.

Oscar stumbled. The runaway cutting head smashed into a rolldown door like a battering ram on a drawbridge. Shock ripped up Oscar's hand as if the bolt cutters had clipped a third rail.

Loud. The sound was so loud Oscar's left ear just shrieked like a cheap alarm clock. The echoes rolled away down the infinite tube and came back mushy and mingled with shreds of the blood-curdling falsetto scream he'd let out.

And then, just as it occurred to him that he was still running backwards, he tripped on something stretched across the floor. His feet flipped out from under him and he flew ass-first into the dark. His arms flapped up to shield his head just as the floor cracked his tailbone and compacted his lungs into the back of his throat.

Rolling into a broken ball like a drowned spider in a bathtub, he could not defend himself, let alone speculate upon what had attacked him. A burning breath like a draught of liquid oxygen made him cough and retch on the concrete.

Someone in a nearby space shouted at him to shut the fuck up, they had to work in the morning. He gasped an apology before he remembered his own troubles.

Something had attacked him in the dark. His mind told him it was a dog, emphatically pushed pictures of big black Rottweilers snarling and baring yellow teeth, and it would be easy to accept them. It was no less terrifying, but it added up. The storage place had bought some dogs, or strays had wandered in, or—

No. What he saw, however briefly, overwhelmed any reflexive rational explanation. It wasn't a dog, or a man, or anything like anything he'd ever seen, before. It was something *Not Of This World,* as the born-again Yuppies said.

And it was still somewhere very close by.

Nothing was broken, thank God for small favors, but he wouldn't be sitting in chairs for a week. He rolled onto his knees and dragged himself upright, clutching the wall and wheezing. By the murky lamplight, he saw that he'd tripped over his own extension cord, and the bolt cutters lay splayed open on the floor about eight feet away. *You old fool,* he scolded himself, *you've got yourself all wound up over nothing...*

Something darker than darkness lay or squatted at the very edge of the lamp's feeble corona. The light glinted off something. An eye... No, it had no eyes. Only teeth.

His knees shook. He was too terrified even to run, but when he finally took a step, it was towards the thing, and another, slowly, testing every inch for a sign of life. At last, he bent, head swimming, to grab the bolt cutters. The prone figure hissed at him and backed into the curtain of opaque shadow. Coward, he thought, but he crept backwards with the bolt cutters brandished like a cross against vampires.

He went to his own storage space and picked up the lamp, switching on the blazing white fluorescent lamp, and the blinking red emergency light at the other end. The lamp hurt his eyes. How long had he been in the dark?

It was harder to pry himself out of his own space again. His hand caught the leash and started to pull the door down. A man was in the next space, and he needed help. They were discarded and damned, but they were yet human beings, and to ignore another would only prove that he was not fit to save, himself.

Outside his space, the corridor felt hotter. He went to #368 and held the lamp up to the soiled padlock, then set it on the floor to apply the bolt cutters. The serrated teeth nipped through the cheap aluminum lock like it was made of cheese. Something banged into the door just opposite his face. Oscar fumbled the bolt cutters then held them up like a club as he squatted to grab the handle and threw the door up as hard as he could.

It jerked to a stop at chest-height. Oscar took a step back. A palpable flood of stench rolled over him, like mildew and carrion and raw sewage poured into a space heater.

The dingy sheet-metal walls were plastered with clipped photos and maps from *National Geographic,* along with the pages of a Gaugin coffee table book. Everywhere, the sunny, honey-colored windows into another world gazed down in blind disgust upon this one.

His neighbor lay on a Coleman air mattress with his head at Oscar's feet. In a red UCLA T-shirt and red pajamas, he looked like someone sleeping in their own home, and for a moment, his beleaguered, lost stare was enough to make Oscar back away and apologize as he reached to close the door.

But then, no matter how much he wanted not to, he still saw the things that crouched over the art lover, and brazenly continued with the business of eating him.

They were two or three feet tall, but hunchbacked and bent on all fours. Their skin a glossy, bubbling black like roofing tar; long, crooked limbs dragging bloated bellies and propping up wobbly, ponderous heads, which were nothing but bulging jaws and teeth.

He could see no eyes, ears or nostrils. Huge incisors and tusklike canines as broad as Oscar's palm were jammed into the huge jaws like a drawer stuffed with meat cleavers, and as they busily gnawed and nipped chunks off the man, they made that insidious clicking sound that he'd heard night after night. The sound of them gnawing, eating their way through this building, and through its nameless, faceless tenants.

"Go away," the man moaned. "It doesn't hurt..."

Two of them dismantled his legs, while two more gnawed on the exposed bones of his arms, and gobbled the loose, weathered skin of his neck.

Long, warty black tongues flopped out to lap up the sluggish blood flow, and somehow, Oscar's reeling mind supposed, they must be drugging him. Their saliva was some kind of anesthetic, perhaps, for how else could he still be alive and trying with a skeletal vestige of a hand to wave Oscar away?

Repulsion drove a hot steel rod up his spine, turning fear to fury, as he accepted them. They were something unacceptable, but they were most definitely of this world. They were the very essence of the goddamned place.

A fifth creep that he hadn't seen squeezed out from behind a tumble of art books and growled at him, extending its quivering tongue like an invitation. Maybe it didn't hurt. Maybe after everything else he'd been through, maybe being eaten, becoming nothing, felt good.

I doubt it, thought Oscar Gurewich. He swung the bolt cutters in a reckless downward smash that crushed the head of the advancing creep into its sunken shoulders. The others gasped and clicked and leapt over the prostrate feast with bloody, fat-marbled muscle in their teeth.

Oscar turned and banged his head on the rolldown door, raced blindly back to his space through a flurry of stars. Stumbling over his turntable and falling into the opposite wall, he rebounded and reached for the door leash. They came surging in before he could close it, and set to work on his legs.

He kicked out at an impossible jolt of agony, throwing a squealing creep into the rotator for Elaine's old Leslie organ with a thick strap of Oscar's outer thigh meat in its mouth. He dangled on the edge of shock, but the pain was like a knot that simply untied itself. A cold, tingling euphoria suffused his trembling flesh with the promise of escape. It wasn't so bad, after all, to be eaten.

The others climbed him, and he sagged almost willingly, under their rubbery weight. He felt claws at his neck and fetid breath stirring his thin, silver hair, and teeth shredding his clothing, yet he couldn't move a muscle.

It figured that something like this would be the end. The world had been taking bites of him for so long, stealing his wife and his livelihood and his home. At every turn, he had clung all the tighter to his things, to the false cocoon he'd secreted around his raw, unfinished form.

Elaine had loved him so much it killed her. He knew that, always had, but never admitted it. His clinging to his records, his books and his junk had smothered her spirit, and when he could not tear himself away, she had sickened and died before he even realized he was losing her. He hated himself for the relief he'd felt, when he realized he wouldn't have to abandon all that stuff, to live in the camper.

He barely felt the teeth clamping down on the crown of his skull, skating across bone as they peeled off his scalp. But he felt his heart breaking, and his tears came flowing down so thickly he couldn't see where he was swinging the bolt cutters. In his head, he heard only the invincible rhythm of Verdi's *Anvil Chorus.*

The fanged cutting head demolished an orange crate filled with Wagner and Handel and sent a creep spinning. The creep on his back shredded the sleeve of his cardigan sweater and tried to chew off his arm, but he flung it headfirst into the cinderblock wall and chased it with the cutters, smashing its crooked spine out between its chattering teeth before it hit the floor.

Spinning on his heel, greased by blood streaming down his leg, Oscar chopped down a stack of Elaine's old novelty records. Yma Sumac, Martin Denny and Spike Jones took wing like clay pigeons. The bolt cutters spun out of his grip and caromed off the wall. There were still more of them than he could count, and more dropping out of the open duct overhead. Out of every crack and cavity in the sad tomb of his life, they slithered and skulked, snapping their cleaver-teeth and crowding him into the narrow, coffin-shaped bonus space.

His life was forfeit long before they showed up, but Oscar Gurewich was nobody's food. He looked around at all his things, all the music that had both set him free and buried him, all the heavy, dusty things he had mistaken for the stuff of life itself. All the terribly flammable shit he'd surrounded himself with…

In his pocket, he thumbed the lid off his monogrammed silver Zippo lighter. A silly affectation he'd found in his stocking one Xmas, though Elaine loathed the smell of his pipe and cigars. He struck the flint and tossed it into a crate of sheet music.

The antique yellow paper ignited like potassium powder. The creeps cowered, hissing, as he flung flaming paper into every corner of the storage space. He kicked a creep away from his wounded leg, then heaved a tower of ancient Mozart limited pressings on top of the snarling abomination.

The fire took root among the crates and oiled cases and bloomed in earnest. Creeps melted like wax and burst in the flames, or scrambled back up into the duct with their asses ablaze. Alarms rang in the corridor and sprinklers spurted unevenly outside his space. The vents sucked smoke and fluttering embers into the central duct.

Oscar looked around him. He didn't feel like he was burning, but he smelled bacon underneath the reek of broiled sewage. The thought of trying to save any of it made him laugh until he coughed. He didn't belong to any of this stuff. He could remember and play any of it that really mattered. But he turned and reached into the mounds of flame, digging by memory until he found the familiar grip of an old instrument case. His clarinet, the one he'd played in the symphony when he met Elaine.

He snapped up the case and patted out plumes of fire on his sweater. Backing away from the furnace roar of his life burning up, he noticed that he'd grabbed the wrong goddamned instrument. The grubby, rubber-banded grip was attached to the case for a beat up old tenor saxophone that Elaine had bought for him at a yard sale back when they courted. A loud, vulgar horn that Mozart might've loved, but which had always seemed to Oscar to be the flatulent, razzing death-knell of the classical era. Well, to hell with it. He had to play something.

He picked up the bolt cutters and shambled down the corridor past bleary-eyed refugees in thermal longjohns, down the stairs and out past the front office of Xtra Space Self Storage, oblivious to the security guard who tried to stop him, but then screamed, "Jesus, you've been scalped!" and puked on the sidewalk.

Sirens wailed and blared as fire engines and police converged on the storage complex. They'd be busy for a while, maybe all night, if they found the nest of creeps.

Feeling neither the cold nor the pain of his many wounds, Oscar Gurewich tossed an imaginary dollar into an imaginary swear jar and walked down Sepulveda to go get his goddamned camper back.

The Glitter of the Crowns

CHARLAINE HARRIS

Helen Dismuss looked out the living room picture window at the back of the two story house on Valley Vista Road. Trees and mountains stretched westward as far as she could see, with only a hint of other human habitation here and there. They'd picked this side of the mountain, the side facing away from the chichi skiing resort, on purpose. Helen Dismuss and her husband had worked to climb to this house—both figuratively and literally—and Helen was conscious of a little thrill in a very private place every time she surveyed her kingdom.

The view when she turned to face the room was just as good, but for other reasons. Though the majority of the Dismuss trophies were downstairs, the ones that meant the most to Helen were in a display case placed in a proudly obvious position in the family room.

In the closest house to the Dismuss's, which was none too close, Fran Silvertoe was looking out her east-facing front window, but not to admire the view. The older Dismuss girl, Cyndi, was due to arrive with Fran's two children, Anton and Olga. Fran was sure that Cyndi was a responsible driver; but still, the girl was only seventeen. It had seemed like a great arrangement, the year after Cyndi had gotten her driver's license. Since Fran Silvertoe worked at home in web design, if Cyndi took Anton and Olga to school and brought them back it saved Fran over an hour of productive time. Cyndi made some money; Anton and Olga didn't have to wait outside for the school bus to wind its way up the mountain.

Fran had some cause for worry today. It was beginning to snow, and she'd planned a special night for her son that might be spoiled by the weather. And it seemed almost certain that Ivan's plane would be delayed, so her husband would be spending this important evening in a motel near the airport outside of Houston. He'd rely on Fran to take pictures and provide a full account.

Fran was not normally a high-strung woman, but she would be the first to tell you that once every month she got pretty antsy. This afternoon, watching the big flakes swirl out of the sky, Fran paced in front of the large windows in her living room, which faced out over the valley and its population. The sight of the homes of the people below, of the vehicles and tiny pedestrians, gave her a feeling of comfort.

At last, Cyndi's Toyota 4Runner came into view on the curve below, passing the Frankel house. Mr. Frankel, as usual, was out in his front yard smoking, and he waved to the kids, who waved back politely. Fran was glad to notice that Cyndi was driving at a responsible speed, and her headlights were on. Fran stood close to the glass and looked up. The snowflakes were falling faster and faster. There'd already been one snowfall, and its remains were still sitting a foot deep in the forest. The few families on Blake Mountain hired a guy who lived at the base to clear their roads every snowfall, but he wouldn't work through the night. The mountain people might very well be snowed in by the morning. Ordinarily, this wouldn't be such a big deal, since today was Friday. But tonight, the weather and Ivan's absence created serious obstacles.

At least Fran's children were now home safely. Fran felt a frisson of horror at the thought of them trapped with some other family down in the valley.

Anton got out of the front seat of the 4Runner, looking back to laugh at something Cyndi was saying. Anton was tall, with light brown hair and a runner's build. He was on the track team and the debate team, and he was a popular boy. Fran's heart expanded with pride as she watched him call a final comment to Cyndi and her sister, who must be in the back seat with Olga.

Fran wondered, for a moment, if Anton had a little crush on Cyndi Dismuss. She was realistic enough to know that no matter how wonderful she believed Anton was, a fourteen-year-old boy didn't have a chance with the sophisticated and very popular Cyndi Dismuss—or even with Bethanee, Cyndi's thirteen-year-old sister. Ivan had dubbed Bethanee "Cyndi Junior," and Olga had taken to the nickname with glee. Olga and Bethanee would never be friends.

Olga was wiggling out of the 4Runner to land on sturdy legs, sliding her backpack onto her shoulders, her round face partially obscured by the dark brown hair that swung forward as she looked down to be sure of her footing. If Fran had worried a bit that Anton might have a crush on one of the girls, she worried even more that hanging around the Dismuss sisters would give her own daughter a permanent feeling of inferiority.

As Olga and Anton trudged up the driveway to the house, Fran realized their forms were actually obscured by the fast-falling snow. She hurried from the front window to the kitchen door, pressing the button to raise the garage door. They'd have to remove their wet shoes in the garage. Then they could have a snack, but not until after Fran checked her son's temperature.

Helen was on the phone with her husband when she heard Cyndi and Bethanee come in the Dismuss kitchen. Cyndi had her own garage door opener, and she always parked under cover. The girls were talking and laughing as they hung their coats on hooks by the back door and stowed their shoes under a bench.

Helen smiled. The excellent relationship between the sisters was a huge source of pride for Helen, who had never gotten along with her own siblings. Burke, a first-born child, had always been very different from his brother, too. Helen and Burke were very fortunate to have found each other, they told other couples frequently. And the two felt even more fortunate to have had two beautiful daughters.

"All right, darling," she said to Burke. "Thank God the girls are home now. The snow's getting much worse here, and I'd worry about you every minute if you tried to make it home. Staying in McCarthy is the best thing to do. But I'll miss you!"

"Say hi to Cyndi and Bethanee," Burke Dismuss said. "Remind Bethanee she needs to work on her new routine tonight."

"Girls, I've got your dad on the phone!" Helen said, walking into the kitchen with the phone in her hand. "He's going to be stuck in McCarthy. You have anything you want to tell him?"

Bethanee grabbed the phone first. "Hey, Dad, I made an A on my algebra test!" she said.

Helen could hear Burke saying, "That's my girl. We studied hard for that one. Now you can focus on that dance routine, huh?"

"Sure, Dad." Bethanee made a little face. "How many times?"

"Do it five times for Mom," Burke said firmly.

"O-kay," Bethanee said, dragging out the world. "Here's Cyndi."

"Dad, I have a date with Jeff Ostrander for homecoming!" Cyndi said. "He broke up with Marcia to take me."

"Honey, that's great. The Ostranders are nice people. Marcia taking it okay?"

"Oh, she boohooed at school today, but I took her in the girls' bathroom and I told her how sorry I was, and she kind of cheered up. Gradually."

"Keep that smile going, honey," Ivan said. "And look out for your mom and your sister tonight. I worry about you all when I'm not there, especially during bad weather. Remember your training!"

"We'll do the safety routine," Cyndi promised. Ivan could tell from her poorly-suppressed exasperation that Cyndi thought he was a total alarmist.

"Cyndi," he said, with an *I'm-not-fooling* edge to his voice.

She widened her big blue eyes at her mother. "Okay, Dad, okay! We'll take care of everything here! Don't worry, and get back home soon. I've got the Miss Snowy Peaks pageant in two weeks, and you know that's the gateway to Miss Colorado!"

"All right, you focus on that competition. I already told Bethanee she had to do her dance routine five times tonight. You'd better help her out and work on your own singing."

"Sure, Dad. As soon as we eat dinner and watch a movie..."

"Cyndi!"

"Just kidding, Dad. It *is* Friday night."

"Oh, gosh, that's right. Why doesn't my kitten have a date?"

Cyndi could hear Burke's frown, even over the telephone. "Daddy! I was going to the movies with John Agostino, but he broke his ankle at football practice."

"Weak excuse!"

Cyndi laughed. "Yeah, I know, Dad. But he can't drive with a broken right ankle, and I don't want to go get him in this weather. I'd have to listen to his mom giving him a list of dos and don'ts, and then I'd have to cope with getting him into the movie theater with the crutches...no, I don't think so!"

"I wouldn't let you go out in this weather, anyway!" Helen called.

"Hear that, Dad? I'm in for the night."

After a little more conversation, Helen retrieved the phone to wish her husband goodnight and to remind him not to eat that chili at the hotel in McCarthy, since he'd had such bad heartburn the last time he'd tried it.

"Duly noted," Burke said. "I can hardly wait to see my three beautiful gals! Don't forget to check the doors and windows, honey."

Helen hung up after saying a final goodbye, a little relieved that the evening could be spent in a low-key way. Not that she didn't adore her husband, but occasionally living with him was like living with a loose power line. He was so anxious for the girls to excel at everything! He drilled them so strictly! But they were growing up to be capable and assertive, which Helen could only approve.

It had been Helen's idea to start the girls in the pageant circuit. She'd been a product of the pageant experience, herself, and in her opinion the process would teach the girls how to compete, how to be disciplined, how to lose graciously and try harder next time. Sure, she and Burke would spend some money in the process, but by the time her girls were ready to leave home she'd feel confident they could cope with college and much, much more.

Burke had observed the girls' pageant progress for a couple of years, and then he'd started adding his own arabesques to the training.

And the girls started winning more consistently.

Cyndi's room was rose pink. The walls were covered with pictures of Cyndi and her friends, Cyndi in her Junior Homecoming Maid evening dress, Cyndi accepting an award for community service, Cyndi with her first hunting trophy.

Bethanee's room was lavender and ruffles and lace. She still liked horses, and there were several pictures of her with her favorite at the valley stable. She had some framed awards for her bow-and-arrow accuracy in her age division at the state tournament. Her junior high cheerleader uniform was hanging on a special hook on the wall so she could enjoy it constantly.

All the rest of their trophies were downstairs in the training room.

While Helen was indulging her daughters by heating up a pizza, Fran Silvertoes was taking Anton's temperature for the second time.

It was rising. Like her own.

Anton was twitching with nerves. "I knew it," he said. He was sweating and his eyes were a bright brown, almost mahogany. Olga held her brother's hand. Ordinarily she was very offhand about her big brother, but this evening she was conscious of a great surge of fear for him. She looked from her brother to her mother, mutely seeking reassurance.

"Anton, listen," Fran said, forcing her voice to be even and calm. "We're going to go over it all again. It's killing your dad that he can't be here for tonight. He's already called four times. But with Dad or without, you'll get through this just fine. Thousands of kids do this every year."

"I'm hungry," Anton said.

"I know. You can go out to find something to eat in an hour or two." She smiled at him. "This is going to be a great night for you, son."

"Can I fix him a hamburger?" Olga asked. "I want to help."

"He can't eat that tonight," Fran said, trying to make her voice gentle. "You know he can't. He'll go out soon. So will I. You have to be brave, sugar."

"The weather's so bad, Mom." Olga looked at the driving snow and shivered.

Fran knew that Anton could hear her: he would be one big nerve all over his body, by now. "Don't worry about your brother. He'll do just fine," Fran said briskly. "Now, go get some water for him to drink."

Olga sped off to the kitchen, and Anton opened his eyes. He was drooling. The condition was a powerful thing, and not always a beautiful one, especially for the first change.

"Mom, tell me the rules again." His eyes fixed on her face with a frightening intensity.

"Okay." She took a level breath. "Tonight's your night, you must not fail," she said, nearly chanting. "No matter rain, no matter hail."

"Or snowstorm," he whispered.

She smiled, but she still looked quite serious. "The spirit cares not what your plight," she continued.

"Fresh blood must cross your lips tonight," Anton finished. "It's not Shakespeare, huh?"

She laughed. "No, it's not, but it gets the point across. Tonight you have to get a deer or a rabbit or a squirrel or *something*."

The "something" was what they didn't talk about.

"It won't be long now," she told her son. "I wish your dad could have been here. He'd be so proud." The phone rang. "I'll bet that's him now, wanting to know how you're doing," she said, and rose to answer it.

Olga crept in while her mother was talking in the next room. Anton was shivering uncontrollably. "Does it hurt?" she asked. Even in his distress, Anton could tell how frightened she was. For the first time in his life, the boy envied Olga for a split second. She would never have to go through this, since she was the second child.

"It feels like fire running through me," he said. "Like my blood's boiling. Yeah, it hurts." He arched and gasped. "But it's pretty exciting." He growled.

They looked at each other, surprised at the ferocious sound, and then they both laughed. But then Anton growled again, and his mouth began to change in shape.

His mother braced herself against the wall in the living room. Outside of Houston, her husband had already gone into the woods behind his hotel and removed his clothes. He was about to put the garments and his cell phone into a plastic bag, which he'd lodge in the nearest tree. The weather down there was cool and windy, but clear. There would be something to kill, something easy to find. Anton's change could not have come at a worse time.

In the basement practice room, Bethanee had performed her dance routine five times. One wall was mirrored, the floors were laminate wood and otherwise bare, and two walls were lined with glass cases containing the girls' crowns, sashes, scepters, trophies, and other pageant regalia. A couple of pieces of training equipment stood enveloped in custom pink-and-gold covers dotted with fleurs-de-lis.

Cyndi and her mother, seated on the squashy old leather couch, evaluated each performance with discerning eyes. Neither of them was bitchy in their comments, because they'd been on the receiving end of such critiques many a time. When Bethanee was exhausted, the three women did one of their favorite things: they posed in front of the mirror wall. Three blondes, three beauties.

"Mom, today when Marcia was crying in the bathroom, she told me that some day I'd get payback," Cyndi said. She was looking over one shoulder provocatively, the effect somewhat dissipated by the fact that she was wearing pink sweats.

"What's with the fat pants?" Bethanee asked.

"I started today," Cyndi said. She felt achy and a little bloated, but posing was always fun. Bethanee was lying on one elbow, giving her reflection a haughty look. Helen, between them, had chosen a classic model pose, designed to look as though she were walking down a sidewalk and just by chance happened to look spectacular. She could still pull it off.

"Payback?" said Bethanee, returning to Cyndi's previous words. "What the hell does that mean? Is she talking, like, Karma or something?"

"Language," said Helen automatically. "No one likes to hear words like that coming out of a lady's mouth."

"Oh, Mom. You should have heard Marcia! Dad would've made her spend an hour in the penalty box!" Cyndi switched poses, crouching at her sister's back to look challengingly at the mirror.

"So she was hoping something would go wrong for you simply because you've been so blessed?" Helen said, not a little indignant. "It's not like you haven't worked for it. At least you didn't have to get instructors. My training took care of most of your pageant events, and your father's taken care of the rest." Burke, in charge of the extra training and the discipline, called himself "fair but firm." In her private thoughts, Helen had always considered he came down pretty heavily on the "firm" side, but she couldn't deny that between them they'd raised two attractive, competitive, multi-talented young women. She reached out to knock on the wood of one of the training devices as she passed on her way to the stairs.

As the Dismuss family separated—Helen to watch a couple of recorded episodes of "Toddlers and Tiaras," Cyndi to begin a paper that would be due on Tuesday, Bethanee to spend some time on Facebook—the Frankels were getting increasingly worried by the weather situation. Paul and Rebecca Frankel had lived on the mountain before anyone else had built there, and their house was older and smaller than the suburban monster houses the other families had constructed. Paul and Rebecca were the oldest residents, too.

Tonight, they were having one of their frequent arguments.

"It's too cold outside, Beck. I'll just stand in the garage. I can't go out in the snow. You remember that couple who vanished last year in the snowstorm?"

"Paul, you promised me. When I had to quit two years ago, you swore you would never smoke in the house again. The garage counts." Rebecca wisely ignored the mention of the missing couple. She had her own ideas about what had happened to them, ideas she hadn't shared with her husband.

"Beck, I'll freeze my balls off in the yard!"

"Then don't smoke," Rebecca Frankel snapped. "My lungs are more important than your addiction." As if to punctuate that idea, she left the room and Paul heard the familiar sound of his wife's using her inhaler.

Ten minutes later, they'd reached a workable compromise. Paul would stand under the shelter of the garage, but he would push the button to open the garage door before he smoked.

While the Dismuss family was peacefully engaged in their various pursuits and Paul Frankel was blissfully inhaling, the Silvertoes family was going through hell.

Olga was holding Anton's hand, when he would let her. The girl was crying openly. If Ivan had been at home, he would have stayed with Anton while Fran consoled Olga in another part of the house, with the door firmly shut, until the time that the inevitable happened.

Fran had called Ivan when Anton's transition had made the boy more and more miserable, catching Ivan just as he was about to drop his phone in the bag for safekeeping. "I'm so sorry," Ivan said helplessly, repeating himself. Fran sighed. "You can't help it," she said, exercising great self-control. "But let me tell you, when Olga starts having her periods, you get to carry the ball on that one!"

He chuckled weakly. "You got it," he said. "I'll take her to the store for her pads. You'd better get back in there. Bye, honey. Good luck."

"Talk to you later," she said, snapping the phone shut. In her brief absence, Anton's condition had gone from bad to worse. His back was arching, and he'd rolled off the bed onto the floor. "Olga!" Fran said sharply. "Off to your room. Lock the door."

Olga, looking down at her brother with a sad mixture of fear and concern, scrambled out of the room.

Fran knelt by her son. "Anton, downstairs," she said sharply. "Otherwise, we'll never get the stains out." She helped the boy to his feet, but even as she gripped his arm she could feel the muscles and bones writhing underneath his skin in a way that was all too familiar. She urged him forward, cursing her decision to let him begin the transition in his own room. She'd thought vaguely of the possibility of visitors, of the comfort of familiar surroundings, but she knew now that she hadn't been thinking clearly. No one was going to come calling in a snowstorm, and the whole house was familiar.

The mother and son lurched unsteadily from side to side as they descended, Anton panting heavily and hardly aware of what he was doing, Fran trying to hold onto her son and her calm. When they'd almost reached the main floor, Anton's legs crumpled and he crouched on all fours.

"Not now! Anton, come on, just a little more!" Fran grabbed his arm and tried to tug Anton upright, but he growled at her. Fran instantly backed away. He might be her beloved son, but he was also not responsible for his actions tonight. With some difficulty, Fran got past the crouching form and opened the front door. The freezing air gusted in, burdened with snow. Anton raised his snout to scent the fresh air. After he'd sniffed its wildness, the change hit him full force. A full-size wolf shook himself and launched his gray lithe form out the open door.

Fran slammed the door shut and bolted it. She collapsed onto the wet floor. *I'll have to get the mop*, she thought. But her legs wouldn't cooperate. That had been a very close call. *I'll get it in a minute*. Then a new realization hit her and she said, "Oh, dammit!" She'd forgotten the camera, still on the table by Anton's disordered bed. Well, they'd missed their chance. All things considered, she didn't mind living with that. Ivan would be sorry, though. After a few more moments of recuperation, Fran's legs began obeying her commands again, and she got up to get the mop. "Olga, you can come out now!" she called up the stairs. "I've got to go out, too. You need to mop while I'm gone."

Olga crept down the stairs, looking over the railing. "Is Anton really gone?" she said.

"Yes, honey. And you know I've got to go. The sooner I get out, the sooner I come back. Remember the special code?"

"Three fast knocks, two slow."

"You're a great kid, Olga," Fran said. She smiled fondly at her daughter, but the same change that had agonized Anton was claiming her flesh and bones. "I might as well go out the front, too," she said, while she was still capable of human speech. "Lock the door. Don't be careless. Rememberrrrr..." she growled.

Olga opened the front door, and her mother licked Olga's hand as she slunk past. She waited to hear her daughter shut and lock the door. Since the tourist couple had gone missing last year in conditions like these, she'd reminded her daughter to be extra careful.

Out in the howling wind and the snow, young Anton was having the greatest experience of his life. Fully wolf, he ran as he'd never run on the high school track. The new layer of white stuff made it hard to find an animal scent, though, and the bit of Anton that remained self-aware began to feel worried. He was hungry, hungrier than he'd ever been in his life. He wanted something warm and soft and crunchy, all at the same time, and he knew eating such a thing was vitally necessary. The young wolf began scouring the winter woods for some trace of a living thing. He'd know it when he found it. The first few moments of the search were disappointing. Then he smelled a rabbit, and he threw back his head and howled in indescribable delight.

Rebecca opened the door to the garage to call to Paul, "Did you hear that?" She was wrapped in a blanket, and he saw that her hands were shaking.

"I sure did," he said, stomping on his cigarette. "You think it was a dog? The Browns have a big dog."

"They have a standard poodle," Rebecca said. She stepped back inside the house. Paul followed her. "I don't think I've ever heard that dog make a noise like that. That sounded more like a wolf."

"I guess it could be," Paul said. "We keep the doors shut, they'll stay away. They're more scared of us than we are of them."

Rebecca was making hot chocolate. She seemed to be trying to put their previous squabble behind her. Paul took a cup gladly, and he fantasized for the hundredth time about quitting smoking. Maybe he'd already smoked his last cigarette!

At just the moment Rebecca joined Paul in the garage, Cyndi Dismuss was asking the same question Rebecca had. "Did you hear that?" Cyndi said from the door of Bethanee's room. Bethanee looked up from her laptop. "Hear what?" the younger girl asked. "Hey, did you see what Marcia posted about you on Facebook?"

Cyndi said, "I'm not worried about it. You snooze, you lose. She snoozed on Jeff. She lost." Cyndi gave a flick of her fingers. "Bye-bye, Marcia! He's mine now, if I want him."

Bethanee grinned. "I hope I grow up to be just like you," she said.

"Watch it, Sis," Cyndi said, grinning back. "Everyone thinks we should be fighting all the time."

"Not us," Bethanee said. The two sisters gave each other a fond hug.

Fran Silvertoe had made her kill in record time. She hadn't spared a moment to enjoy the freedom that came from running in her wolf form. She'd followed a very fresh scent trail and come upon a coyote. The fight had been fierce but short, and Fran had eaten the skinny creature very quickly. She scouted around for her son. She wasn't supposed to help him. He had to make his first kill by himself. Fran finally found traces of Anton, and she started to follow him…but she forced herself to go back to the family home. Olga was by herself, and she owed a duty to her daughter, too.

Much further away from the Silvertoe house, Anton huffed in exasperation. His breath made a plume of smoke. The second rabbit, like the first, had been faster than he expected, since he wasn't used to floundering through the rising snow. The hunger was gnawing at him. On the wind, he caught a trace of the most delightful smell…blood, human blood. It was overlaid by something horrid, but the lure of it was magical. Anton plunged through the drifting snow and the trees to the Frankel home.

Paul Frankel had lasted maybe twenty minutes with his quit-smoking resolve. Despite the nasty look Rebecca had given him over the top of the glasses she wore to knit, he'd headed back out into the frigid garage and raised the door again. It made a rattling sound that seemed to travel forever through the darkness. Paul lit up. He felt almost as virtuous as though he had actually quit, and was only smoking one last cigarette for old times' sake. So it wouldn't go to waste. So it wouldn't hang around to tempt him.

Anton crept closer and closer. He could locate the human easily. The aroma of the blood called to him. Blood and warm flesh were just within his reach in that garage; and miracle of miracles, the door was raised about two feet, enough for him to slip underneath! Anton gathered himself and wriggled on his belly into the relative calm of the garage. A single vehicle, an aging Ford Explorer, concealed Anton from Paul's view. Anton slunk, quite instinctively. He'd almost gotten around the body of the Explorer, when he saw the cigarette land on the garage floor and watched a foot casually rub out the ember.

Having quit again, Paul turned to go inside, when—quite suddenly—he was sure he was not alone. Though he tried over and over to explain to himself how he knew this, he did know it. He gauged the distance from himself to the door, thought of how long it took him to turn the knob, leap inside and slam the door behind him and lock it. And the time was too long. His aging bones would never make it. The car was much closer. Had he locked it? He wasn't in the habit of doing so since they kept the garage door closed. Just his luck, he might have had a senior moment and locked the damn thing.

All these thoughts travelled through Paul's head with amazing speed. Once he'd made up his mind, he thought through the procedure, and then he took two quick steps to the Explorer, opened it, launched himself into the driver's seat, and slammed the door.

There was a snarl and a snap and he looked into the face of a wolf at the car window.

He began sounding the horn.

This was a move he hadn't thought through. He was shocked at his own stupidity when his wife flung open the kitchen door to find out what the hell he thought he was doing. The wolf changed targets in a heartbeat, and launched himself at Rebecca, who was clutching something. Paul had a second to realize she had her knitting, when Rebecca flung up her hand, and the overheard fluorescent light glinted on knitting needle. She sank it into the wolf's shoulder.

Anton howled, and howled again. No one had ever hurt Anton on purpose before, and he was shocked and astonished at how much the stab of the needle hurt. Rebecca pulled out the needle and stabbed again, and Anton knew he had to retreat. He skidded under the door and was back out in the storm, not only gnawingly hungry, but now humiliated and in pain.

The young wolf found a copse of young trees and he rested there for a few minutes, trying to recover his nerve. By now the need for blood and food was consuming him, and he had to conquer his driving impulse to try the Frankel home again. The woman had been terrifying, the man quick-witted. He couldn't risk a return, and there had been that disgusting smell overlying the delicious blood scent.

He began working his way around the mountain. He gave chase to a rat, but it eluded him. In his limited awareness, Anton began to be seriously worried. His future as a werewolf was over tonight if he didn't cross his lips with blood. He would be a disgrace to his parents rather than a source of pride.

Anton began zigging and zagging through the snow, trying to pick up a scent. He was getting further and further from home. On the slope above the Dismuss home, Anton smelled something foul and rotted. He flinched back and moved forward. Then the best scent ever wafted to him on the bitter wind. It was blood, female blood. Anton felt a surge of elation.

There was plenty of bloody-soft-crunchy, only a few yards downslope.

Anton began working his way down, glad to escape the foul smell and increasingly excited by the very good smell. He was so thrilled that he yipped.

From her seat on the slipper chair in her sister's lavender bedroom, Cyndi heard the small sound, muffled by the wind and the house itself. She'd been painting her toenails while Bethanee flirted with a classmate on Facebook. They could hear the television downstairs, and their mother's laughter. Helen hadn't heard the same thing they had.

After a long minute of listening, the sisters rose without a word. Cyndi closed the nail polish and heel-walked to her room, hoping her toenails would have time to dry before she put on her boots. Bethanee had closed down her laptop and was scrambling for her closet.

Five minutes later, the girls were downstairs. Their mother looked away from the TV set as they came into the room. "What's going on?" she said. "Is this a drill?"

"No, Mom. Just stay where you are. We'll handle it." Just like their dad had taught them.

"You sure, sweetie? I can go get...."

"Nah, we got it." Bethanee was actually pretty excited at getting to implement some of her dad's training, but she was trying to maintain a stoic face.

"All right," Helen said, smiling and smoothing her blonde mane. "I'm bait, then." She opened a drawer in the table next to her corner of the couch, extracted a Sig Sauer, and put it under a bright turquoise throw pillow at her right hand. She resumed watching her show, but her attention wasn't on the screen any longer. She patted around for the remote control, stopped "Toddlers and Tiaras" and switched to regular programming. She didn't want to miss anything.

The wolf sniffed around the base of the house, more and more excited by the nearness of easy prey and the failure of the early part of his hunt. The part of him that was still Anton felt vaguely sorry that one of the Dismuss women would have to die, but if he didn't kill and eat something tonight, he'd be a failure the rest of his existence, which wouldn't be long. If he went home without being bloodied, his mom would have to declare him non-pack.

And one of the women smelled so intoxicating!

The wolf peered through the window into the family room. He could see Helen smiling at something on the television, her hands resting at her sides. She would be so easy! But going through the glass...not so easy to survive.

Increasingly frustrated, he continued his patrol around the house. The front door was thick and strong, the windows high and hazardous, the lowered garage door metal and therefore out of the question. No obliging smoker was going to open it. There was one lightweight wooden door, though, from the back yard into the garage. The wolf paused indecisively. The rich odor of blood and his overwhelming hunger took away what little sense he retained. He charged. The door splintered. The wolf found himself in the relative quiet and dark of four walls, out of the blinding snow, and only one kitchen door away from the Dismuss women. He was so *hungry*.

He was sniffing at the bottom of the kitchen door—the intoxicating scent was rolling out from under it!—when he heard movement on the other side of the only barrier between himself and his food, his life-saving meal. The wolf froze, listening to the small movements, and finally, oh joy, the snick of the lock being disengaged came to his ears. They must be so curious they were going to open the door to peek out!

Stupid women, always talking about pageants and dresses and entry fees. His contempt blazed, though he'd thought seventy times about either Cyndi or Bethanee when he was alone in his room at home with the door shut. They were...yummy.

And dumb, because the door was opening just a bit. Into darkness.

He sprang with the force of a battering ram, his mouth open and ready to bite, but just as he skidded to a stop on the kitchen floor, the light came on and the Dismuss sisters were facing him.

He froze.

The girls were now wearing camouflage and Kevlar vests and high-laced boots. There was not a curve in sight.

And the mouth-watering aroma of succulent woman was overlaid with the taint of gun oil. Cyndi had a shotgun, and Bethanee had a .357 Magnum.

"Down on the fucking floor," growled Bethanee, her gun never wavering in its aim.

"Language," came their mother's voice faintly.

"It's okay, Mom, you can come in," Cyndi called. "Sorry about the language," she added, giving her sister a stern glance. "Stress of the moment!"

Mrs. Dismuss came in, gun in one hand, remote control in the other. She regarded the wolf with some astonishment. "I wonder who this might be?" she said. "I don't think it's just a wolf. A real wolf wouldn't have obeyed your commands."

Anton whined.

"Nah, I don't think so either," Bethanee said. "I think we got a real werewolf." Her grin spread from ear to ear.

"He broke into our house, so he's okay by the rules. But don't play with him here. Down to the basement," Helen Dismuss said.

With guns at the ready, the Dismuss sisters let the wolf know in very simple terms that he was supposed to go down the steps. This proved surprisingly awkward in wolf form, and Anton had a difficult time paying attention to their orders. Their wonderful smell was just as enticing, even though circumstances had changed completely. If he could just graze one of them with his fangs, if he could just get a drop of blood...but a big mouthful would be so much better. His teeth were so ready to clamp down on the muscular arm holding the shotgun! Inevitably, his self-control snapped like his teeth wanted to, and he leaped for Bethanee's throat since she was a bit shorter and her firearm was smaller.

But the years Burke had worked with Bethanee paid off, and she fired. The bullet went through the wolf's right rear leg, and he went down.

Neither of the girls broke discipline in their excitement, though their hearts were pounding at furious rates. They watched with stern faces while the wolf yipped and thrashed and bled. When he was exhausted he lay panting, his blood spreading over the laminate wood flooring. Under their fascinated gaze, Anton once more became human.

It is not possible to be more humiliated than a naked fourteen year old boy whose lust object has just shot him and is standing looking at him, fully clothed. But as Anton lay shivering and shaking, at least the wound in his leg began to feel better, and he knew it would heal.

"Hey, dickwad," Cyndi said. "How long you been a werewolf?"

"Tonight was my first night out," Anton said.

"You didn't do it very well," Bethanee said, and she sounded simply disappointed. "On the other hand, we've known you for at least five years, and I didn't have a suspicion you would turn into an animal."

"I didn't think you would shoot me," Anton said. "Why'd you do that?" But even to his own ears he sounded unconvincing and weak.

"Oh, come on," Bethanee said with considerable indignation. "You were going to eat me."

"I have to have some blood," Anton said. "We have to taste blood when we change the first time. If we can't do make that happen, we won't be in the pack. We'll be cast out the rest of our lives."

The girls regarded him skeptically. "Right," said Cyndi.

"Please," Anton said. "Can I just bite one of you? Just enough to get a little blood on my teeth? It won't make you turn into a werewolf." As a matter of fact, Anton wasn't sure about that. Since he'd planned on killing one of them, their future hadn't been a big concern.

Cyndi looked at Bethanee quizzically. "So what do you think will happen after that, after we let you bite one of us?" she asked Anton.

"Then I've got a drop of blood down my throat, you and your mom are fine, and I run home."

Cyndi glanced down for a second so Anton could not read the amused smile on her lips. Bethanee giggled.

"What?" Anton said, though in his heart was dark and growing suspicion.

"Why do you think we'd let you go?" Cyndi said, not hiding her smirk now. "You did your best to kill us. Now it's our turn." She stepped aside, revealing the stocks. "Just put your head in the middle hole," she advised Anton. "And we'll go from there."

"But you know me," Anton said. "You know my mom. You know my sister."

He was still boy enough to think that would make a different to the two lovely blondes. He was beginning to see that they were much, much more.

Cyndi jabbed with her shotgun, and he shuffled over to the stocks (what the fuck did they want stocks for? Who kept stocks in their basements?). His leg was healing, but it was very sore. Just to keep the girls calm while he figured out what argument to use, because after all they had to let him go, Anton complied. Stocks, he discovered, are very uncomfortable.

"So, you have to change into a wolf at the full moon, huh?" Cyndi said.

"Yeah, that's true," Anton said, though the angle of his neck made conversation awkward. "This was the first time. The snow was so heavy, I couldn't catch a rabbit."

"Oh, so rabbit was first choice and we were second," Bethanee said, and since he was sure she was teasing, Anton made himself chuckle.

Even holding a shotgun, Cyndi was standing with her shoulders back, chest out, right foot slightly in front of her left…a pageant pose. It was reassuring to Anton.

"You know what would be fun?" Cyndi asked her sister. "What if we could keep him alive for a month, and get Marcia down here? Let him loose on her?"

"That *would* be funny," Bethanee said. "Of course, cleanup would be a bitch."

"Language," Helen Dismuss said gently, from halfway down the stairs. "I've been on the phone with your father, girls, and he's so proud of you."

Cyndi kicked an empty flower pot over to the stocks, which were positioned in the middle of the room. "There, in case you need to pee," she said to Anton.

"When are you going to let me go?"

"Oh! That would be—never!" Bethanee said, and giggled. "Sooner or later, you'll join a couple of people we know." And the girls laughed, while Helen shook her head in gentle admonishment.

And the three women trooped up the stairs, leaving the light on...at least for a while. The naked boy thought about the snow covering up his tracks and his scent, wondered when his mother would begin searching for him, wondered if the snow would wipe out all trace of his scent. He wondered if she would find the bodies of the missing couple from last winter, the ones buried upslope of the Dismuss house. He wondered what would happen to his mother when her nose led her to this house.

Then all he had to do was look at the glittering crowns.

Doll's Eyes

TIM BRYANT

"I'm interested in paying you to have sexual relations with my wife," you said, following the script as if you were interviewing someone to work at Nourish Plant Nursery, the business you've owned and operated for the past five years. You'd been through this enough times that it didn't faze you, and you were almost taken aback when the man sitting across from you flinched. You were both sitting in your dining room, a room off of the kitchen that held a heavy oak table that, until recently, had seen little action. The walls were white and mostly bare, except for a clock that you could hear ticking. It was a clock that Rachel bought on your honeymoon, which means it had been ticking away there for just over nine years. Rachel was upstairs in bed, flipping through channels on a TV that you could also hear faintly. You wondered if the man across the table realized how close she was, hovering just above the two of you.

"You wanna videotape it or something?" the man said. He was just a little bigger than you, maybe six foot, and built like a Mack truck, which was fitting. He was a long haul driver from halfway across the country—you think he said Iowa or maybe it was Ohio—and he had lumbered right into your path at the truck stop on the interstate just west of town. He seemed to fit just about every requirement on your list.

"It's not like that," you said. "We have legitimate reasons."

You made no show of sharing any of them. They were none of his damn business. You wanted him for one thing, and one thing only. To produce the healthy son that you could not, and to do it quickly and quietly. If he passed your screening process, he would do his job and be on his way, never to return. Fuck 'em and forget 'em. What more could the guy ask for?

It's not that you didn't try. God knows you did. Six unborn fetuses over the course of the past four years. Almost as many fertility doctors, who poked and prodded and pointed the finger at you. You kept it up as long as you could, until you could scarcely look at yourself in the mirror in the mornings. Each one of the babies had been fawned over, prepared for, little creatures to carry your name and standing further up the ladder, another generation along the chain. It's what you told Rachel, and though she might have known better, she also knew not to push things.

Truth is, it ate at you, the way one doctor had looked at your wife, shaking his head as if to suggest that she could have done better for herself or, worse, that he could have done your job better. The way the one down in Metarie, the asshole who had his own helicopter, had cracked the joke that you were supposed to be a seed man. Each of the babies had arrived much too early, monstrous things that mocked you and your imperfections. The more you were told to relax, the more stressed you became. You had, at last, looked away from yourself completely and had begun the process of finding a suitable replacement. One that no one but you and Rachel would ever need know about.

"I do want to be there," you said. At first, you had been ambivalent about that part and embarrassed to admit it. Made a big play that it was only for Rachel's protection. After a couple of tries which didn't take, you had decided that you should at least pretend to enjoy it as much as Rachel did.

The Nourish Parrish Sheriff's Department was making its second trip to your front door, and the deputy didn't appear happy to be back.

"Mr. Creach, you have just got to do something about these goddamn plants in your yard," he said. "We've had two more complaints about neighborhood dogs getting into them and getting sick. Dr. Donnel down at West Street Vet says you've already killed one of 'em."

"I won the Best Kept Yard award from the Civic Club two years in a row," you said.

You shut the door behind you and walked out into the bright day. The manicured front yard gleamed green under a series of strategically placed mimosa trees, and its coolness on your bare feet was stark contrast to the heat rising from your collar.

"They're supposed to keep their goddam dogs on a leash, you know," you said to the deputy, who was walking around to the side of your house, swinging a flashlight as if it weren't ten o'clock in the morning. Damn neighborhood regulations only seemed to work against you. People didn't like you. They were jealous. You wondered how close the deputy was to using the flashlight against your skull.

"Those plants are taking over your yard," the deputy said, "and, from what I hear, they're straight poison to dog and man alike. I might be willing to look the other way, but you get some kid out here, you gonna wind up in trouble like you ain't never seen. You don't get out here and dig 'em up, I'm gonna have to send someone out to do it myself."

You knew that, whatever happened, you could not dig up the plants. "I'll do it tonight," you said.

You made a living with your hands, digging in dirt, digging in books, learning everything you could about plant science, botany and arboriculture. You got your PhD in horticultural science from LSU and had run your own retail plant nursery, specializing in native Louisiana plants and seeds. You hadn't become wealthy, but you paid your bills, had a nice home in a newly built subdivision and could afford two or three vacations per year. You enjoyed your work and were proud of the repeat clientele you had managed to build up.

Doll's Eyes. You recognized the plant that sprung up in your back yard, in that area between the back corner where the lawn equipment was stored and the small green house which had the tomatoes, peppers, cucumbers and aubergines that you loved on one side, and Rachel's geraniums, poinsettias, and celosias on the other. The damn things sprung up and bloomed into clusters of white berries. Each berry had a single dark spot, a feature reminiscent of porcelain doll's eyes, hanging on blood red stems like raw optic nerves. You shuddered to look at them.

There in that empty space, midway across the yard, where the grass always grew sparsely due to rain water washing it down the gentle slope toward the whitewash fence that marked the property line, you'd dug the very first hole. You'd dropped the baby, the fetus, in, almost as if you were planting its little body by moonlight. You'd stopped to remember the Farmer's Almanac that hung on the nail on the wall in your grandparent's little farmhouse kitchen. How your grandfather had always checked its Astrological Timetable before doing planting of any kind. You wondered what the Farmer's Almanac would have said about what you were doing on that particular night. What your grandfather might have said.

You packed the red clay down tight and then added topsoil to blend it in with the surrounding area. Then, standing directly over the spot where the eyeless little form shrank into the earth, as if it were returning to its natural mother, you did a little dance. Not a ceremonial dance, for you saw no reason for ceremony, but you felt like some Native American Indian, dancing from one foot to the other, all in an effort to pack the earth down tight, where no animals would come sniffing around and cause trouble.

You wondered how soon the Doll's Eyes had begun to grow out of the spot. You had stood in the kitchen window, within easy view of it, over the course of four or five days, but you could never bring yourself to look up from the dishes to see the little piece of ground. By the time you finally looked, the plant was a good foot and a half high. You knew it was growing fast. That wasn't all you knew.

Rachel had had the miscarriage almost five months into the pregnancy. You wanted a son. Of course, a girl would have been fine too, and that first baby had been a girl. Not fully formed at all, it looked more like an animal to you, a fact that made a difficult situation easier. Most of all, it reminded you of squirrel hunting as a young boy. You could still see the skinned squirrels that you and your grandfather had piled up on the old metal table in the shed behind their old farmhouse when you were a child. How old had you been then? Ten, twelve? The twenty years between hadn't pushed the memory out of your mind. But the body you wrapped in an old oil-spattered towel from the garage had definitely been a girl. That you would also never forget.

Rachel had sunk into a depression immediately after the episode. Not that there was any huge difference. She was always moody; melancholic, as she called it. She had gotten to the point where she lived her life inside the walls of your home. It was a good home, in a good neighborhood, she said. She was happy enough to stay there the rest of her life. And it seemed she meant it literally.

Looking back, you now wonder if you had become so desperate at feeling those walls closing in, your life slowly slipping away, that you had forced the issue of having a child. You'd already tried the extramarital affair route, with the college girl who worked part time for you at the nursery. It had gone nowhere, with you too timid to come out and announce your intentions and her too unworldly to have taken you up on the idea anyway.

Only weeks after the first miscarriage, you talked Rachel into trying again. With the second pregnancy, everything seemed more normal. Rachel wasn't as worried and had actually gotten out and sat on the deck, sipping sweet tea and watching as you did landscaping work in the yard, tending it all the way back to where the tall oaks took over, with their Spanish moss and singing cicadas. She lost the second child, another girl, in the sixteenth week of pregnancy. That one you talked to as you shoveled a new hole three or four feet from the first, probably because Rachel and you had already picked out a name. *Belinda, why the fuck did you leave me here?* you said. *You never even grew eyes to see this dreary fucking world.*

Once again, you finished your work and slid Belinda down into the cold, damp ground. This time, when you danced your dance, you sang a soft song under a cloudy, moonless sky; a song that sounded like a baby's cry. You heard coyotes howl along in the neighboring woods and felt as if they understood something that even Rachel did not.

In the weeks to come, the plant nursery fell into a long lull. Seasons began to turn, and you were too tired to keep up. The college girl graduated and moved out of state, and instead of hiring a replacement, you let the store level off to a point where you could handle things with no assistance. You didn't always return calls from perspective new clients. You turned down business opportunities. You started thinking about selling the whole enchilada and moving. Maybe with Rachel, maybe not.

Rachel went through three more pregnancies. There was a boy, born dead in the sixth month of gestation. Again, his little body had all the features that you had. He was Gary Creach, Jr. but with no eyes and no heart working inside of him. And by the time you buried the fourth, another boy, the space in the backyard was starting to get overgrown. You stopped giving them names.

Of all the goddam things, you had said, shaking your head in disbelief, after the second, third and fourth plant sprang up. Doll's Eyes climbed out of the ground everywhere, fanning out just above your secret spots and making a claim for that corner of the yard. It was if they were watching you. You dreamed about them at night, couldn't get them out of your mind in the day. You brought out your old school books and researched them again and again. Got to know them. They were indigenous to North America. A member of the Ranunculaceae family. Flowered in the summer. Grew one to two feet tall. They were poisonous. Very poisonous.

Finally, you had taken the gardening shears and cut them all level with the ground, bagged them up and tossed them into the trash. Two days later, they were back in twice the numbers. Each time you got rid of them, they doubled up and reappeared. Each night, after Rachel went to bed, you would step out onto the patio. It began to feel like a stare down. Then the patch of plants began to offer up prizes. A nutria, then another. A rattlesnake. And then the neighbor's Jack Russell terrier. You diligently disposed of each, wrapping the dog in a tarp and carting it down to the twenty-four hour Stop 'n' Go, heaving it over the side of the dumpster when no one was looking. Of course, after the Sheriff's Department got involved, it became obvious what you had to do. And you knew you couldn't slip around at night to do it. You would have to see what you were doing.

On a hot and humid July morning, you half-heartedly consulted the Almanac, which told you nothing, then dragged a shovel out of the shed and across the lawn to the wild and wooly patch of Doll's Eyes. Again, they seemed to watch, following you as you approached them. Like they knew what was coming. It took almost an hour to cut through them all, and when you finished, the heap of eyes was waist high. Then you began to dig.

Roots had taken over, pushing the red clay out of the way as they twisted and turned beneath the top soil. You had to bring out a hatchet and a pruning saw, and on you worked, until the sun was directly above you and steaming down. You had been steeling yourself for what lay beyond the roots, but the babies confounded you, fusing with the roots of the plants to become one great tangled mass, dug deep into the earth on one side and reaching up and out on the other. Roots grew directly out of eye sockets. Joints twisted in nonhuman ways. Epidermis mutated. As you hacked through limbs and branches, they seemed to flex and recoil. You did the same.

Finally, you picked up the shovel and used brute force, bringing it straight up over your head until its blade came down across your lower back. You slammed it into the hole before you, never realizing that your back had split open and dripped bloody sweat. After a minute of aimless barrage, you fell in a heap at the side of the grave, your upper torso dangling into it like a lure in the mouth of a dry fish.

The session with the truck driver had been a success, and you and Rachel busied yourselves with the daily minutiae once again. You never discussed the man or the night that produced the new baby. This time there was a palpable difference. For all of your fretting about your lack of success in the babymaking department, you were also happy to know that the scheme had worked. You began to spend more time with the business again. You started taking applications for help in the coming fall.

Then the unthinkable happened. Three months into the pregnancy, Rachel awakened in the middle of the night in a cold sweat, shaking like a wet dog. The bloody sheet welcomed the arrival of the seventh child, another boy. Another fetus with no eyes.

"It was your fucking fault all along," you screamed at Rachel as she lay on the bathroom floor, sick at one end and bleeding a trail from the other. "You're the one who's to blame."

You felt absolved, but it brought no peace. A darkness rose up inside of you, a darkness that Rachel recognized.

"I will never have a child who has to look at you and call you a father," she said. The way she looked up at you made you want to rip her eyes from their sockets. She was pitiful, and yet you felt no pity. Her words had no air in them, no real conviction behind them. They sounded like dying words to you. The kind of thing you would say when you knew your time was up and any blowback was inconsequential. You backhanded her across the mouth hard enough to scatter teeth across the floor like dice on a craps table.

By the time you made it down the stairs, through the kitchen and the dining room, onto the back patio, you weren't surprised to hear the Sheriff's Department roll up the driveway. At this point, you thought, nothing much would surprise you. And, anyway, it was your own damn fault for not thinking to take Rachel's cell from her while she was down. You had it coming.

You slipped to the corner of the house and thought momentarily about trying to make a break to the back of the greenhouse. Where would you go from there though? Over the fence into another yard that might have looked identical to an untrained eye but without the plants, the careful cultivation, the lifetime of work. It flit through your mind that the greenhouse was divided between your stuff and Rachel's, just as everything in the house was, just as your lives were. If your wedding day had been about uniting, then every day since had been about dividing back up again. This was what it had all been leading to. You slinked down behind the crop of Doll's Eyes, which seemed plenty thick enough to hide you from whoever might be coming. You glanced down and those big eyes seemed to be saying, *come down here, come down here with us. We will protect you.* And you began to dig.

You feel bigger than ever before. You feel powerful. When you breathe, everything breathes around you, through you. You watch with new and infinite eyes and bide your time. You watch a man who is not a Sheriff's deputy walk in to your back door like he knows exactly where he's going, and you grow. You watch an ambulance haul Rachel away, with the man standing over her, rushing the paramedics along the way. You recognize the man as the truck driver from Ohio. The ground grumbles, you twist and you grow. You grow hungry, and you feed on mice. Squirrels. A dog. Later—maybe much later—you watch the man sit on your deck with Rachel and laugh over glasses of wine. You hear him talk about changing the whole backyard, about tearing the greenhouse down and replacing it with a pool, a Jacuzzi even. You watch the way you watched them in the bedroom upstairs. Your seed spills into the soil, and you grow. The cicadas scream relentlessly in your ears. You grow and you grow, you twist yourself into knots and you wait for the man to come close.

Bloaters

NEAL BARRETT, JR.

Juker's Road past Brunkit half a mile, sharp turn left where every cop in town's on hand plus Pucker, Hix, Stix from the Highway Patrol, Sheriff Huckin and his re-tarded (wups) intellectually im-paired deputy Snum. Cars jammed this way, cars jammed that, blue lights red lights headlights flash bringing spasms, seizures midnight fits to every epileptic for twenty miles around. Thirty-two radios barking, howling, hissing at one another while all these mothers from law and order stand staring in a ditch, three throwing up, two already down.

Officer Billy Kaup makes his way through the crowd with a lurch with a waddle with a stagger with a stomp, a perilous load for a *WALK-O* leg on sale at Bogger Drug, not truly built for 487 pounds of Oklahoma lard.

"Loo-tenut!" Billy shouts, straining to overcome the bluster, the chaos, the goddamn racket all around. "Loooo-tenut, over here! I'm right over—"

"Billy. Shut the fuck up."

Billy turned, looked into the barrel of Lieutenant Dark's Czech KORO BRNO .38 revolver with the long barrel, solid steel frame, special ergonomic hardwood grip. He knew all this by heart. Dark muttered them every minute of the day, even in his sleep.

"Sorry, sir, hard to see a thing in all this darn hubbub, you know? Figured you was somewhere, sir, knew you'd want to get on the scene, find all the facts, put your ex-pertise to work soon as you—huh?"

Dark was already out of sight, heading through the crowd, taking his time, as Dark ever did. No one got in the way of Police Lieutenant Cheyenne Dark. Last of an unbroken line of a famed Lakota-Sioux beauty and a Buffalo Soldier, Dark was a big man with night-black hair flowing down his broad shoulders, solid granite chin, nose harking back to the pharaohs, eyes that scared birds off the trees. His skin was the color of road tar, hot and shiny just before it hits the street. He wondered if he'd ever shoot Billy or just pretend. He could tolerate whites, but Billy

Kaup was an exception to the rule. Too fat to eat, a habit he'd never acquired, and too damn heavy to carry off.

Cop folk scattered, jumped aside to let Dark through. Dark took them in, named them in his head: Good. Rotten. Nowhere in between.

"Never seen nothin' like it," said Doc Josack. "Not in all my years in the healin' pro-fession."

"Damn certain," said someone in the crowd.

"Sure as hell not," said another.

Dark stepped up, looked where the flashlights went. Ditch full of weeds. Beer cans. Butts. Bananas. Pages from *Yummy Boobs*, Baby shoes and socks. Everything soaked from rain the night before. Condoms, floating about like sailors lost at sea. And, as the main attraction, a man some six-feet long. Skin slightly worse than a Fifth Degree burn. Head, belly, every limb swollen the size of basketballs. Not the little ones, regulation size.

"How you figure it, sir?" asked Mackie "suckup" Monty from the crowd.

"Shit. Fella got bit by the biggest damn skeeter in the world," said Officer Tack.

"Lennie, don't open your mouth till Christmas," said Dark.

Billy Kaup threw up, followed by Highway Jockey Stix. Dark gave them both a dreadful eye. "Anyone know this dude? Look like he come from 'round here?"

"Looks some like Troy Rake," said Sherrif Huckin. "Running Back for the Voles. Got that leg broke in '94 'gainst the Mahookie Mice."

"Did," said Deputy Snum. "Seen him do it I did."

"Could well be," said Doc Josak real quick. Didn't like at all they were drifting into body talk.

"Spite of the victim's condition, you can see that kinda twisty scar about the knee. Patched that leg myself."

Doc bent down, probed the late star's knee. "Think we got a medical Eye-D here, fellows."

"How's that?" said Dark.

"What I'm thinking, is," Doc said, reaching in his jacket, coming up with something shiny bright, "Let's just see what we got here, boys..."

"*Doc-Doc!*" Dark went at him fast.

"*GODDAMN IT DOC DON'T DO THAT!*"

Troy Rake exploded. Blood lifted lawmen. Tossed them about, slammed them into trees sent them sprawling all about. Finally, the horrid geyser paused, knew what ought to come next, broke into a roaring red tsunami that buried every cop, every car, every leech every louse every possum every pig for half a mile around.

Lieutenant Cheyenne Dark took a sacred Lakota-Sioux vow to burn, flay, slowly dismember Doc Josak soon as he could find another fucker dumb enough to live in Pluck City, Oklahoma.

Pluck City came to a halt some four miles out past Mom's Motel, (Whores R Us) Jimbo's Gas & Guns, the grave-yard and the dump. Melvy Geets' home was somewhat farther than that. Just passing by, you'd figure a whole trailer park from prehistoric times had fallen from the sky, jammed, crammed, huddled up tight, settled in to breed little Geets to loose upon the world.

Melvy, bald at 39, was Pop. Cele, fatter, somewhat younger, was Mom. Cerlew, Ribby and Node were blessings conceived by *Jug-Rite* wine. Mostly, the Geets slept in. Melvy was looking for a job, waiting for something right to come along: Billionaire, world president. The pay for either was fine, but he'd pass them both by for The Power to Cloud Girls' Minds.

Cele's back was acting up. She never rose till noon. The kids stayed home. The school board said they'd shoot them on sight if they ever came to class.

Everything was fine at the Geets' until 12:04 and the news. That's when they broke into *LUCY ALL NITE*. Melvy didn't have a fluff, didn't have a fleck atop his head, but all his body hair turned white.

Cele thought the Bog Lake Banshee had come to life again. She'd heard Melvy scream, heard him yell, heard him howl when he caught his parts in the zipper one time. Still, she'd never heard a sound like this. She backed against the wall as Melvy raced by, saw him disappear through trailer 22, bowling down the kids in Number 9. Heard him tumble down the stairs, heard a screech that sent every beetle, every rat, every roach fleeing through the walls.

Melvy had known what he'd find the instant he'd seen the news. He'd hoped, for an instant, he was having a stroke, losing his mind, anything but this. No such fucking luck. There was Daddy Gramps, lying peaceful in his bed.

Shrunk. Shriveled. Flat. Empty as a Safeway sack. Melvy felt the blood rise to his head. Felt the anger, felt the rage. Felt the fear he'd known when Freddy Frok knocked him cold in Seventh Grade.

"BASTARD! ASSHOLE! NO GOOD GODDAMN SON OF A BITCH!"

Melvy wanted to kill him right there. Should have before. Never did. Instead, he ran up the stairs. Grabbed the first kid he could find. CerlewRibbyNode. Whatever. Never could tell them apart. All looked exactly like Cele. Wasn't a Geets ever had six toes, ears like a cat. Grabbed one up, shook it till its tongue hung out.

"What did you do," he yelled, "Go to sleep? Play with yourself? Didn't fix him, just let him *go*? Didn't have *time* from doing nothing at all?"

Melvy shook whoever till it burst into tears. Cele stepped in, grabbed the child away.

"Just stop it, Melvy. It's over, hon. Nothing you can do about it now."

"Nothing? Can't do *nothing* now?" Melvy gave her a look that lifted her out of her shoes.

"What we can *do*, you stupid bitch, is start packing. Stuff we gotta have, nothing that we don't. We going, not coming back."

"Melvy—"

"Shut up. They'll know. They'll *all* know. Got their nose in everything. Cops, FBI. Fucking CIA. They'll sniff every corner, they'll know it was him."

"He's your Grandad, hon. Not mine."

Mervy reached for her neck. Cele screamed and ran, pushed the kids aside.

"You." Mervy glared at CerlewRibbyNode. "Feed the dogs and the cat. Shoot 'em outside. Man's running for his life don't need a bunch of pets..."

Mary Sue and Mary Jo hit Tulsa in the A.M., 1:49. Walked through the airport, wheelie-bags behind. Cute little bunnies, frisky little colts. Even at this godawful hour men were struck blind, stupefied, stunned by the sudden rush of unrequited lust. They were twins, breathtaking beauties with long, impossible legs, skirts so short you *knew* you could, you know, reach up there, just a few inches more... Firm little butts that jiggled with a rhythm of their own, tilty-perky-turned-up tits, *snooty* tits not for mortal man to know.

And, if you had time for faces at all, a fine Scandinavian nose, wide Italian lips, black, black espresso eyes from harems of the East. After they were gone, men said they could taste their presence in the air. Nearly all of them stopped somewhere for a drink.

Mary Sue liked big cars. Mary Jo rented a Honda no one would notice anywhere.

As they headed south on 75, another car followed, a 1958 Mercedes, Midnight Blue, in-line, 4-cylinder, ivory dash, interior unborn lamb. Driving this buggy was Johnny D. Pius, founder and minister of the Reborn Church of WAB, Wipe Out Bad, located south of Oak Ridge, Tennessee. The congregation had grown from only 32 "wipers" to 4,006, thanks to RENDER-TO, a PR firm that knew how to drag the mothers in.

"I'm flat *star-ving*," said Mary Sue. "I am so weak I can hardly keep my eyes open, Mary Jo."

"Close 'em. Nothing you need to see."

"I could drive. That'd keep me awake awhile."

Mary Jo moaned. "I'd as soon give the wheel to a monkey on speed. Shit, girl. Don't even think about it."

"I could fucking die."

"You know better than that."

"Well I *feel* like I could, all right?"

"We'll eat when we get there."

"When's that?"

"You'll know when we do."

"Yeah, how?"

"I'll stop the car and say 'Here we are, Mary Jo.'"

"You think that's cute? It's not cute at all..."

Mary Jo felt a craving too, but greater problems were on her mind. She had that all too familiar feeling, that growing sense of peril, the insight common to her kind that said danger was coming closer with every mile. And, along with this apprehension, the puzzling notion that a wondrous chance to sate her hunger was also up ahead. She paid no heed to the latter. What happened was real or her tummy calling its need.

She'd come to Oklahoma because the feeling of disaster was too strong to ignore. She knew, even then, that another entity was aware of this imminent event. And, the moment their plane set down, that presence struck her like a fiery stroke inside her head. Now, on the road, whatever it was followed close behind. This didn't seem to bother Mary Sue. In some ways, Mary Sue lacked the talents of her sister. In others, she scared the crap out of Mary Jo.

"I'm staying," said Cele. "This is mah home, Mervy. I am not leavin' every time you get all worked up."

"Worked up?" Mervy glared. Wondered, not the first time, how Miss Pin Oak, 1993, had somehow changed into the Dough Boy's daughter in a few short years.

"Worked up, Cele, is trying to save our lovely family from on-coming disaster. We got to stick together. I cannot handle all this by my fucking self."

"We could, you know, kinda leave him, hon."

Mervy slapped her, missed by a mile. Always did. Cele bawled. Mervy stomped off, rushed through Number 9. Down the stairs to chaos below. The smell was awful. A stink, a stench, an odor foul beyond compare. A reek bad enough to gag a goat. And, the ever-present gag of pinky-mist in the air.

Mervy yelled at Node. Words drowned out by the hum by the thrum by the slam of wheezy pumps, by the thrash of old engines, the clunk of pounding gears.

Ribby was somewhere, Cerlew at the pumps.

Little bastards, if they'd been on watch we wouldn't be in this mess...

Mervy stepped down in the pit, studied Daddy Bob. He was deflating some, not near fast enough. Blood was rushing out of his great enormous heart, pulsing like an Oklahoma well. Pumps sucking fast, moving the stuff through the network of pipes that led to the bottomless pit in Mervy's backyard. Mervy knew it didn't end. If it did, the whole county would be foot-deep red by now.

"How you feeling, Daddy Bob?" asked Mervy.

"How you think I am? I'm fine as ever, boy."

"Well ever'thing's not so fine, case you didn't know. You got us on the goddamn tube with that stunt up Juker's Road."

"Sorry. Man can't help doin' what a man's got to do."

"Yeah, well. It was the kids messed up. I ought to tell you that."

"Who'd I bite, anyone we know?"

"They're saying on morning news might've been Troy Rake, running back for the Voles."

"Kid broke his leg in '94 'gainst the Mahookie Mice. Damn. Sorry 'bout that."

"Thing is, Daddy Bob, we got to re-locate. Packing up now. Want to get moving 'fore the law starts nosing around."

Daddy Bob frowned. "Law don't have no reason to nose around. Haven't done nothing wrong. Not till now."

"See, that's the thing. Now they do got something. Gonna start looking around, anyone's not their kind, folks got a lifestyle don't fit your av'rage norm. People got a different kind of cast."

"Guess that'd be us."

"Figure it'd be."

Daddy Bob suddenly looked alarmed. "You got to do it, boy. Get the family safe somehow. I don't mind too much. I had a long an' active life."

Melvy saw Daddy Bob was draining fine, smoothing down to a semi-normal form.

"Jesus," Melvy said, "don't even think about that. Got it figured real good. Ordered me a pump, oughta be here now. Thing'll fit right in the van. Got your air-powered double-diaphragm, self-priming, trouble-free guar-an-tee. Got your stainless steel frame. You'll be fine as you can be."

Daddy Bob's face was too flat to cry. "None of this is your fault, boy. None of it's mine. What I got, it's in the family jeans. Nothing you can do about that."

"Just settle down, all right?"

"No, it'd be best to leave me, son. I can handle that."

"And when the cops come 'round, find you still here?"

"Shoot, like I said, I truly don't want to go anywhere but here."

"Well, thing is, I truly don't want to go to the fucking penitentiary. Just bleed, old man, and do what you're told..."

Cheyenne Dark didn't care much for folks of any sort, starting with whites and working down. The blacks, Asians, Mexicans and ay-rabs he knew didn't show him much at all. And, if there was anything that brought his inbred savagery alive it was assholes from papers, magazines and TV shows descending on the town. Once the business on Jukers got out the crazies were swarming like rats on cheese. On top of that, Captain Eddie D. Smitt was off on semi-permanent leave at the East Tulsa Home for the Silly and Inept. If something got done or didn't, it was up to C. Dark. Shit. What was he doing here anyway? All he could figure was the miserable pay and nothing to do for 90 miles around.

One thing he liked was intimate lust with female women who shared his own desire. There were plenty of grown-up girls in Pluck City. Maybe two were pretty as Afghan hounds. Some of the ladies at Mom's (Whores R Us) would do fine. Trouble was, all those females lived right here, and he did too. You couldn't have a job and pussy too in a small Okie town.

It was on this thought that someone tapped upon his door. He didn't allow but one person the right to do that, and he told her to come on in.

"Lieutenant. Hope I didn't pick a bad time," she said.

Dark had to laugh. "You think of a good time 'round here and we'll have a parade, Ellie May."

Ellie May Stinte pulled up a chair, took out her famous Big Chief antique tablet and laid it in her lap. Ellie May was 86, overly slim, spry as a new-born colt. She liked to tell everyone the 80s were the new 90s, and she fully intended to stay and find out.

"I got NCIC, InterPol, every site on Crime you can pull up on the web. I mean, stuff you'd never figure, even if you knew where to look."

She pushed her glasses down her nose, started to read her notes. "Fourteen cases of inflationary deaths. That's the U.S.A. and everywhere else. Three in this country: Montana, Idaho, Louisiana. 1835-1946. Two in France. One in Spain. All the rest guess where: Romania. Eight cases there."

"What you figure that means?" asked Dark.

"Got no idea. You know when the first case was? October 6, 1742."

"Jesus."

"You know I don't care for that, Dark."

"Sorry. Not myself today."

"I figure you likely are. Don't let it happen again. Other seven cases: 1700s to 1901. We got us a weird one here, chief. And nothing I found gives a clue how this kind of thing comes about."

"They couldn't figure it in 300 years, don't guess we will either."

"Now I don't know that, Dark. We got ways now they didn't even have twenty, fifty years ago."

"Uh-huh. I hope you got a couple good ideas where to start. I'm feeling dumb right now, and—"

Billy Kaup burst through the door, stomping on one good limb, shakin' with his *WALK-O* on the other, near five-hundred weight of pure disaster on the run.

"God-*damnit*-Kaup!" Dark came out of his chair, fury in his eyes. Nothing bothered Ellie May Stinte, she didn't budge an inch.

"You better have some awful good reason for being in my office, or your sorry ass is on the street, boy!"

"Pardon the protrusion, Lootenant, I wouldn't invade your presence if it wasn't po-lice business, no sir, I would not do that," said Kaup. "I got somethin' of great import, I surely do."

"You got 'bout eight seconds to show it 'fore I put a ounce of lead through your fuckin' fat head. 'Scuse the language, Miss Stinte."

Officer Kaup slid aside, let somebody squeeze through. Somebody 'round seventy-two, 93 pounds, nothing on his head, white whiskers on his chin.

"Who the hell's this?" said Dark.

"Sir, this here's Pro-fessor-Doctor Wilhem Schongeharten-Schmidt, re-tired. Used to teach back east 'fore he settled here."

"Teach what?" asked Dark. He could hear the chaos, the blare of horns, the shouts of folk jamming the streets below.

"Sir, I do not know vhy I am here," the man said, in a tone some stronger than his size. "I haff done nothing. I do not know vhy I have been dragged to this place against my vhill."

Dark looked puzzled. "Why the hell is he here, Kaup?"

"Tell him what you told me," said Kaup.

"In my academic life, I haff been a scholar of legend and myth. Verevolfs, demons, suckers of blood. Other transformational effents."

Dark stood up straight. "And this has got something to do with what's going on here?"

Professor-Doctor Schmidt turned red. "No, it does not! I haff told this oberlehausengrater fool that myth is not ze same as truth. He vill not listen to me!"

"Begging your es-teemed pardon, sir," said Kaup. "You *told* me you'd hearda this stuff before. You've talked to other folks about it too."

Schmidt gave him a nasty look. "Of course I haff heard of dhiss thing. I haff heard of dragons, death dogs, devilcats and flying pigs. I haff teached these thing. I do not *believe* they are true." He glared at Kaup. "Only Ghestakerleben fools do that!"

"Listen, what's that mean," said Kaup, "that uh Ghe-what you call it."

Dark looked at Ellie May Stinte. The lady looked back. "You can say it," she said. "Just this once."

Dark nodded. "Get this motherfucking nazi asshole outa my sight. And I'll see you, Kaup, after you've shed about three-hundred pounds. Shouldn't be hard without six months pay."

"Sir—!" Kaup lost the power of speech, as he saw Dark's hand slide to his belt, saw his fingers touch the ergonomic grip of his famous revolver, the Czech KORO BRNO .38. Long Barrel. Sold steel frame. He flattened Professor-Doctor Schmidt on his way out the door.

////

At 3:32 A.M., Mary Jo checked into a bad motel some twenty-two miles from Pluck City. Her extraordinary senses told her the follower was there somewhere, but its presence promised no danger. Later, yes. Great danger indeed, when the purpose of her trip was revealed. Whatever that might be. Even Mary Sue was troubled, aware, though she lacked the great power of her twin.

Once inside, Mary Jo brought covers into the dank bathroom, forced sheets under the door, until the place was totally sealed from light. Then, along with Mary Sue, she drifted quickly into sleep. Daylight would come and go and blessed night would come again. Then, once more, the two would be safe in the realm where they belonged.

Night came early that time of the year. Mary Jo made certain the day had fled, then ventured out of the tiny bathroom, sat on the bed, turned on the tiny TV. Her heart near stopped. Which, of course, it simply couldn't do. It had come close twice, but that was long ago.

"Mary Sue, get your butt up here. Guess what we found, hon!"

Mary Sue flopped down at her side. Stared at the news, lovely mouth wide, eyes big as gold doubloons.

"Great Green Goats…I'm seeing what I see?"

"Sure as hell are."

"*Bloaters!* BLOATERS!"

Mary Jo laughed. "When did you last see one of those, sis?"

"Uh, October 6, 1742. We spent a week in Bicaz—On the Bistriti River…"

"Romania, right?"

"*Not* right, love. It was Moldavia then. Not till—"

Mary Jo gave her a hug. "Can't fool you. Nothing wrong with your memory, Mary Sue I swear."

"So I can eat now?"

"You surely can, dear. Son of a bitch. Bloaters! We have struck the mother lode, girl!"

When you can't have a really good meal, go with what you've got. Don't have a New York Strip, Bad Mac'll do fine. Mary Sue distracted a doc, two guards. Skimped around naked, fiddled with their heads. Mary Jo hit the blood room. Piled her goodies in a wheelchair out to the car. The guards, the doc, woke in good time. Marveled at the finest orgy they'd ever had.

Professor-Doktor Wilhelm Schongeharten-Schmidt never opened the door. Not ever. Many times, this practice had saved his life. Once, just south of Hagers Grove, Missouri, a fire of unknown origin gutted his house to the ground. Herr Doktor escaped with minor burns, but he *never* opened the door.

It was, then, to his great surprise and horror, to turn from his kitchen to find the man sitting in his best easy chair.

"DAHMT-DEHEISIN-FOKKER!" Schmidt shouted, leaping half a foot. "Who are you! Vhat are you dohing here! Ghet out! Ghetinzee OUT!"

"Take her easy now, friend. Ahm meanin' no harm. Just want to talk a spell."

"I don't know you, don't vhant to know you," said Schmidt, guessing how long it would take him to get to the poker by the fire.

The man was lean, pushing on scrawny, scraggy and gaunt. He wore old overalls, hightop kangaroos, circa 1902.

No shirt, no socks, country jaw and bushy beard, hair right out of a thrashing machine. Eyes the shade of water in the still of a swamp. The eyes scared the shit out of Professor-Doktor Schmidt.

"You'll excuse the in-trusion, sir," the man said. I don't mean to take up your time. I am Johnny D. Pius, founder and minister of the Reborn Church of WAB, that's Wipe Out Bad, south of Oak Ridge, Tennessee.

"Don't bother tellin' me who you are and ain't. We knowed about you some time. Know you're not into 'legend and myth' like you told that loon with one leg. You've dipped your toe into things inhuman more'n once, old man, nearly got it bit off."

Schmidt shook his head. "That iss not so! I haff never—"

Johnny Pius grinned. "Funny thing is, I come here chasin' a pair of en-tirely different frights. Then had me a talk with that gimp-legged tub works for the police. Found something I didn't know but you did."

Pius leaned forward in his chair. "Seems y'all got a *bloater* problem in town..."

Schmidt's face went white. "I told that fool such things vere foolish stories, nothing more!"

"But they ain't, are they? What I think, Doc, you got a special eye for the foul, for the damned, the unclean forces in the world."

"No," cried Schmidt, "This iss not zo. I do not deal with things that are not real!"

"*You mean like us?*"

Schmidt turned, felt his heart leap up into his throat.

They were there, WHOOSH! with the smell of sulphur and Chanel, sleek, shiny, naked as newborn babes, babes made to make a man cry, and a really big surprise.

"Well I'll be whacked," laughed Pius, slapping a hand across his knee, "lookie who we got here!"

"Figured it was someone like you," said Mary Jo, "I can smell a Bible thumper a mile away."

"Get OUT of here," shouted Schmidt, "I cannot abide creatures of dark demonic nature. Satan's whores!"

"Watch it, bud," said Mary Sue.

"Told everyone we weren't real," said Mary Jo, "didn't have baby Jesus here fooled.

Man knows his fiends when he sees 'em."

Mary Jo's bright blue eyes turned red. She pointed a sharp black nail at Schmidt. "What we were thinking, a fella like you'd have a sense about folks of unusual nature in town. Bet you got a good idea where a bloater-maker'd live around here."

"No. I know NUSSING!"

Schmidt went cold as Mary Sue cuddled up behind him, gave his neck a lick or two.

"God in Heaven!" cried Schmidt.

"Doubt he'll listen to you," Johnny Pius said.

"Can I have him, sis, just a little bit, huh?"

"A nip, honey, the man's good a bad ticker, I can hear it from here."

"Oh, all right. A nip it is, I guess."

Schmidt felt something cold, something sharp, something awful at the tender flesh of his throat.

"All right—all right!" he yelled, a scream so shrill it shattered a mirror in the hall. "*GEETS! GEETS! GEETS! Hell with 'em all!*"

"Guess we'll run into you later," Mary Jo told Pius. "Better read a verse or two, while you got the time."

"I shall pursue the cursed undead with all my—"

Something fluttered, something squeaked, something dark took wing and flew out the open door...

Dark woke from a dream, from a fancy, from an apparition of the night. He never answered the phone. Something told him this time he should.

"Some big hubbub out on Tenth, Lootenant," said Billy Kaup. "All kinda yellin,' screaming, all get-out. I'll get a squad and—"

"You get your big ass to bed, Kaup. I'm takin' this one myself!"

He was in his black-black shirt, his trousers and his boots, his Czech .38 as ever by his side. Racing down the street, waking up frogs, drunks, flea-bag dogs, hair climbing up the back of his neck. He raced through the night, big hands gripping the wheel with all his warrior might.

Chaos at the Geets. Cerlew-Node-Ribby squeezed in the van, huffing, puffing, wheezing in a frenzy, pumping in desperation to empty the flood, the rush, the gush, the torrent of blood bursting from Daddy Bob into the pipes that sent this red abomination into the alleys, into the streets.

Cele, screaming at Melvy, tossing bags in the van: shoes, socks, toasters and clocks.

"Cele, we are on the fucking run! We cannot TAKE all that shit!"

"You can just leave me here, Mervy, I am not goin' to leave my precious prosessions behind!"

"GodDAMNIT Cele—Huh? What? Whu? What the hell's that!"

Bats! Bats! Of a sudden they were flitting-flapping this way and that. Screeching, squealing, darting all about. Mervy grabbed a net Cele had sneaked in the van. Cele liked to eat little yellow butterflies.

"Son of a bitch," Mervy yelled, slashing his net about. "Get off my FACE, get outa here!"

The touch of silky locks, the scent of golden thighs. WHOOSH! Mary Sue, Mary Jo, naked, lovely, angels of the night.

"Lord help us," cried Cele, "we got young children here!"

Mervy gaped. Blinded by the glow, by the wonder of the sight.

"This'd be the Geets place, right?" said Mary Jo. "You folks goin' on a trip?"

Dark saw it coming, coming on fast. Big, hot lights in the mirror, then—"Shit!" All of a sudden it was past. He could scarcely believe his eyes. The thing was a monster. Big Mercedes, 1958, Midnight Blue, likely 4-cylinder, blasting through the night. He caught a look at the driver, then the big bullet was past. Country jaw, eyes like something out of the nuthouse for the night.

"Kaup," he shouted in his radio, "got a crazy on my tail. Big Mercedes, 1958. Find this fucker, lock him up tight."

"Will do, Lootenant. Found that Pro-fesser fella naked in a Safeway store. Said there was spiders in his head, couldn't get 'em out."

"Lock him up too. Get this fruitcake off my back, Kaup, get him off now!"

Dark slammed his foot down hard, caught the big car up ahead, did a special left-rear-fender-slap and ran him flying off the road.

"Do not fuck with me, white man," he muttered, and whined on ahead.

"Oh, *my*," cried Mary Sue, peeking in the van, "never seen anything yummy as this." She patted Node's head, gave him a little kiss. "Oh, hi, little boy, you're a cutie you are."

"Demon!" yelled Cele, "get away from my boy!"

Mervy felt a knot rise up in his throat and everywhere else. "You'll, uh—have to get outa here. We're in some hurry an' we got no truck with your kind."

Mary Sue giggled. "Don't got a truck, hon, got a van. Isn't he something, love? What I think—"

"Hold it, sis," said Mary Jo, "trouble on the way."

"I *hear* him," said Mary Sue, sniffing the air, wetting her crimson lips. "What a nice man. Smells like a big ol' Injun to me!"

Dark came over the hill, slammed on the brakes, nearly rammed an eighty-six rusted out van.

"What the *hell* is goin' on here? Who are—"

Dark froze. Couldn't breathe, couldn't move. Couldn't recall his name. Oh, lord they were soft, lovely, slick as otters, bare as baby butts, the very best dream he'd never had, the very finest sight he'd never seen. They were everything there wasn't in Pluck fucking City, Oklahoma—housewives, whores, hags in rubber shoes. They were all he'd ever wanted—and *what were they DOING out here...?*

Dark slid out, planted his boots on the ground.

"Well hey, what's up, big man?" Mary Sue did a bump, did a grind, did something naughty, something plain obscene.

"Don't know what you ladies are up to," said Dark, "you're both real fine but you can't do that out here. You—Huh? Who the hell you supposed to be?"

"Mervy D. Geets," Mervy said, "ain't done a thing to bring the law."

"We'll see you did or not. This your vehicle? You got a license, friend?"

"Just like ever'body else. You got no right to—"

Mervy's words were lost as a rattle, as a roar filled the night, shook the van on its wheels.

"What's that, what you got in there?" Dark sniffed, as a terrible odor filled the air...

Then, in a second, maybe half of that, last night's supper started climbing up his throat. Football star...guy in a ditch...all swole up, red shit flying everywhere... Dark went low, drew his big Czech gun, aimed it at Mervy Geets' head.

"Ever'body, hands up high, don't give me no trouble, do it now!"

"Hey, *you*," said Mary Jo, "lookie here, pal!"

"Huh?"

A lovely foot hit Dark in the middle, sent him flying, sent him sprawling to the ground.

"Ribby, hit it—Now!" Melvy yelled.

A door slammed shut, the van roared to life. Dark tried to pick himself up. A rush of wet-sticky-awful-stuff nailed him down again.

Dark gagged, pulled himself up, slid into the car.

PLUSHA! PLUSHA! PLUSH! Arterial disorder in the thirty-third degree hit the windshield with a whack. Dark turned on the wipers. Got a quick look before they ripped their roots and tore away. The van was fading fast, nearly out of sight.

"All units," Dark shouted in his obsolete cop radio, "Get your butts outa here, black fucking van, no plates, down Ragger Road, left on the pike. Get movin' now!"

"Out right *now*," howled Cele, "we got chil'ren in here!"

Mary Jo pushed her gently aside. "Mister whatever, you don't want us to go. That two-bit pump, it's not going to last. Me and Mary Sue, we can handle your excess fine. We drain, no pain. Deal or what? Like the misses says, you got a family here. That cop brings you down, you're going away for hard time."

Mervy shook his head. "Damn, honey, this pile of crap won't make it out of town."

Mary Jo smiled. "Hey, we can fix that."

Drawing her sister close, she stared past Cerlew, Ribby and Node, pressed her hands against the windshield, made a funny sound. Mervy felt dizzy, thought he'd be sick.

Something bright and shiny lit up the night.

"Lordy, what's that!" Mervy said.

"That's a Veil of Unreason," Mary Sue said. "Neat, huh?"

"Our kind of folk, we've got shit people never seen," said Mary Jo. "We're going to be just fine."

"We're God-fearin Christians," wailed Cele. "We don't want your kind here!"

"Can it," said Mervy. "See you got anything to drink back there."

Dark saw the van far off, saw the bright funny light. Somehow, the road up ahead didn't look like Oklahoma anymore.

"Kaup," he said, flipping on his radio, "Tell Captain Eddie D. Smitt, he gets outa the loony bin, I'm taking perma-nent leave. Tell him I'm sick of this job, sick of ugly women, sick of this goddamn town. Over and out, lard butt, have a good time."

"Lootenant!—"

Cheyenne Dark cut him off. He wondered why he hadn't thought sooner, how pretty and fine the girls were up in Lakota Sioux land. Figured it was way past time he had a look again...

Detritus

CHET WILLIAMSON

He'd become aware over the past few days that he was sharing his room with a disturbing amount of dead tissue. The realization had started the first day, with his flaking scalp, but it was on the second night in the hotel that he saw the hairs on the wall of the bathroom, eye level as he took his shower.

Keene had been mentally exhausted from another day of doing nothing but staring at the nearly blank screen of his laptop, waiting for words to come, waiting for that *one* word to bear fruit.

It was, he recalled, his wife's idea for him to get away, to force a change of scene so that he could write. He hadn't published anything in years, and his department chair had suggested in too obvious tones that it might be time for the college's poetry professor to actually write some poetry again.

The evening after that confrontation, he'd told his wife that he was afraid the well had run dry, and that when he *did* get an idea for a poem, it seemed trivial, an unworthy subject to write about, or dealt with an emotion or situation he had treated previously in verse when he was younger, his mind sharper, more vicious and intent. Get away, he'd heard her say. Go to a strange town, somewhere he'd never been, and where he knew no one. He could hole up in a hotel, walk around town, talk to people he'd never met, find what the poet Richard Hugo, under whom he'd once studied, called "the triggering town," and let it trigger his own creativity.

It seemed a good idea. Whenever they'd traveled, Keene had always brought something back—memories, sensations, emotions—that he'd been able to transmute into words. He asked her where she'd like to go, and she demurred, saying nothing, which he interpreted to mean that this should be *his* trip, that he should go alone, with no companion and no goal other than changing his scene, allowing whatever muse might be given rein to guide him in whatever way possible, without her intrusion.

The thought of being alone in a strange place was in itself enough to spur his imagination, and he set himself to the pleasant task of finding somewhere in the country to which he might retreat for two or three weeks. It would have to be now, for he was teaching no sessions this summer. And it would have to be a place that was completely unlike his native New England, an *orbis novus* in which he would be alien.

That left out the northwest. He'd been to California too many times, and the desert southwest as well. The South would be simmering in summer, and at any rate he had a natural political and philosophical antipathy to everything from the Mason-Dixon Line down to Florida. The Midwest he saw as an unending flatness, devoid of interest. And then he thought of Texas.

Keene had loved westerns when he was a kid, and he had never been to Texas, not once. He went online and started educating himself about the state. On the map, West Texas looked frighteningly open, mile upon mile without a town, and he kept picturing desert wastes, but without the awe-inspiring rock formations that the high desert of Arizona and Utah boasted. He looked toward the east then, toward the Louisiana line, and his eye fell upon the name of a town that he recognized, just north of Lufkin.

He recalled the name, Nacogdoches, because it was so distinctive, a Spanish name, he assumed. He had first become aware of it when another professor had introduced him to the work of an author who lived there, not a poet, but a genre writer who nonetheless had a vivid and distinctive regional voice, and whose work was even more popular in certain European countries than in America. He'd read some of the writer's short stories and two of his novels, both set in East Texas during the 1930s, and was charmed by the poetry he found lodged in the frequently crude language. Perhaps, he thought, if Nacogdoches could so sweeten the prose of a writer of tough-guy and horrific fiction, some of its poetry would rub off on him.

He found the town's website, and was surprised to learn that it was the oldest town in Texas, and had begun as a Spanish colonial outpost. Within an hour, he had made a reservation for a two-week stay at the Hotel Nacogdoches, a downtown establishment which had been built in the early 1900s on the site of a far older inn on the *El Camino Real,* which passed through the town.

When Keene told his wife of his chosen location, her reaction was so oblivious that he didn't even ask if she was sure she didn't want to come with him. He was certain she would say she didn't.

The flight from Boston to Houston was grueling. He was in the middle seat of the back row, flanked by a businessman who had his laptop and what appeared a month's worth of papers spread out in thick clumps over his tray table, and a rotund Indian man, fifteen per cent of whose bulk involuntarily intruded into Keene's already confining space. Not a word was spoken by any of them the entire flight, not even at the end, when rough skies took their toll upon the Indian, and he vomited into his airsickness bag. The businessman, one body width away, ignored it, but Keene silently handed the Indian the bag from his own seatback pocket. The Indian nodded thanks, and, a moment later, used that bag as well.

At least, Keene observed after the long shuffle off the plane and onto the jetway, no stray gobs of vomit had gotten on him. His rental car was waiting for him, and, after waiting for the GPS to get its bearings, he started driving north on 59.

The day was lovely, though hot, and the kind of puffy white clouds featured in so many John Ford westerns floated in the blue sky. Off to the west, Keene saw what looked like a dark thunderhead, but he would learn later that it was the smoke from a series of wildfires that had been plaguing East Texas. The area had had no rain in weeks, and the prairies and forests, of which there were a surprising number, were tinderboxes.

As he neared Nacogdoches, Keene pressed a button on the GPS to raise the volume of the robotic voice, and as he brought his hand back to the steering wheel, he found that something small and dark clung to his finger. It seemed to be a dried bit of detritus, like something one might pluck from one's nostril.

With a soft hiss of revulsion, he flicked it down onto the floor, on the passenger side, where he wouldn't have to step on it. God, didn't they clean the cars when they got them ready for the next driver? Someone had been digging in their nose or ears or who knew where else, and then used the GPS button, leaving whatever was on their finger for him to touch. Disgusting.

He looked with suspicion at the steering wheel that he'd been holding for the past two hours, then steered with his left hand as he rubbed his thumb over the fingers of his right. He increased the pressure and saw small gray fragments form, thin strands of dirt and tissue made from the stuff on the steering wheel that had adhered to his hand. He slid his fingertips hard across the leather that sheathed the wheel and felt what had been clinging to it peel off and cling instead to his flesh.

He voiced another brief sound of disgust and wiped his hand on the passenger seat, looked at it, and drove on. His hands sat on the steering wheel gingerly, and when they started to sweat, even a little, he wiped them on the cloth of the passenger seat.

Nacogdoches came upon him slowly in a string of strip malls that little prepared him for the downtown area. In spite of his knowledge of its history, its quaintness surprised him. The buildings appeared old, almost in places like a wild west town in the movies, with the occasional false front at the top. Many of the streets were red brick, and the sidewalks were frequently disjointed, the separate blocks several inches above and below each other, as if from an earthquake, and Keene wondered if they simply followed the levels of earlier board sidewalks for some reason.

The hotel might have been nearly a century old, but little of the original building seemed to have survived. It appeared to have been severely remodeled in the 1950s or 60s, with a newer six-story tower and restaurant wings encasing and erasing what was left of the earlier edifice. Here and there parts of the old building seemed to pitifully stick out like the limbs of a man crushed by a falling house.

Keene was ensconced on the third floor at the end of the hall in a corner room from which he could see both northern and eastern views. No bellman saw him to 301, so he took his time entering and observing the space in which he hoped he would once again find his muse. It seemed humble enough. A recessed closet with no door was on the right as he entered. Straight ahead was a queen-sized bed with a small bed stand next to it, and, as he came into the room fully, on his right was a low dresser with a TV locked into position on top, and a round table in the corner by the large east window with an easy chair that could double as a desk chair. The smaller north windows, high on the wall, paralleled the bed. A large recessed shelf with a wide mirror faced the north window. On that shelf was a small coffeemaker, an ice bucket, wrapped coffee cups and glasses. Keene expected to find a hand sink, but there was none, only a smooth expanse of green faux marble. To the left as he looked in the mirror was the bathroom, small but functional, all white, with a wide, curved double shower curtain.

He noticed that the fittings of the pipes below the sink seemed old, and there were red-brown streaks on the wall beneath them where rusty water had once leaked. Still, everything seemed clean enough, and the white hotel linens were fluffed and welcoming, the washcloth tucked into a pocket made from a hand towel, which was a nice touch.

Keene quickly unpacked, tucking his clothes into the two wide drawers provided, and hanging his shirts and the summer blazer he had brought in the open closet. He had packed just enough clothes to last the two weeks, so decided to keep wearing the shirt in which he had traveled, after giving it the sniff test and detecting nothing offensive. Still, he brushed his teeth, then took a washcloth, unwrapped a small bar of soap, and washed his face and neck thoroughly.

He wrung out the washcloth and straightened it prior to hanging it on the rod, and when he did he noticed the stain. It was red, right in the center of the foot-square white cloth, a streak about an inch long and half an inch wide. The instant he saw it he glanced in the mirror to see if his nose was bleeding or if he had somehow ripped his lip or eye on something. But his face stared back at him, unmarred, rubbed pink and clean. Still, he put a finger beneath his nose and sniffed to see if any blood sprayed out. There was none. Nothing. Not even mucus.

What then? Lipstick? Or someone else's blood which hadn't been laundered away? He'd had the cloth all over his face, for God's sake, at his eyes and his mouth. Someone else's blood had come so close to him? Blood which could have come from *anywhere* on someone's body?

In spite of the urge to toss the cloth into the tub, he examined it again. It was impossible to tell what the stain could be, except that it was red, or once had been. It was really more pink, he thought. He tried to make himself relax. Even if it was stained, weren't hotels obligated by law to launder their linens at a temperature that would kill any germs? He couldn't imagine it being otherwise.

He draped it over the edge of the tub with the stain outward, so that the maid would be sure to see it when she cleaned up the next day. It wasn't worth a complaint call to the front desk, but at least someone would know about it.

Keene went down to the hotel bar, a dark cozy room with Texas memorabilia hung on all the walls. A cheeseburger and two beers later, he went back to his room, where he stripped and took a shower, then set up his laptop on the round table. He also laid out his yellow legal pad and several pens and pencils in preparation for the next day. He quickly linked to the hotel's Wi-Fi and checked his email and Facebook page, then powered down again. After a perfunctory call to his wife, he crawled into bed with his book, a suspense novel by the Nacogdoches writer whose work had in part brought him there, and read until he felt sleepy enough to ignore the constant cycling on and off of the air conditioner.

He quickly learned that he wasn't tired enough to sleep through the noise, in spite of his weary muscles. A slice of light from the hall came through the bottom of his door, and he kept watching it until he closed his eyes again and turned away toward the wall. Then he thought about the sheets. The sheets and the bedspread.

The sheet had slipped down a bit so that the bedspread was in contact with his cheek. He thought about the stain on the washcloth and pulled the sheet up, doubling the top of it over the bedspread to break the contact of the rougher cloth with his flesh. How many people, he wondered, would tenant this room before that bedspread was laundered?

He lay there a moment longer, then got up and yanked back the spread so that it was covering only the bottom half of the bed. Then he crawled under the sheet and closed his eyes again. He didn't know when he finally drifted off to sleep, but it was a long time after midnight.

Still, he awoke shortly after dawn, as the strange light pressed through the thin skin of his eyelids. It was, he saw, creeping around the edges of the thick curtains, low bright sunlight making its way in. He pulled the sheet over his head, but could not sleep, so he got up, made the in-room coffee, and shaved. Then he dressed and went down to the lobby.

Breakfast in the hotel dining room was hearty but pricey, so Keene decided to wander into town and find some future options. As it turned out, there were few. Though the hotel was only a block from the main street, the only eating establishment on that street was The Olde Towne General Store, a luncheonette with a counter where you ordered and a kitchen in the back. The food was served with disposable plates and utensils, but the prices were low and the people friendly. Keene had only a cup of coffee while he read his complimentary local newspaper, whose stories were limited to those of the Nacogdoches area and the state of Texas.

When he walked back onto the street, the damp Texas heat hit him again. Still, he explored, finding a multitude of antique shops, every one of which had a garrulous proprietor, and eventually he learned to allow for at least a half hour's worth of conversation as he entered each. That was all right, he reminded himself. It was all material, all potential triggers for his work. So he chatted and listened and made mental notes about each character he confronted, in case he might find them useful. He learned much about Dr. Pepper bottles, World War II ordnance, and fluorescent minerals, whatever each proprietor felt most passionate about.

He had a leisurely lunch at the Olde Towne, and watched the patrons come in and out. Then he went back to the hotel.

The maid had been there in his absence, and fresh towels hung on the rods. He was tempted to spread them out to see if there were any stains, but resisted the impulse. There were three large bath towels, two washcloths, and two hand towels, so if one did happen to be soiled, there were others in reserve.

He sat down at the table, pushed the laptop back, set one of the blank legal pads in front of him and picked up a pencil. He sat there an hour, but nothing came. He scratched his head frequently. It didn't itch, but he'd discovered a small spot on his scalp, under his hair, that was slightly upraised, almost scaly, and his fingers naturally strayed to it, as one's tongue predictably slid to a small cut inside one's mouth, seeking out the rough upon the smooth, the imperfection upon the otherwise immaculate surface.

When he looked away from the blank paper that had demanded all his attention, he saw a minuscule assortment of whitish flakes, tiny pieces of dandruff, remnants, he supposed, of his own flesh. There they lay, a small constellation upon the dark sky of the tabletop. And then the first word came, and he wrote it down:

Detritus

That was a strange one, he thought as he sat and looked at it. Detritus. A Roman gladiator. The name of a star. A genus, a class. It sounded like it could be anything.

But that was what the little pile of white dust before him was, wasn't it? Detritus. How it was defined? Dead organic material. The stuff that had once been part of a living organism, but which had been sloughed off, expelled, drained away, detached from its owner, its host. Something that had lived, but lived no longer.

Almost like a ghost, he thought.

He looked at the small pile of white flakes, then he rubbed his index finger over it and looked at it, now a white line across his flesh. He lowered his hand to the floor and quickly rubbed his thumb across his finger until it was free of the organic dust, then looked at his finger and down at the carpet.

Keene couldn't see the bits of what had come from his head on its thick surface, even though its color was dark. Where had it gone? Into the carpet, he supposed, down among the tufts and individual fibers.

He dismissed the thought, refusing to follow where it led, and looked back at the word on the paper. Detritus. Maybe he could do something with that, with the way that the mental detritus of those long dead still somehow inhabits the living, whether socially, politically, or emotionally. There was a great deal of scope in the concept. It was certainly worth thinking about.

Perhaps that was enough for one day. No use pushing too hard. After all, he had two weeks. Two weeks of nothing to do but relax and let his mind take him where it would. This was at least a start. One word, but a rich one, yes? Detritus.

He got online, checked Facebook and email, wrote a few replies and comments, and called home and told his wife he'd begun to work, though it was coming slowly. Then he went down to the restaurant and had dinner.

Back in his room he watched some television, then stripped and stepped into the bathroom to take his shower. He flicked on the light and the exhaust fan, and slid a bath towel from the rod, then opened it and examined both sides. It seemed unstained, though there was a small hole in the one corner. Keene took a washcloth and a plastic bottle of bath gel and stepped into the tub.

As before, the stream of the shower was forceful enough, almost painful on the more sensitive parts of his body, but it was just that, a stream, with no spray to speak of. He automatically tried once again to adjust it, and once again found there was nothing to turn. He wet his hair and shampooed it, digging in with his fingers to eject the scaly flakes from his scalp, the *detritus*, and he said the word aloud.

As he did, he turned toward the wall, and there he saw several hairs plastered to the tile by the hot dampness. They were only a few inches in length, but they were black, and his hair was brown with a great deal of gray. There were, he thought, three of them stuck to the wall, clustered together so that they made a kind of *kanji*, a pictogram, but of what he could not say.

Where had they come from? They hadn't been there when he'd showered that morning, and he had certainly not been in contact with any black-haired individual. Though they could have been some of his wife's dark hairs, he hadn't been near her for several days now.

A maid? All those he'd seen had been Hispanic, but how could a maid have gotten any of her hairs stuck to his shower wall? Surely they didn't help themselves to a shower in a guest room? What if the guest returned when they were in the bathroom fully nude? No. That was impossible.

But still, there were the hairs, right in front of him.

With his hand, he redirected the water so that it struck the hairs and washed them down the side of the wall, into the standing water the slow-draining tub had collected. Keene looked down at the soapy, cloudy pool in which he stood ankle-deep, thinking that those black hairs could now be against his bare skin, and he rinsed his hair quickly, and just as quickly rinsed his body, holding first one leg and then the other under the powerful stream as he stepped out of the tub and onto the mat.

When he was finished toweling himself off, water was still running down the tub drain. He flipped the damp towel over the shower curtain rod and stepped back into the main room where he slipped on a clean pair of briefs. He stood there for a moment, then sat down at the table again, determined to change his mood by surfing the Internet and seeing what he might find.

But while he was sitting in the easy chair he'd been using, it occurred to him that there was only a thin layer of cotton between his buttocks and the seat of the chair, and he wondered how many other people, men and women and hygienically careless children, had sat in it as well.

How many of them had sat in it without any clothes on at all?

And how often did the housekeeping staff bother to clean the seats of chairs? Even if they did, wouldn't it be merely a perfunctory swipe of the vacuum cleaner?

Keene imagined everything that people did in hotel rooms, and he thought of all the asses and testes and penises and vaginas with which this chair seat could have been in contact, and of all the traces, albeit small, of feces and urine and semen and menstrual blood that might have, over months and years, oozed into this fabric on which he now sat.

He looked down at his own semi-nude body, felt the bare skin of his back starting to sweat against the back of the chair, and he leaned forward, only to feel the tops of his thighs and his genitals squeeze more firmly against the chair seat. He closed his eyes and slowly stood up, leaning on the table as he did.

Standing, he looked down at the seat, reached down and gingerly touched it. Then he got to his knees beside it, and ever so delicately sniffed at the fabric, sniffed once and once only, then recoiled.

In his nose clung a mixture of something dead and something else that reeked sourly and horribly of all life's vivid processes of elimination and decay. He blew out violently, so that a bolus of mucus, both moist and dried, shot from his left nostril and pasted itself to the carpet. He stared at it for a moment, fancying it the *anima* of the odor he had just experienced, the physical manifestation of that rank, deep smell inhabiting the seat of the chair.

Then he shook his head and told himself that surely the smell could not have been so strong, that if it had, he would have noticed it long before, as soon as he had entered the room for the first time. He took a few deep breaths and leaned once more toward the chair, further away this time, and sniffed again.

There was nothing. He moved closer, an inch away. Still nothing. He let the tip of his nose touch the chair again and inhaled, lightly, then more aggressively. There was a smell of something musty and sour, but nowhere near as strong as before. Had he grown used to it so quickly? Or had that first sensation been due to imagination, to the anticipation of smelling something awful, and his mind giving him the expected response?

Whatever the answer, he retreated, backing away from the chair until the bare backs of his legs struck the bed. He clambered onto it, pulling back the bedspread as he went, until he was crouching on the white sheets. Then he got a glimpse of himself in the mirror over the wide shelf that held the coffeemaker.

He laughed. He looked so absurd, as if he were about to start a sprint as soon as the gun fired, but with a wild, fearful look in his eyes as though tigers would be chasing him. He looked frightened and naked and vulnerable and altogether ridiculous.

All right then. Maybe it was true that the chair seat was less than pristine, but that could be remedied easily enough.

He stepped off the bed and walked into the bathroom, where he got a clean bath towel, folded it double, and smoothed it over the chair seat and up onto its slanted back as well. He sat back down, and was relieved to find that, even wearing only briefs, not an inch of his bare skin touched anything except the clean towel. At least he *hoped* it was clean.

He placed his left wrist on one of the two flat spaces between his laptop's touch-pad and took the mouse in his right hand. As he negotiated his way around the

Internet, he became aware of just how much his upper wrists were in contact with the edge of the wooden table, and while he surfed he couldn't help but think about how many people who had stayed in the room before him might have leaned against the edge while in various states of undress.

He told himself that it was wood, not cloth, but as the images continued to roll through his mind, he finally sat back and observed the edge of the table for a moment. Then he spat on his finger and began to rub it across the edge, back and forth, lightly at first, then with more pressure, until he felt a slight tackiness to the wood, as though a thin surface was peeling away bit by bit, an organic layer of... *detritus* troweled onto the wood, composed of sloughed off flesh and sweat and hair and anything else the human species was capable of exuding.

There it was, right there on his finger, a thin strip of...other people, or other people's *leavings.* It was barely a sixteenth of an inch across at its thickest, and the ends tapered to near invisibility. But small as it was, it held the souvenirs of life, the organic residue its owners had left behind, replete with how many strands of DNA, how many histories of living or even now dead creatures?

The concept amazed and sickened, awed and disgusted Keene. He tried to hurl the thing from him, but it clung, transferred from finger to thumb as he'd tried to snap it away. He looked at it in horror, as though it were a scar or a brand on his flesh, a tumor born from the whorls and loops of his own thumbprint. The thought occurred to him to stand, go to the bathroom and wash it away, or push the chair far enough so that he could reach the tissue that drooped from the built-in holder on the wall. But those actions would take time, and the contact with the thing was unbearable.

So Keene leaned down and rubbed his thumb into the tufts of the dark carpet at his feet, rubbed and rubbed until he was certain the strand of detritus was crushed, disintegrated, totally and incontrovertibly annihilated. He held his thumb and fingers a few inches in front of his eyes and looked long and hard, but could see nothing. Maybe part of the thing had been forced into his very pores, but if so it was invisible to him. Still, he scurried into the bathroom and washed his hands with soap and hot water, scrubbing with the washcloth until he was satisfied that not a trace remained.

He looked at his face in the mirror until it lost its attitudes of tension and panic. Then he took a deep breath, hung up the washcloth and dried his hands with an unused face towel.

Keene decided to surf the net no longer. Careful not to touch the edge of the table, he powered down the laptop and got into bed. It was early, barely nine o'clock, but he thought that perhaps television would relax him, and then he might read for a while until he got sleepy.

The remote sat on the bedside table, and he picked it up and looked for the power button, then pushed it. He held the remote in his hand, his head propped up against the pillows. He had made certain that the open ends of the pillowcases were doubled over, and the weight of his head now kept them in place. There was a news program on, and he clicked the channel advance button, but nothing appeared that captured his attention.

He picked up a card upon which the remote had been sitting. It listed the channels available, and he scanned it, finding the usual cable fare. There was, however, a small, light brown stain at the bottom right of the card, and his attention fixed on it.

Keene turned over the card, but the stain had not penetrated through the heavy paper. Then he looked at the stain again. It was only a half inch wide, and was at the bottom right corner. Coffee? Cola? Or maybe blood, or juice from a burger, but that was the same thing, wasn't it? Blood, but cattle instead of human.

He dropped the card back onto the bedside table and looked at the remote he still held in his other hand. Between the various buttons that peppered its front was a light coating of dust. He held it over the side of the bed and blew on it, but saw nothing drift away. Then he ran the edge of his little finger between the rows of buttons. The dust came away, adhering to his finger, but not all of it. A thin circle surrounded each round button like a gray halo, and there seemed to be some deposit of what he had thought of as dust that simply would not come off.

Not dust then. What?

He brushed the dust from his finger and thought about it. The remote control was used most often where? In bed, just as he was using it now. And in bed guests were undressed, their hands going to touch themselves, scratching, adjusting, or just rubbing for the pleasure of it.

And when there were two of them, touching each other, one thing leading to the next, the remote still on the bed, but forgotten, and the hands and bodies exploring, touching moistness, fluids on fingers, hands, then, afterwards, finding the remote and touching it with those fingers, turning off the TV, putting the remote back on the table, with those same fluids drying on its plastic surface, the dust adhering to it, and the next day the maids cleaning the room simply pick it up and put it where it's supposed to be, for the next guest.

For him.

Keene moved very slowly, reaching over and setting the remote on the bedside table as though it were a snake that might at any moment bite him. Then he got up, washed his hands again, more thoroughly than before, and, using a towel from the bathroom, pulled the TV plug from the wall socket rather than use the remote to turn off the set or press the power button on the TV itself.

He walked back to the bed and climbed in, pulling the sheet up to his chin. For a long time he simply lay there, trying to make his hands stop shaking, to force his breathing to be less shallow. After a time, he relaxed and looked up at the ceiling, the one place in the room free of detritus, the place no one had touched. He thought maybe he could read now, and picked up the book. It was clean. He had bought it new and had never loaned it to anyone, so he opened the pages and was, for a few minutes, able to lose himself in the story.

But he felt unaccountably warm, and when he lifted the book and looked down the length of his body in the bed, he saw that the bedspread was further up than it had been before.

Was that possible? Had his movements somehow pulled up the spread?

He lay down the book and, taking the edge of the spread delicately between his thumb and forefinger, sat up and tossed it further down toward the foot of the bed. Then he looked at it and wondered again how often they laundered the spreads. Certainly not every week, not even after every guest, probably. It was a *bedspread*, for god's sake, and his wife never laundered them at home, at least he didn't think so. She probably just shook them out, and he remembered her occasionally putting them in the dryer on no heat just to beat the dust out of them.

Did they do that here? They would have to do more, wouldn't they? Think of all the people who came in and, as he had, threw their suitcases on the bed to open them and put their clothing in the drawers and closet. Those suitcases had sat in god knows how many filthy sidewalks and backs of taxicabs and even restrooms, because you had to take your carry-on into the stall with you if you had no traveling companion to watch it.

And as if that wasn't bad enough, there was the scenario of two lovers, or a man and wife, or, even worse, a hotel guest and a *whore* forgoing the pulling back of the spread and just having sudden, impulsive sex right on the bed, on the bedspread itself, and—

And then he remembered the TV reports he had seen about hotel cleanliness, and how they tested bedding and found that many of them showed traces of blood, semen, and other body fluids, and he tried to remember *how* they tested for those things, and he thought he remembered them showing photographs of the stains glowing, glowing blue, blue in the darkness.

Black light, is that what it was called? No, *ultra-violet*, that was it. They shone an ultraviolet light on the fabrics, and the organic material showed up as a glowing stain.

An ultra-violet light, like the man in the antique shop who had all the fluorescent stones had talked about. And Keene wondered what such a light would show on *his* bedspread, his sheets, the pillowcases where he lay his head.

Best not to think about it now, and he tried to put it out of his head, lay down on the bed, but lightly, lightly, as though trying to levitate his body to make it float just above the surface of white cotton. It did no good. He felt the contact of flesh on sheet as clearly as he heard the pumping of his own heart in his ears.

Relax, he told himself. Breathe deeply. In, out...in, out...in...out...

He closed his eyes, and in a few moments was calm again, or at least more calm than he had been. He would sleep now, and in the morning...well, he would do something.

Keene opened his eyes and reached up for the switch to turn off the bedside light, but stopped. He took a tissue from the small pile he had put on the bedside table, put it over his finger and thumb, and turned the switch, letting the tissue fall to the floor in the darkness.

The next morning he awoke early again and sang old songs to himself as he performed his morning ablutions and dressed. He thought they would keep him from thinking about things he didn't want to think about. He sang "Runaway," "Blowin' in the Wind," "My Funny Valentine," and anything else he could come up with. It was a strange medley, but it accomplished its task of diffusing his attention until he was dressed and out the door.

He ate breakfast at the Olde Towne and then walked several blocks to the antique store that also did a trade in luminescent rocks and minerals. It didn't open until ten, so he sat on the bench outside and waited. A few minutes after the hour he heard the unlocking of the door and went inside.

The proprietor recognized him and welcomed him back. They talked for a while, and Keene told him what he was looking for.

A few hours later Keene went back to the hotel and set the light on the bedside table, next to a pair of scissors he had bought at the same shop at which he had gotten the light. It wasn't dark enough to try out the light. He would have to wait till night. In the meantime maybe he could work on his poetry.

The maids had been in the room, so there were clean towels again. He took one and spread it over the round table like a tablecloth. Then he put his legal pad on top of it and picked up a pencil and looked at the word he had written...when? The day before? Two days? He couldn't remember how long he had been there, or even what day it was. It couldn't have been that long, could it?

Detritus

There it was, as alone on the paper as he was in the room. That one word.

He sat there looking at it, thinking about the word and its connotations, its various levels of meaning, of the directions in which he might be able to take that single word. Detritus.

The inside of his left ear itched, and he picked at it with his little finger, but that only seemed to make it worse. In spite of all the warnings, he dug a bit deeper until he snagged a bit of what he assumed to be wax with the edge of his fingernail and pulled it out. Pale yellow, the bit of ear wax clung to his nail, and before he could even think about it, he flicked it onto the floor, over near the wall, where it disappeared into the tufts of carpet, just the way he had discarded the bits of white scale he had picked from his scalp on that first day.

As soon as he had done it, he regretted it, for it made him think of all those who had sat there before him doing the same thing, extruding bits of dried effluvia from ears or mouths or noses, those bits that people excavated from the mines of their body cavities and snapped away unthinkingly. How many bits of *detritus*, of ear wax, scabs, scale from dry scalps, and dear Christ, what his grandfather used to call *boogers*, horrible *horrible* word for dried nasal mucus—how much of that had worked its way into this hotel carpet over the years, filtered down through the tufts, beyond the reach of the vacuum cleaner, to lodge itself permanently into the backing, resistant to even the carpet shampooer that they *might* have used once a year to clean it.

As though drawn by the thought, Keene got out of his chair and went down on his hands and knees, and looked closely at the surface of the carpet. As he ran his fingers along the surface, he could see that each individual tuft was twisted, and the image struck him of thousands of small worms or cilia side by side, their heads up as if waiting to be fed. Though he pressed down the tufts, trying to part them, he still couldn't see the carpet backing, only the tufts, as though their depth was infinite.

He had another image then, one that almost brought back the panic of the previous night: that the surface on which he was kneeling was made up of the heads of hundreds of thousands of these worms, and that only their concentrated strength held him up, and that if they were to sway to one side or the other, he would slip down into their midst, lost forever in the darkness, dying, sinking further and further down until he was just one more piece of detritus, of dead organic matter in the sea of it that would engulf him and make him one with it all.

He closed his eyes, breathed deeply until the image passed and he could open them again. Then he got slowly to his feet and stamped his right foot lightly on the floor as if to ascertain its solidity. He forced himself to smile, but he knew he had to leave the room.

Keene walked across the carpet as though across quicksand, and stepped into the hallway with relief, closing the door of the room behind him. The click of the lock sounded like a litany. He went down to the bar and found it empty, only natural in the midafternoon of a weekday. Sitting at the end of the bar, he ordered a local Texas beer and sipped it slowly, not looking at the pint glass in his hand for fear of finding it soiled. He kept his attention fixed on a baseball game on the large screen TV and watched with an intensity that suggested a life or death interest in the result, though he wasn't familiar with even the names of either of the teams.

He stayed there for hours, drinking beer, ordering a sandwich, and then drinking scotch until he could see through the single window of the bar that it was growing dark outside. After he signed his tab, he stood up and realized that he had had more to drink than he'd thought. His last trip to the bathroom had been some time before, and his legs swayed slightly under him. It would be all right. He could walk to the elevator easily enough.

Still, he had to stop in the lobby and sit down on one of the couches. His head seemed to be floating. The woman behind the desk looked at him oddly, and he raised a hand in reassurance. He was all right. Just a little too much to drink.

He sat there until he could see, past the bright gleam of the hotel's outside lights, that the sky was black. When he stood, he felt steadier on his feet and realized that he'd been sitting there for a long time.

He took the elevator to the third floor and walked down the hall, stopping at the door of his room. It was silent, as if there were no other guests at all. No sounds of voices or television or music. Nothing. Dead quiet.

The green light appeared when he slid the keycard in and out, and he pressed down on the door handle, opened it and entered. It was dark inside, and he realized he must have pulled the curtains closed before he'd left the room, though he didn't recall doing so. Fine. He would leave the lights off. He would have to anyway for what he wanted to do. He kicked off his shoes so as to not drag any more filth into the room, and let the door glide shut.

There was enough light coming in from around the edge of the curtains to let him see the shapes of the pieces of furniture. He remembered leaving the light on the chest of drawers, so he made his way to it and felt along the smooth, polished wooden top.

There it was, and he wrapped his hand around its cylindrical mass. It was battery powered, so he didn't have to fumble around in the darkness trying to plug it in. This would tell him, wouldn't it? He would know whether all the things he had imagined were true, or if he was just being stupid and childish, a baby afraid of, literally, boogeymen.

He picked up the scissors as well, with the idea of actually cutting out a piece of the bedspread if it proved to be contaminated. The bedspread was what he would examine first, and he took the light and the scissors and stepped toward the bed until he felt his shins bump into it. Then he found the switch on the light he held and turned it on.

The entire bed seemed to burst into a violet flame, intensely bright. Only a very few patches were dark. His eyes squinted against the sudden light, and he dumbly realized what it must mean. The vast expanse of the bedspread was coated, literally *sodden* with detritus, accumulated over a period of months or even years, be it semen or other less likely organic spillages.

Vomit lurched into Keene's throat, and he tasted again the scotch and the beer and the supper he had had, made vile and bitter by bile. He felt it rolling through his lips and over his chin, and he saw what came out of him gleaming in the light as it descended, a waterfall of violet fire.

The vomitus landed on the bed, and seemed to meld into the violet stains already there, assimilating into it with a ferocious glimmer, glinting and coruscating and nearly blinding Keene. He turned away, and the light in his hand involuntarily followed and shone fully down onto the carpet of the room.

He saw a pool of violet light.

As though the floor of the room itself was a living thing, the light not only glowed, it pulsed in a rhythm akin to that of his own swift heartbeat. In the seconds that followed, the certainty sheared through his mind that the blazing light was proof that lodged within the carpet, the spread, dear god, probably the table and chair as well (and he ran the light over table and chair and the vibrant glow proved him right) was such a wealth of dead, shed organic matter that each object consisted more of detritus than of its own original materials.

He shone the light around in a panic, and saw that every inch of the floor, including that on which he stood, burned with the same violet light. Trembling uncontrollably, he felt his gorge rise again, and he spewed a lilac stream of phosphorescence from his throat, closing his eyes with the effort to bring it all up, to violently add his own contribution to the charnel house full of dead matter that he had once thought of more happily as just a hotel room.

When he opened his eyes, it was with a shock that he knew the matter might not be dead after all.

He had thought he had seen the surface of the carpet pulsing, but now he saw that it was more than that. It was actually heaving, as though something underneath were struggling to come out. And then it did.

As absurd as it seemed to Keene, he couldn't help but think of a mesh netting stretched over the surface of a large bowl of pudding, then pressed down into it from all sides, so that the mesh vanished beneath the pudding, which rose up through it. Only in this case the carpet was the netting, and the detritus the pudding. And it was pudding only if pudding was composed of bits of dried mucus, flakes of scalp to which hairs (straight and curly, black, brown and gray) still clung, a mass of exudation whose natural yellow and gray and white and brown all turned to sickly shades of lilac in Keene's light.

And this organic stew, once living, then dead, and alive once more, churned up in great thick froths from the carpet, hiding the tufts beneath its irregular, blotchy, ever-changing surface, breaking in waves at Keene's feet as though he were an island surrounded by hurricane-driven surf. It wasn't until he saw the thing start to flow over the toes of his shoes, flow and ebb, leaving bits of itself behind, that it occurred to him to flee.

But there was nowhere to go. The roiling mass was all around him, fully covering what had been the carpet, and now the stench of it scurried into his nostrils like a mole into the earth and made him dizzy and even sicker than before. It was the smell of shit, rot, blood, decay, of pus festering in a boil for months before finally being pricked and freed. His stomach twisted, but there was nothing more to come up.

He looked about frantically for a route of escape, but ten feet lay between him and the door to the hall, ten impassable feet composed of squirming, churning detritus, with bits breaking loose from the whole, snapping into the air like violet fangs, falling back again to mingle once more into the dead-alive stew. Then he thought of the bathroom, a dark, gaping mouth in the purple cave of the room.

He tried to shake the clinging human debris from his foot, then took two large steps, crying out with each one as his feet came down onto and into something that both crunched and yielded wetly to his weight, and then with the third step his foot landed on the hard tile of the bathroom floor, and he swung around and tried to push the door closed with his shoulder, but it only went partway, then stopped.

Keene looked down and moaned when he saw the detritus pushing its way in through the gap in the door and beneath it as well, the crawling, oozing matter illuminated by the light still clutched in his hand. He flicked on the bathroom light with his fist, thinking that it would help somehow, would save him from this violet mass pursuing him. It only made it worse.

Now he could see the details of his nemesis, each flake, scab, glob, every piece of *stuff* now all too visible, every bit of it joined to every other in impossibly appalling ways. The bright, glaring light made what he had seen in the violet light calming in comparison.

His moan turned to a cry of terror as he stumbled backwards, his legs hitting the hard bathtub so that he fell back against the shower curtain. Both layers, the outer cloth and the inner plastic, gave way, and he tumbled into the dry tub, striking his head against the porcelain hard enough to make him dizzy but not stun him. When his vision cleared, he saw that the cloth outer shower curtain on which he now partly lay was also teeming with life, its undulating surface only inches from his face.

He tried to push himself up, but his stockinged feet slipped on the smooth surface of the tub, and he could gain no traction. He could only watch, the light and the scissors still clenched in his white-knuckled hands, as the moist yet somehow calcified mass of tissue continued to lurch into the bathroom, under and around the edges of the door. Keene opened his mouth to scream, but the sound locked in his throat when he saw a fibrous, greenish-yellow strand of what looked like mucus, thick as a finger, slide over the edge of the tub and down it toward his bare arm.

Another followed, and another, outrunners of the whole, and in another few seconds what seemed a blanket of congealed human debris was in the tub with him, around him, and he felt himself sinking into it, pulled by clutching tendrils that wound about his bare arms, encrusting them as the sticky strands flattened and dried instantly upon his flesh.

Keene looked down and gasped, taking into his nostrils and lungs the sheer overwhelming reek of the thing that was engulfing him. For a moment the smell of it stole away what little sanity he had left, and when he looked again the layer of detritus was covering his wrists. He had to get it off of him. That was the only thing he knew, the only thought that made any sense in this insane nightmare.

He dropped the light he'd been clutching and opened the scissors so that the blades were exposed, and then he began to scrape frantically at the crust upon his arms. He used the blade like a razor, slicing down as though trimming the hairs on his arms, cutting away the layer of filth clinging to him. But the more he sheared off, the more seemed to come into the tub and onto his flesh.

So he began to hack as well as slice, stabbing at the creature or creatures that were invading and occupying the sacred country of his body. He ignored the pain, ignored the blood, thought only of expelling this thing from him, cutting it away like the cancer it was, banishing this *detritus*, now and forever, lost, lost…

And as he worked, as his arm flailed and blood flew and spattered the gray-white-yellow-green beast with red, the idea for the poem burst into his head, full-blown and, it seemed to him, perfect. And it sang in his head as he worked, sang to the rhythm of the movement of his arm, sang him into the safety of the dark, sang him away from what possessed him, sang him into the silence deep, deeper than he had ever known.

The next morning the maids found, in the otherwise empty bathroom, the male guest lying dead in the bathtub in a pool of his own blood. Strips of his flesh surrounded him like ribbons, floating in the blood. In his hand was a pair of scissors which had caused the self-inflicted wounds. Next to the body was a small plastic flashlight, still turned on, powered by two double-A batteries.

When the name of the guest was cross-checked with police records, it was found that he had only that day been listed as a suspect in the murder of his wife, a cancer patient found dead in their Massachusetts home the day before, five days after the now deceased suspect had received news that his academic tenure at the small liberal arts college at which he taught literature had been denied, that he would not return for the fall semester, and that his and his wife's medical coverage would cease within sixty days.

Following the investigation of the death scene, which included a thorough ultra-violet light examination, and after the body was removed, the medical examiner privately congratulated the hotel manager on the immaculate cleanliness of the room.

Monster

ANNE PERRY

Monty stood in the middle of the floor and gazed around the bookshelves that lined the walls and crowded the floor, making navigation around them awkward. At least three hundred of the books would never sell. Not that Cambridge wasn't an excellent book town, none in England better. It was the books themselves that were wrong, and the way the whole shop was laid out. As the new part owner, Mr Wingfield had just said, it was old-fashioned.

"The best ones are old books," Monty had retorted defensively. He could not afford to be rude. Mr Wingfield's very large investment would save the life of the shop, and he seemed a decent man, a genuine booklover, not a rich man looking for somewhere to invest his money. But no one with an ounce of intelligence thought that second-hand books were a way to make one's fortune. And Mr Wingfield looked sharp enough, if a little gaunt, as though some permanent worry rode on his shoulders and made them stoop.

"Old books," Mr Wingfield agreed. "But not old-fashioned, not without a very definite place in the history and passion of mankind. We have some very fine books, but they are lost amid the pedestrian. We need order, and more space so they can breathe."

"I've already tried to buy more space," Monty replied. "One side's a house, and they're not going to sell. The other side is a tailor shop, and they've been there for a hundred and fifty years, as they never forget to tell me."

"We can create space in here with a little rearrangement," Mr Wingfield explained, stepping forward to stand beside Monty. "Or maybe quite a lot of rearrangement," he amended. "And the illusion of space with more light. We must direct the customers' attention where we wish it to go. If we got rid of say three hundred books, we could do without that whole shelf there." He pointed to the middle of the room, and instantly Monty realized how much better that would be.

"And move this one," Mr Wingfield went on with growing eagerness. "Put a large mirror there," he added.

"A mirror?" Monty could not see the purpose of such a thing.

"Light," Mr Wingfield said gently. "Reflect and magnify. A mirror there will catch the light from the door and make it seem as if there is another whole room of books just beyond that corner. And you should have an armchair, an old leather one..."

"It'll take up space," Monty argued reluctantly, it would have been a nice idea. Armchairs suggested time, and comfort.

As if he had seen the idea in Monty's eyes, Mr Wingfield smiled. "Exactly," he agreed. "We want them to think that we have time and comfort to spare for them to meet all the greatest minds of the past at their leisure. We must redecorate the place. And in time I will find more books, rare and precious ones, full of adventures of the heart and the soul, deep thoughts of the mind, laughter and every-day life of people since the dawn of time. There are wonderful discoveries of the things we take for granted in our world today which is dying of a starved imagination, and lack of wonder."

"That will take ages," Monty felt a strong need to bring him back to the practical.

"I plan about two to three weeks," Mr Wingfield replied.

"And what shall we do in that time...?" Monty was anxious.

"Well...I have booked a short cruise around the Mediterranean. There is plenty of room for you, if you care to come. I thought we might discuss various possibilities at greater length, and of course in most pleasant surroundings. I have many ideas for widening our range of older books and manuscripts, and I would very much appreciate your own ideas before we commit to anything."

Monty was stunned. It took him completely by surprise, and yet instantly his imagination was filled with images of dancing blue water, white sails bellying in the wind, islands like jewels in the sun. Ancient legends became immediate, cities with history that wove through the legends of the past.

Mr Wingfield's voice interrupted his thoughts and brought him reluctantly back to the present—a dusty, over-filled bookshop in Cambridge.

"Will you come?"

"I...I'm not sure that I should..." Temptation pulled hard.

"I would regard it as a favour. My wife died a short while ago. My daughter has not yet truly recovered from the loss. You would be company for her."

Conscience was satisfied. "Thank you," Monty accepted. "I suppose I really would be no use here."

That evening Monty sat in his favourite pub having an excellent supper. He felt both nervous and excited as he told his closest friend Hank, about his sudden change of plans. Hank was a professor of mathematics at one of the colleges at the university, a charming man of wit and learning, and almost immeasurable practicality. He had been Monty's sounding board, and anchor in sanity, in several of his recent adventures where crime and the inexplicable seemed to have crossed into a mutual territory of horror. It was in one such adventure that the previous owner of the bookshop had been murdered. It was an ugly loss and the memory of it still hurt. There were aspects of it which had been only Monty's over-heated imagination, and he knew that without Hank telling him. But other things were still unexplained and sometimes in the middle of the night, Monty found himself still troubled. Hank had known it, even though Monty had not said so except obliquely.

"Excellent," Hank said enthusiastically. "Get away from the bookshop and everything to do with it for a while. Gain a little perspective."

"You still think I imagined half of it, don't you," Monty said a little peevishly.

"No." Hank was as always, perfectly reasonable. "More like three-quarters." He smiled. "But not all. There'll be an explanation, and when we find it we'll wonder why we were ever blind to it. But as yet I don't know what it is. Go to the Mediterranean. I envy you. It'll be gorgeous this time of year. Long before we get any real warmth here. You'll be back in time for the hawthorn blossom. The hedges will be mounded white and the air will smell like heaven. If you're not too blasé with Sardinia, Naples and the Greek Islands, or wherever else you go!"

Monty grinned. Hank was right. It was a marvellous idea. "Why don't you come too? I imagine there'll be room."

"Because I have a job to do," Hank said drily. "If I disappear off into the Mediterranean they might discover they can do without me—then where would I be?"

Monty received his first real shock when Mr Wingfield met him in the dockside.

"There she is," Wingfield said with something approaching pride. His thin, dark face was lit with pleasure at seeing Monty, as if a great weight had been lifted from him. He was pointing not at the small passenger cruiser moored closest to them, but at a marvellously graceful two masted yacht fifty yards beyond. Its sails were furled at the moment, and no doubt these days it had some form of engine as well, but clearly its main source of power was the wind. Everything about its long, clean lines said that it was designed by men who knew the sea, both its danger and its ease.

Monty opened his mouth to say something, then realized how foolish he would sound, and merely let out a sigh.

"I thought you would see its beauty," Mr Wingfield said approvingly, exactly as if Monty had spoken. "There's a four-man crew, plus a cook, of course. And there will be five passengers, apart from ourselves. Come, let's board and get you settled. We leave on the tide."

Monty obeyed and followed him along the dockside. It was a surprise, but really it made no practical difference. Perhaps it added a little to the glamour of it?

As soon as he trod on the deck Monty felt the total difference from being on land. It all moved, the wood creaking, the deck altering his balance as it pitched very slightly under his feet. He looked up at the mainmast soaring into the sky, its tip weaving tiny circles on the clouds. The rigging was like black pen lines linking everything to everything else, mainmast, foremast, bowsprit, booms. If one of them were to catch you as it swept across the deck when you came about on the other tack, it would carry you into the sea, if it did not crack your head open first! Or perhaps they were too high above the deck for that? Somebody would have thought of it.

He was led below and shown to a tiny cabin, just large enough for a bunk and a cupboard, and room to stand if he did not take more than two steps in any direction. But then he need do no more than sleep here. He unpacked the few things he had brought, only the necessities, and fifteen minutes later he was up on the deck again looking around.

Two men in their early thirties were standing near the rail. They looked alike in build and features, as if they were brothers. One, perhaps the elder, was both heavier and darker. He was busy pointing out various buildings on the shore. The younger merely nodded, almost as if he dared not interrupt. Neither of them turned to look at Monty, although they must have heard his feet on the deck.

"The Trevellyn brothers," a woman's voice said from somewhere behind Monty.

He turned around quickly and saw an elderly lady with a curious, intelligent face and wind-whipped white hair, although there was in fact no wind at all. She smiled. "Mrs Worth," she introduced herself.

"Montague Danforth," Monty replied. "But please call me Monty. How do you do, Mrs Worth."

"How do you do, Monty. I think we shall have an interesting voyage, don't you?"

'Interesting' was an odd choice of word, but it would be rude to point that out.

"Indeed," he said with a smile. "I am looking forward to Sardinia, and even more to Naples. I have heard it is unbelievably beautiful."

"Oh indeed," Mrs Worth agreed. "But I always find people even more interesting than places, don't you?"

Monty could see nothing interesting in the two young men a few yards away from him, leaning on the railing. Perhaps she meant the people of Naples.

A few minutes later a man and a woman came across the deck. She was very elegant, but she did not appeal to Monty. This girl looked as if she would break under the least pressure. The young man with her was protective, an arm around her, which was quite unnecessary, the deck was clear and the ship running smoothly, sails billowing white against a cloudless sky.

Beside Monty, Mrs Worth watched them with intense interest. For the life of him, Monty could not think why. From the way the girl displayed the diamond on her ring finger, and its accompanying wedding band, they were obviously on honeymoon. Even so, she wore a vaguely petulant expression as her husband introduced her to the brothers.

"Very interesting," Mrs Worth murmured to Monty. "Barry and Avice Kendal," she added. "A young woman who has achieved what she set out to, and is finding it surprisingly lacking in flavour."

Monty had no idea why she should think such a thing. Poor soul must have had a life devoid of passion or interest other than in her fancies of the lives of others. He ought to be nicer to her, but it would not be easy. He was here to discuss the new plan for the bookshop with Mr Wingfield, and to be pleasant to his daughter, so very recently bereaved of her mother. He was not particularly good with children, but judging from Mr Wingfield's age, she might be fourteen or fifteen, probably as awkward and self-absorbed as most teenagers. All he could do was try.

Perhaps it was not such a wonderful idea to have come? It had sounded like a good adventure, not to mention temporary freedom from the cold British spring and the chores of overseeing the bookshop renovation. Talking about ideas was often a lot more fun than dealing with the practicalities of workmen, costs, schedules, who does what.

But long days at sea with newly-weds already disillusioned, Tweedledum and Tweedledee brothers, a gossiping old woman and an erratic and bereaved teenage girl might not be as exhilarating as he had imagined.

Dinner was very pleasant if a little dull. Neither Mr Wingfield nor his daughter appeared, having taken something very light, in their cabin instead. Those who were present all sat at the one large table. There was no room for anything separate, and Monty was relieved. It made conversation a choice rather than a necessity, and he would have been miserable alone.

They discussed the various places the ship would call in, and to Monty's surprise Mrs Worth seemed to be quite familiar with all of them. She also gave detailed and affectionate descriptions of Constantinople, Haifa, Alexandria and various other great cities of the past.

"I can't think how you fitted so much into one lifetime," Avice Kendal said a little waspishly.

"Perhaps she's a flying Dutchman," John Trevellyn suggested with a glint in his eye. "Doomed to wander from place to place for eternity. Has anybody ever seen her ashore?"

His elder brother gave him a crushing look, opened his mouth to speak, then as John stared at him, he suddenly changed his mind and laughed a trifle artificially.

Barry Kendal changed the subject, asking Monty what he did, and the conversation turned to books. All the same, Monty was uncomfortable. Ghost stories, even legendary ones, reminded him only too vividly of his own unusual sensitivity to the powers of supernatural evil and the hideously close brushes he had had with it in the very recent past.

He was glad to escape to be alone for a while on deck in the brilliant moonlight and watch the endless beauty of its reflection across the glittering expanse of the water, the pale canvas billowing, the mast weaving its circles among the stars.

It was not sure how long it was before he realized he was not alone. There was a young woman only a few yards away, standing motionlessly. The slight breeze ruffled her dark hair and blew her dress against her slender body, outlining the delicacy of it. She had wide eyes black in the moonlight and an extraordinary face. She was not beautiful in the traditional sense, but there was a power of emotion in her that was compelling. Monty could not look away from her, however intrusive it might be to stare.

For several moments neither of them moved, then she turned to look back at him and smiled very slightly.

"You must be Monty." Her voice was soft and low, very beautiful. "I'm Lenore Wingfield."

There was no one else she could have been, but he was still stunned. It was a moment before he could frame words to reply, even then he stammered.

"There is no need to look for something nice to say," she assured him. "There really isn't anything. I would far rather have the truth. Tears are better than a painted smile, don't you think? I hate clown masks. I think lies in the face are as bad as those with words."

It was an extraordinary moment, especially to a stranger, but she seemed to be expecting some kind of reply.

"I don't like clowns much either," he agreed. "Although quite a lot of them have pretend tears..."

"Isn't there enough real grief?" she asked. "Does mockery make it any better? The darkness is not a game."

He felt a sudden chill pass through him, as if there were ice in the wind. Memories returned, the stench of blood and mould, the knowledge that there were powerful things which could not be explained.

"Yes," he said gravely. "I do know."

She came a step closer, looking at him in a different way now, as if she saw more than an unremarkable young man who sold rare books.

"Perhaps you do," she agreed. "I'm sorry. I thought my father would choose somebody bland, without dreams—or nightmares. How clever—how very clever."

He had no idea what she meant, and before he could ask she flashed him a dazzling smile, then turned and walked away with a grace so easy and fluid that she seemed to melt soundlessly into the shadows of the deckhouse.

The next day they were well on their way south and the wind was considerably more brisk. No one else was on deck except Monty when Mr Wingfield appeared. He was well wrapped up and his face looked weary and pinched. Perhaps he was not as good a sailor as he had expected. Monty was concerned for him.

"I'm fine," Wingfield answered, his tone dismissing the subject. "The air will be good for me. Lenore tells me you met on deck yesterday."

"Yes..." Monty wanted to say more, but he could not think exactly what. His thoughts were disturbed, confused. He knew Wingfield was watching him and waiting.

"Did she mention her mother to you?" he asked at length when Monty had said nothing.

"Only obliquely," Monty replied. "I'm not even sure how the subject arose, but she spoke of clowns, painted smiles, and how the darkness is real."

Wingfield shuddered, his eyes fixed on some far distant white crest in the sea. "Indeed it is. But it is not always where you expect it to be. Nor is its shape what you think."

"I know," Monty said quietly.

"Do you?" Wingfield asked, searching Monty's face anxiously. "Forgive me, but I doubt it. Lenore is…troubled. She and her mother were close. She has not accepted her death yet. She has very dark imaginings that it was not a natural death."

Monty felt the chill again, like a cold hand touching his skin. "Not natural?" he asked.

Wingfield sighed. "Not supernatural! Just…tragic. She is concerned it was suicide. My wife had a wasting disease. Very distressing to watch, and we were helpless to prevent its course. One is reluctant to admit such things. One never gives up hope of finding a cure…until, of course, it is too late. Lenore is still imagining we might have found something."

"I'm sorry," Monty said sincerely. That explained it. The darkness that had brushed him was helplessness, even a misplaced guilt, an overwhelming despair. All very human.

"I'm so sorry."

Wingfield smiled bleakly. "Let me turn to happier things, and more useful. Let me tell you some of the places I mean to acquire books. I have in mind certain avenues…"

They passed through the Straits of Gibraltar and into calm seas. It grew noticeably warmer, everyone spent more time on deck. Monty was talking to Lenore, trying to draw her into happier thoughts, without being too obvious about it, when they saw the newly-weds standing side by side near the railing, looking towards the faint outline of the coast to the north.

Lenore shook her head, the ghost of a smile on her lips.

"What is it?" Monty asked.

"See how they stand," Lenore replied. "His body is curved away from hers, and she is so stiff I half expect to see ice crystals on her."

"I think she is not finding sea travel as easy as she thought she would," Monty pointed out.

Lenore laughed, amusement without joy. "How polite you are. Do you ever say what you mean, Monty? Or are you like most people, and actually you don't mean anything?"

He was stung. It was unfair. "I don't know why she's unhappy," he replied fairly tartly. "And I think interfering is more likely to make it worse than better."

"Bravo!" she exclaimed. "That at least is honest. Mind your own business, Lenore! Can you mend my unhappiness, Monty? Or do you listen to me because my father owns your bookshop, and he asked you to?"

"He only owns half of it," he corrected her tartly. "The other half is mine. We need new investment to survive. And what are you really asking me? If I like you?"

"Oh!" Her eyes widened.

He felt himself blushing hotly, but she had asked for that, and he was not going to back down.

She began to laugh, a harsh, jerky sound full of despair.

"I'm sorry," he said quickly. "Yes, I do like you. And I can't imagine how awful it must be to fear that someone you loved deeply was in such pain that they took their own life."

Quite suddenly she reached out and touched his face gently with her white finger tips. It was delicate, intimate, and her skin was like ice.

"Maybe Dad's not so dusty after all," she said softly, then laughed and turned away, sauntering off along the deck, looking ahead into the wind.

They reached Sardinia and went ashore for a few hours. Monty joined Wingfield and Lenore and to begin with it was highly enjoyable to explore the old city of Cagliari. The streets were narrow and steep and full of character. Wingfield seemed happy to let Monty and Lenore lead the way. A few times he stopped and told them to go ahead, and come back for him. He looked oddly guilty as he did so, as if he were letting them down, but Lenore seemed to understand and Monty felt it would only add to the discomfort of it if he were to comment. Wingfield was obviously tired, and not as strong as he had first led Monty to believe. Perhaps his pallor was not natural, but that of an invalid?

Eventually Monty became worried.

"Are you sure he's alright?" he asked Lenore. "I think we should go back and help him. He must be feeling rotten."

She smiled. "He doesn't want to spoil our pleasure. But if you think I should, I'll go back for him. He wouldn't want you to know he can't make it alone."

He started forward. "You can't help. I meant physically, not just encouragement."

"I said I'll go!" she was firm.

He took another step forward and her hand shot out to grasp his arm. Her fingers closed on him like a vice, bruising his flesh. He cried out with the stab of pain that went through him, pulling away, but he could not move.

Then just as suddenly she let go. "I'm sorry. Really—he would be embarrassed. I know you mean well, but there are things about my father that you don't understand. I can help him, I always have. Please..." She smiled at him, pleading.

He had no possible alternative. "Of course. But if I can help, just call."

They got back to the ship exhausted and Wingfield retired to his cabin, not even reappearing for dinner. Lenore was quiet, and Monty guessed that she was worried. When Wingfield had spoken of his wife's death his whole concern had been for his daughter. Never once had he mentioned his own grief, and only now was Monty beginning to appreciate how deep it must be. No wonder the man looked drained. He had to do more to help. His absorption with his own occasional discomfort was an appalling selfishness.

Accordingly the following day he was on deck with Lenore as soon as breakfast was finished.

"I think he's better, thank you," she replied to his enquiry. They spent the morning talking of many things. He was surprised how widely knowledgeable she was and they were laughing at an obscure joke they both understood when Mrs Worth joined them at the railing, peering into the distance to where Italy must lie beyond the blue line of the horizon.

"I am looking forward to seeing Naples," Monty said enthusiastically.

"And Vesuvius," Mrs Worth added. "Of course I have seen it before, but one cannot see too much of a place so beautiful."

"They say 'see Naples and die,' don't they?" Lenore asked, looking a little sideways at the older woman. "Is it fatal, do you suppose? Or only the ultimate experience?"

Mrs Worth looked at her with a long, penetrating gaze. "I expect it is fatal for some," she answered. "But they bring their death with them, it is not Naples which kills them. But then I imagine you know that." She said it with a waspishness that took Monty by surprise. Then quite suddenly she turned and walked away briskly, even though on the confined deck she would go no more than a few yards.

Monty started to go after her and ask for an explanation of her rudeness, and an apology, but Lenore put out her hand onto his arm and the strength of her grip brought back the memory of pain from the time she had touched him in Cagliari.

"Don't," she said gently, relaxing her grip. "She doesn't like me. It is understandable. I remind her of death, of her own mortality. She is of an age when that has a pain all its own."

Monty was startled. "That's ridiculous! Why on earth should you remind her of death?"

"Because I am alive, and I will be, long after she has gone." She smiled, a curious, energetic expression, one Monty found impossible to read. It was uncomfortable, and yet also exciting, as if she knew something marvellous that he did not. He stared at her. For all the darkness of her immediate past, the loss and the grief, there was something in her fiercely alive. Perhaps that was what Mrs Worth had seen, and envied.

"I believe you," he said simply. "I would like to think of you always alive, as much as you are right now."

She took his hand. "Oh, I will be, I promise you. Come, let's watch the wake of the ship. Do you see how the gulls in the air behind us exactly mirror the V of the waves astern? Even the air is blue and from here the power of the sea is hidden, and unimaginable."

He felt the power again that evening, after dinner, but in a completely different way. They had spent the afternoon in pleasant, idle conversation, sharing memories, laughing easily, as if for a brief time even death could be ignored. Lenore was funny and charming and Monty realized with surprise how much he liked her, was even attracted to her dark, brittle beauty.

At dinner Mrs Worth was silent, her usual interesting conversation vanished. The newly-weds were sulking, the brothers politely contradicting each other.

Mr Wingfield looked as if he had recovered his strength. There was even a little colour in his rather gaunt face. He told stories about the history of Naples from its original Greek founders, through the Romans, the French kingdom of the Two Sicilies, up to the present day. Afterwards he walked on the deck in the clear moonlight with Monty. Lenore was ahead of them, seemingly lost in her own thoughts.

"Thank you, Monty," Wingfield said quietly, his voice only just audible above the sound of the water and the ship's hull and the sigh of the wind in the rigging above them. "Your kindness has made all the difference in the world to Lenore. I'm...very grateful."

"It's a pleasure," Monty said honestly. "She is most attractive..."

Wingfield caught his arm, holding him so hard he was swung around to face him, standing still on the deck.

"But she can give you no more than this," Wingfield said urgently, almost as if he were angry. "After this voyage, you will not see her again..."

Lenore could not have heard their words, but she turned suddenly to face them, her eyes wide.

Monty felt a wave of horror pass over him, as if he were in the presence of overwhelming evil, an endless hunger that could have devoured everything inside, leaving nothing but a husk behind. He was choked by it. Even the vast emptiness of the sea and the night had no air for him to breathe, the light was sucked from the sky.

Lenore was coming back towards him.

The evil vanished and the moonlight returned, bright and dancing on the water.

Wingfield's grip loosened on his arm.

Monty struggled to pass the incident off as nothing, as if he understood, but no words came, except to excuse himself, and stumble for the hatchway, and go below.

He lay on his bunk, not expecting to sleep, but unconsciousness overtook him, rife with nightmare, huge shapeless things, impossible to grasp. In the morning he woke exhausted. He could not concentrate his mind and his legs felt like rubber. He tried in vain to remember how much wine he had taken with dinner. He had been warned that it was potent. He should have listened. Now he had made a fool of himself.

He skipped breakfast, and up on the deck he felt a little better. Lenore teased him gently, but there was a persistent anxiety in her eyes. He could not shake the impression that she knew something he did not, something important and perhaps dangerous. It was there in the things she started to say and then stopped herself, hinted at obliquely, then changed the subject. Finally he could bear the tension no longer.

"What is it?" he demanded. "Your father thanked me for trying to take your mind off your...bereavement, even for a while, and now he says I must not see you after the voyage. Is that your choice?"

"No, of course it isn't," she said softly. "He is afraid that I will tell you too much. He always is, whenever I find a friend. Perhaps he thought that because you are partners with him in the bookshop, and you will need his help, that you will...will be easy to manage—you won't ask too many questions."

"About what?"

"About my mother's death, of course."

"Why would I? It would be...cruel..."

"She took her own life," she said almost under her breath. "It was the only way she could escape from him." She gave a twisted little smile and walked away, leaving him standing on the deck, embarrassed and confused, not knowing what to do.

The climax to his emotional turmoil came a couple of long days later. The weather was quite a bit rougher and no one else was on deck except Monty and Lenore and Mr Wingfield forward of them, gazing into the distance. Half a dozen times Monty had tried to pluck up courage to approach him and ask him for some kind of explanation of his extraordinary remarks about Lenore, but always the right words had eluded him.

Lenore was leaning on the railing when she heard a shout from where her father was standing. She turned, startled, and her foot slipped. Before Monty could reach her, with a terrible scream she pitched over the side and struck the water. A moment later she was already swept astern and Wingfield raced to the stern and plunged in after her.

Lenore and Wingfield were already too far astern for lifebelts to be any use at all.

"Man overboard!" Monty screamed, racing to the wheelhouse and beating against the doors. "Help! Help! Man overboard!"

There was a pounding of feet racing along the deck. There seemed to be men everywhere, hauling on ropes, bringing the huge sails down. Monty was confused, furious, terrified. What the hell were they doing? Then as the deck thrummed with life he understood. Of course—engines. So much more manageable. They could move in any direction. Even so it seemed infinitely slowly that they described the huge arc in the sea back to where Lenore and Wingfield had gone in.

Monty stood at the forward rail, his eyes aching as he searched the water, a lifebelt clutched in his hands. There was nothing, no hands, no arms waving. No shouts above the noise of the wind and the sea.

Then at last he saw them, together, Wingfield struggling desperately to keep Lenore's head above the sharp, choppy waves. He was failing, sinking. By the time the crew lowered the boat and reached them it would be too late.

Monty clung to the lifebelt and leapt over with it. He hit the water hard and it engulfed him in choking, smothering salt. He gasped, spluttered and found his balance, then began to swim towards them, taking the clumsy belt with him.

Later, in the cabin wrapped in blankets and drinking hot whisky and water, feeling the life return to his frozen body, Monty faced Lenore. Wingfield was in his own cabin, exhausted and being tended by the cook, who acted as ship's doctor and general steward. This time Monty would not be fobbed off.

"What the hell happened?" he demanded. "And no more lies and excuses."

"I suppose it's time," she said quietly and looking down at her white hands knotted in her lap over the blankets around her. She faced him suddenly, her eyes wide and black, like holes in her skull. "My father is a monster—not sexually. He has never touched me—that way. It is far subtler. He feeds on my emotions—of any kind—love or hate, terror, despair, anything fierce enough for him to latch onto—like a vampire feeding on blood. He has no passion of his own, he takes mine, as he took my mother's before me. In the end she could sustain him no longer. She was emptied of all that was her inner self. She took her own life, because it was the only escape from utter emptiness. Can you imagine it? Can you conceive of the horror of having nothing inside you—not even dreams left?"

A breath of it touched his imagination like a door opening into infinity, without warmth or light, and he felt himself silently screaming. The evil he had sensed before was back, even closer to his skin.

"How can I help you?" he said when he could master his voice. "You have to escape."

She gave a bleak smile, full of despair. "How? Die as well? I'm not ready to do that—not yet."

"No!" He was appalled. "I didn't mean that!"

She took his arm. "You're very kind, Monty. A good man—but really I don't think you have any idea what sort of power you're talking about. Let's forget it for now. The wind is getting stronger, but it's not cold. Let's go for a walk around the deck. The air is perfect."

The next few days the weather continued to get more blustery. Mr Wingfield came up on deck occasionally but he looked haggard. He spoke to Monty about books, but he did not meet his eyes, as if he were afraid now of what Monty might see in them. What would he see? A vampire starving for food? A cannibal of the soul? The thought was repulsive, and yet Monty could not rid himself of it.

The more time Mr Wingfield spent with Lenore, the worse it became. Finally Monty could bear it no more. The sun was low across the waves and the wind was growing stronger. He could feel it in the pitching of the ship. They were gaining speed.

He excused himself from Wingfield who was sitting in the main cabin, his eyes hollow, his cheeks sunken so that the bones of his skull seemed to stand out, making him look cadaverous. He was a man starving—a monster consumed from within by his own insatiable hunger.

Lenore must free herself from him before he drove her to her death, as he had her mother before. Monty rose to follow her up on deck where he could catch her alone. He left Wingfield without any explanation and started to climb the steep stairs. He must act quickly. No wonder he had had that terrible, consuming sense of evil. He was meant to do something about it.

The ship must have keeled over even further with the wind and he had to cling onto the rails at the sides. He emerged into a wild night. Why on earth was Lenore up there in this weather? Was it the only place she could escape him? How desperate she must be!

It was a moment or two before his eyes became accustomed to the dark, then he saw her. She was standing near the place where the rigging was lashed to the deck, its ropes and black fretwork against the burning colour of the sky. She was beautiful, her hair blowing, long and loose, her eyes wide as if the squall filled her with its own cold energy. He had never seen anyone look so alive.

She was the very opposite of Wingfield. He was the one who was desiccated, sucked dry of all his passion or hope.

And then he knew. It was she who drew the life from him.

He had begotten a monster, and yet still he tried to protect her—and in his own way he had even tried to protect Monty as well. His invitation had been a cry for help, which perhaps he had afterwards regretted.

Lenore was only yards away, watching Monty in the fire of the sunset. She must have seen the realization in his face the moment he understood. She let go of the rail she had been holding onto and came towards him, smiling, a terrible smile, her eyes hollow with hunger.

"You won't beat me, Monty," she said calmly. "I'm far stronger than you will ever be, and you know that already. It will be much easier if you don't fight."

"Is that why your mother killed herself?" he demanded, fury and fear welling up inside him until he all but choked on his own breath. "And now your father?"

"He won't kill himself," she said, still smiling. "He'll never stop trying to save me—or save anyone else from me!"

Monty remembered Wingfield plunging into the water after her, his desperation, and the moment he had hesitated. He tried to imagine what must have been going through his mind. Pity for Wingfield overwhelmed him. Brave, stupid words came to his lips.

"He loves you, in spite of what you are. I dare say you don't understand that, but you know it's true. It's what you use, to save yourself. But I don't love you. And I've seen other kinds of evil. I know what it is."

He heard a sound behind him, and ignored it.

She came forward another step, her hands very slightly raised. He knew the strength in them, he'd felt it before. She was right, he couldn't possibly beat her.

"No, Lenore. Don't!" It was Wingfield's voice behind him. "Leave him alone. Take me."

"I've already taken you," she replied. "You're empty. There's nothing left. I need new passion, new hope—and pain."

Wingfield was level with Monty now, but she ignored him, her eyes still on Monty, her hands loosely at her sides.

Monty stepped towards her, to protect Wingfield, the anger in him at her contempt for the old man blinding him to his own danger.

There was a sudden gust of wind. It screamed in the rigging and the ship keeled over hard. Monty felt himself slipping towards the edge and tried to grasp hold of anything to save himself. He saw Lenore's dress billow out around her as she lost her balance. One moment she was there, wild, outlined against the last light, the next she was gone over into the moiling sea.

Wingfield let out a cry of anguish and Monty caught him as he lunged towards the rail. He held on as if it were to his own life, and as the ship ploughed on through the darkening waves, gradually Wingfield ceased struggling. It was too late. They would never find her now. The storm was rising and would blow itself out before it rested.

Monty eased his hold on Wingfield and straightened up, letting him go.

"There was nothing you could have done," he said gently.

"I know," Wingfield replied. "I just had to try. You can't just walk away from a monster. It's who she was—she didn't mean to be."

Monty did not argue. Wingfield knew his own truth, he just needed a little time to accommodate it.

Orange Lake

AL SARRANTONIO

Halloween!

Halloween is here again.
Dunk the apples,
mow the grain.
Raise a glass
to old Samhain.

Fallow fields
and winter coming.
Beg the old gods
keep Sol turning.

May Day's gone
and dead in ground
But seasons still turn
'round and 'round
'till spring comes back again.

Halloween is here once more!
Dunk the apples,
make the store—
raise a glass
to old Samhain!

PART 1

When the temperature dropped in his office, Bill Grant knew who was coming.

A shadow passed across the single window. The day darkened, the leaves rustled, and the colors turned to deep Autumn. It was nine o'clock in the morning but felt like dusk.

"Samhain," Grant whispered.

The door remained unopened, but the specter appear. His black cloak, hiding an insubstantial body, moved listlessly, as if there was a breeze in the room through the unopened window. Grant shivered, but refused to take his eyes off his old...nemesis? Friend? After all this time he had no answer.

"What can I do for you?" Grant asked, trying to keep his hand from shaking while he reached for the bottle of Jim Beam white label that rested on the corner of his desk. "And how's your little corner of perdition? Still dry as a bone? Or are you ferrying them across the river Styx these days?"

Samhain said nothing, his slitted empty black eyes within his hood unblinking, the red slit of his mouth against his paste-white face immobile.

"Come to hire me?" Grant said, barking a laugh.

"I want to ask a favor," Samhain said quietly, his voice almost a sepulcher whisper.

Again Grant laughed. "Me? You took my wife, nearly killed me—"

"None of that was because I wanted to," Samhain broke in, his voice still soft.

"Get to the point," Grant replied. He had poured two neat inches of bourbon into his Yogi Bear jelly glass and knocked it back. He had done this starting at eight-thirty.

"I don't understand the lure of...spirits," Samhain said, and then, realizing what he had said, almost smiled.

"Something's bothering you," Grant said.

"Yes."

"Spit it out."

The cloak rustled slightly, then was still.

"You will have a visitor. I would like you to take him seriously."

Again Grant barked a laugh, though he wanted to scream. "Who are you—Jacob Marley? I don't want any visitors. Especially at this time of year. In fact, you can leave now."

"A human. A young man. A...client, though he will not be able to pay you."

Grant's hand steadied on the bourbon bottle. "Really..."

Samhain's head nodded, ever so slightly. "Yes."

"And why should I be solicitous to this...young man?"

"Because he needs your help. And so do I."

"Explain," Grant said, his old police detective traits re-asserting themselves.

"There are...certain things I have no control over, even here in Orangefield," the specter said. "What this young man is involved in is one of them. But I think you may be able to help."

Grant couldn't help but smile, though his was even more restrained than Samhain's had been.

"You're kidding."

Samhain shook his head. "You must know by now that I never joke. That is a human attribute."

"And why should I help you?" For the moment, Grant had forgotten about the bourbon and pulled a legal pad, the only other thing on the desk beside a single pen, toward him. He picked up the pen.

"The young man will tell you everything you need to know," Samhain said, by way of explanation. "Only know that your own interests, as well as those of Orangefield—"

"And yours," Grant interjected.

Samhain nodded. "Yes. Let's just say we all need this problem to be resolved."

"And why me?"

Samhain replied immediately. "Because of all the humans I have ever known, you are the most honest and..." He seemed to be searching for a word.

"Stupid?" Grant said. "Incompetent? Drunk? Inconstant? Foolish?" He started to laugh but the specter's demeanor stopped him.

"Trustworthy."

"Well, bully for that." Now Grant did laugh, and spread his hands. "And look where it got me."

"You will help?" Samhain said simply.

"Why should I?" Grant said. "You still haven't told me what this is all about."

The specter seemed to be considering his next words. "Let's say that the Old One has deemed me untrustworthy and is exploring other ways to destroy this world."

"He doesn't trust the Lord of the Dead anymore?"

"No."

The hair on Grant's neck stood up, and he said nothing.

"He is seeking to employ...other means," Samhain explained.

Grant's throat was suddenly very dry. "And there's nothing you can do about it?"

Samhain shook his head slightly.

Grant said, "So I really don't have any choice, do I?"

"You can do nothing, or you can try to help. You will need salt. That's all I can tell you."

"Salt? What in hell does that mean?"

"It means it might work."

"Might work?"

Again the specter shook his head, and now he reached one powder-white hand, little more than a claw, and pushed the bourbon bottle toward Grant.

Grant poured two fingers of bourbon and looked down at it. There was a faint rustle of ice-cold breath and when he looked up Samhain was gone and someone was tramping up the stairs toward his office.

PART 2

He was a young man with old eyes. His thinning hair, delicate as a baby's, looked like it had once been blonde but now was ash-white. He wore the clothes of a college professor – corduroy trousers, flannel shirt. He sat down without being asked.

"I'm not working today," Grant said.

"I can see that," the kid said, looking at the half-empty Jim Beam bottle.

Grant picked it up and tilted it toward the kid

"Little early for me," the kid said.

"It's nine o'clock."

"In the morning."

Grant shrugged, uncapped the bottle and poured two inches of amber liquid into his jelly glass. "It's always nine o'clock."

"The old joke–it's always noon somewhere?"

"No, it's always nine o'clock right here." Grant turned around the Westclox on his desk, which was stuck at nine o'clock.

The kid didn't laugh.

"And anyway, today I had a special visitor. Special circumstances." He took a drink. He looked squarely at the kid. "Are you the spirit whose visit was foretold to me?" he quoted.

The kid said, "Dickens."

"Good. What is it you want?"

"I want to tell you a story about a monster."

Grant's eyes clouded over. "Heard enough of them for one lifetime."

"I'm told that you've dealt with this kind of thing before."

"Yes, and it lost me my livelihood and my wife. I'm the king of weird shit in these here parts."

"So I understand."

"Where do you live?" Grant interjected. Quietly, he had drawn his legal pad toward him and picked up his pen.

"Newburgh, New York. A few hours south of here. I teach high school English at Newburgh Free Academy." He smiled grimly. "For what good it does. I went there myself, and I was the only one in my English class who gave a rat's ass about any of it. Kids these days—"

"Stick to your story," Grant snapped.

The kid nodded and said, "So—"

"How old are you, anyway?" Grant asked.

"Twenty-three. Fresh out of grad school and into the grinder."

Grant wrote something down, harrumphed, and said, "Parts of you look older."

The kid didn't laugh, and Grant leaned over his desk and stared at the kid's face. "Christ, kid, you have the thousand-yard stare."

"I earned it yesterday."

Grant opened a drawer in his desk, took out a reasonably clean jelly jar glass, this one depicting The Flintstones in fading colors. He poured two inches of bourbon into it and slid it across to the kid, who stopped it with his open hand, hesitated, then closed his hand around it and brought it to his lips, knocking back half of it.

"So tell me," Grant said.

The kid put the glass down and stared at Grant, then began to talk.

PART 3

This is what he said:

My buddies and I were looking for an off-season place in the Adirondacks to rent for a week, for a good price. Especially since the weather's been so warm this September. But it was tough going. A lot of the places close up after Labor Day, and a lot that stay open don't rent in the winter. And the real estate agents we tried were either idiots or incompetents, or their listings were so outdated that they weren't any help. We wanted something in the Loon Lake area, either Friend's Lake or Schroon, but kept coming up empty. We'd been staying in a motor court near Loon Lake with our wives, making scouting trips in two separate cars, the girls in one, my two friends and I in the other.

So,we were driving through Warrensburg for the fifth time, looking to gas up, pick up the girls at the motor court and head south, when my buddy Jerry pointed at a cardboard sign stapled to a telephone pole that said 'Richter Real Estate.' It had a crude arrow pointing down a side street.

"I don't remember seeing that," my other friend Paul said, but I had already braked and turned the car.

"Was there an address on the sign?" I asked.

"No."

"I can see why," I mumbled, as the street was completely deserted, tree-lined with empty lots.

"Looks like a dead end," Jerry said.

"It was, and at the end of it was a single dwelling, little more than a summer shack, with another cardboard sign tacked to the wooden screen door that said 'Richter Real Estate.'"

"This is bullshit," Paul said. "Let's just go."

"No," Jerry said, "let's check it out."

By then I had stopped the car and Jerry was already hopping out of the front passenger side.

Paul and I followed, and Jerry was already banging on the door and trying the knob. When he pulled open the screen door the sign fell off.

Paul picked it up and threw it aside.

"This is bullshit," he said.

But the front door opened in Jerry's hand, and as he pushed it open we were confronted by a short, bald, stout man wearing round dark glasses. He looked like Tweedle-Dum. Behind him was an empty room with nothing but an empty desk and chair. The walls were completely bare, not even a calendar. And there wasn't a window or light. The only light that filled the room was what we had let in by opening the door.

"Richter Real Estate?" Jerry asked.

"Yes," the man said slowly.

"Are you Richter?" Paul asked.

The man nodded.

I said, "We're looking for a week's rental, with lake rights."

"That would be fine," Richter said.

"Wait a minute—" Paul began, but Jerry cut him off.

"Where?"

The man said, "Orange Lake."

"Where the heck is Orange Lake?" Jerry asked. "We've been driving all over this area for two days, and we never saw a sign for Orange Lake."

"It's very private, and very easy to get to," the man said. "You won't see it advertised." He had ambled over to his desk and pulled open the top drawer. "One particular property is available on it at the moment. A week's rental would be eight hundred dollars." He pulled out a sheet of paper that looked like a rental contract.

"Eight hundred dollars!" Paul sputtered. We had expected to each pay about that.

"Is that agreeable?" the man said. He retrieved a second item from the drawer, a clutch of photographs, and handed them to Jerry.

"Wow," Jerry said. "This place is gorgeous." He handed the photos to me, and I shared them with Paul. The house was a classic lake A-frame, with a wood burning stove in a great room, a roomy kitchen and a second floor with three bedrooms. There was a dock and a deck with a barbecue.

"Would you like me to show it to you?" the man asked.

Jerry shook his head. "We'll take it."

"But—" the man said.

"I said we'll take it. It's late in the day and the sun's going down. I'm tired and this is what we were looking for." He looked at Paul and I; I nodded and finally Paul said, "Sure, why not?"

"And it has lake rights?" Jerry asked.

"Oh, yes, definitely. There are kayaks stored under the back deck, and a good-sized row boat. The fishing may not be ideal this time of year, but there are pickerel and perch and, of course, sun fish."

"There's a refrigerator for beer?"

The man took off his dark glasses and blinked. His eyes were filmy, almost milk-colored. "Of course." He put his glasses back on.

"Where do we sign?" Jerry said.

The man studied the contract he had drawn out, then handed it to Jerry and pointed. "Here," he said.

Jerry, being a lawyer, read it quickly and then produced his pen. "My God, they don't even require a security deposit." As he signed he said to Richter, "A check is all right?"

Richter nodded. "Or, if you prefer..."

Jerry produced his American Express card. He signed, handed the contract to Paul and I and said, "You guys can settle up with me later. Or, actually, it can be my treat."

Richter took the card, produced a credit card receipt slider from his drawer, and ran a carbon for the receipt. He handed it to Jerry, who signed it with a flourish and then took his Amex card back and returned it to his wallet.

"How do we get there, and where's the key?" he asked Richter.

Richter gave us directions, and handed Jerry a set of keys.

"Call the gals," Jerry said when they got back in the car. "They'll be thrilled to get out of that goddamned motor court."

Paul flipped open his phone and made the call. Jerry handed him the directions and Paul read them into the phone. After a bit he pulled the phone away from his ear and said, "They want to know if they should meet us there or if we should eat first. They're starving."

"Tell them we'll stop at Oscar's and pick up food. We'll meet them at the lake."

Paul spoke into the phone and then closed it. "Done."

"This is gonna be great," Jerry said.

"Wish I was as happy as you," I said, and Jerry immediately became defensive. "What's the problem?"

I shrugged as I nudged the car out onto Route 32. I noticed as we made the turn that the cardboard sign advertising the realtor was gone. "The whole thing just seemed…strange."

Jerry laughed. "So are you." He turned to Paul for support, who was staring out the car window. "What do you think, mealy-mouth?"

Paul shrugged. "Whatever."

"Whatever it is," Jerry said, regaining his humor. He had scored his points.

"What did the girls think?" I asked.

"What do they ever think?" Paul said. "The hubbies are paying the bills. Mary sounded excited. I could hear them talking about finally taking a swim."

"Good enough," Jerry said. "Jane's been talking for two weeks about nothing but diving into Adirondack lake water."

Oscar's was crowded, but the line moved. We picked up ribs and liverwurst and a marinated flank steak, and then swung by the Grand Union supermarket and got two cases of beer and a loaf of rye bread and an onion and assorted chips and dips. The sun was getting low but it was still warm as we piled back into the car. I noticed that even Paul was upbeat now.

"Still nervous, Pervis?" Jerry said to me as I started the car.

Again I shrugged. "It was just a little too easy."

"Sometimes good things are."

With Jerry's help, I followed the directions. Soon we were way off the beaten track, ending up on a gravel road that abruptly turned to packed dirt. The trees hung unnaturally close overhead, their leaves just beginning to turn. Mingled with the oaks were white birches and evergreens.

"Sure looks the way it should," Jerry said.

And then we saw the lake. It loomed up suddenly in the windshield, then filled it.

"It's huge," Paul said.

In the late Autumn day, it was beautiful. The reddening sun speckled the surface, and I swore I could see little jumping fish. The road pulled to the right, and then I saw the house.

"Can't miss it," Jerry said.

"It looks like it's the only one," Paul said.

He was right—there wasn't another structure in sight.

But it certainly looked as advertised. There was a circular drive with a double carport cut into one side of the house. Mary's SUV was parked in one of the spots.

Jerry jumped out of the car as soon as it stopped and called, "Hey, Mary! Jane! Beth!"

There was no answer.

We unloaded the car as Jerry unlocked the door.

Inside it smelled tight and unused but not musty, and looked just like photos Richter had shown up. Jerry started throwing open windows. "Where do you think they are? They didn't have a key."

"Only one place," I said.

We put away the groceries, filled the refrigerator in the roomy kitchen with cold beer, and trooped outside.

Sure enough, three Adirondack chairs were arranged on the end of the dock, with books and towels scattered around them.

But our wives were nowhere to be seen.

"Mary!" Paul shouted into the lowering sun, the water.

There was no answer.

"Either they're walking around the lake, or swimming in it," Paul said.

I kneeled down and dipped my fingers into the water to see how warm it was. It felt odd, and very warm. I quickly pulled them out.

"My bet is they swam to the other side," Paul said.

Jerry was already on the verge of getting mad, tramping back to the house. "Couldn't even wait for us..." he fumed.

"Bring some beers!" I shouted after him.

He brightened a little, and gave me a wave.

Paul opened his phone. "If they went for a walk..."

"Good idea," I said.

After a few moments he shook the phone and looked at it. "Dead spot."

"There are plenty of them up here," I said.

He put it away and stared out at the water. "I don't know about them swimming across. It's pretty wide, and Jane isn't that good a swimmer, is she?"

I settled myself into one of the deck chairs, tossing a copy of *Vanity Fair* magazine aside onto the dock. "Sit down and relax. Beth and Mary are good swimmers and wouldn't let anything happen to Jerry's wife."

Jerry re-appeared with a bucket of iced Coronas.

"We forgot limes!" he said, but he was smiling, already slipping into vacation mode.

I took a beer, settled into the chair, and closed my eyes. "Heaven."

"Something—" Paul said.

I opened my eyes, saw something far out on the water, a brief splash, and heard what sounded like a very faint cry.

"That sounded like Mary," Paul said.

"Take it easy, drink your beer," Jerry retorted. "Your wife's the best swimmer of the three."

Paul frowned, stared at the water, then finally eased himself into an Adirondack chair. "Guess it was nothing."

Jerry laughed, and sat down in the third chair. He kicked at a beach towel with his boat shoe. "They'll be back when they're back. What else is new?"

Paul grunted in agreement and sipped at his beer. "But we're gonna get hell for not buying limes."

We all laughed.

Again there was a faraway cry, which could have been a bird.

"Remember Loon Lake, a few years ago?" Paul asked.

"Yes, big guy, I do," Jerry answered. "No loons to be seen."

"But it was beautiful, wasn't it?"

"That's what made me fall in love with the Adirondacks," I said.

"Me, too," Paul said, wistfully.

Again that slight, faraway sound.

"I think I'll go for a swim," Paul said, standing up. He stripped off his golf shirt and cargo shorts, revealing swim trunks.

"You worried about them?" I asked.

He shook his head, looking distracted. "Just want to swim. That's why we came here, right?"

Without another word he dived from the dock, his long, tall body disappearing into the water.

"He always was like that," Jerry said, putting down his empty Corona and fishing into the ice bucket for another.

I nodded.

"A worry-wart," Jerry said, completing his thought. "Even in high school all he did was worry. And when he met Mary he became a pro."

I was looking out at the water, the sun almost gone below the trees across the lake. I hadn't seen Paul surface.

"Jerry—" I began.

"Not you, too," Jerry said, reading the tone in my voice. He pushed back his long black hair and looked at me through his designer glasses. "Just shut up and enjoy the moment, okay? By the way, I checked out the gas grill, and it's working. Which means we get ribs tonight."

I nodded absently, still waiting for Paul's huge form to break the surface.

Again that faraway call, carried away on the slight breeze.

I opened my own cell phone and checked the signal.

Nothing.

"Jerry—"

"Will you shut the fuck up?" he said, almost shrilly. When I looked at him his eyes were hooded in the near-twilight. "I came up here to be away from all the bullshit," he said, by way of explanation. He looked out at the water. "Including, to tell you the truth, Jane."

Before I could say anything he continued, "We're having problems. Big time. She's pushing to have a kid and I'm pushing back." He drank a long draft from his beer. "I just can't do it."

"Do what?"

"Have a kid."

A sound from across the water. Both of us looked out, Jerry shading his eyes against the red lowering sun. "I thought I heard—"

"It sounded like Paul."

"Was he laughing?"

"It sounded like a yelp."

"A *yelp*?" Jerry laughed. "I don't even know what a yelp is. I'm a lawyer. That's not a technical term."

Again came the sound, more distinct.

Jerry put down his beer bottle, cupped his hands and yelled, "Paul, are you okay?"

Silence.

Jerry picked up his beer and drained it. He reached into the bucket for another one. "Shit, are we gonna hear it about the limes."

"Fuck the limes," I said.

Jerry looked at me hard and said, "Jane and I might be done. Kaput. Finished."

"Just over the kid thing?

"Over a lot of things." He stood up. "I'm going to the deck and fire up the grill. I'll do the cooking tonight."

"Shouldn't we wait for the rest of them?"

"We should, but I don't want to."

He took the bucket with him, and trudged off the dock to the cabin.

The sun sank incrementally below the far pines. I sat nursing my Corona and listening for any sounds. But there were none, except what sounded like a close-by splash of a fish breaking the surface. I thought of my fishing tackle in the trunk but decided to wait until tomorrow morning to haul it out.

And then Paul appeared, hauling himself out of the water at the end of the dock and stretching tall.

"No sign of them," he said, thickly. He looked disoriented.

"Where did you go?"

"I swam..." he said, and then he hesitated. He brought his hands to his head, and then his mouth opened and he tried to scream.

"What's wrong?" I said. His body seemed to be covered with tiny moving *some-things*, which vibrated like tiny hairs all over his visible torso.

"The...entire...*lake*," he managed to croak out. He looked down at his body, and then he looked at me and tried to scream again.

And then he melted away, right down to his skeleton, and fell back off the end of the dock, his bones making clacking sounds as they hit the water below.

I stood speechless, and then I ran to the house where I found Jerry on the back deck, humming to himself over the lit gas barbecue. The remains of two more empty Corona bottles were in the now-empty ice pail.

He turned and smiled at me. "Gonna get shit-faced tonight, my friend."

"They're gone," I managed to get out. "I think they're all gone."

"Who?" His smile was lopsided.

"All of them. Paul. The girls."

"You saw the girls?"

"*You don't get it!*" I shouted. "I saw Paul die, right in front of me, and the girls must be gone, too."

"You saw the girls?" he said, slightly sobering up, locking into lawyer mode.

"No, but—"

"Then they ain't gone." He waved vaguely at the water. "They're...out there. Swimming. That bitch Jane among 'em." He tried to turn back to the barbecue, but I grabbed his arm.

"You're not listening to me. I saw Paul die."

He turned and looked at me, his eyes unreadable in the near dark.

"*I saw him die,*" I repeated. "He just…went away. He turned to bones. Right there on the dock."

He turned off the burners and descended the deck stairs. I heard him laboring under the decking, then saw him pulling out the row boat which was stored there.

"Let's go find the girls," he said.

"I don't know if it's safe," I said. "The way Paul died—"

He continued to labor with the row boat, dragging it toward the short beach.

"You're either with me, or against me, podna," he said. "But I'm going."

I left the deck and joined him, and together we got the boat to the beach, and then into the water.

"Don't go into the water," I said, as he started to walk the boat in.

He looked at me curiously, and then jumped onto the deck before climbing into the boat.

"I don't think the water's safe," I said.

He snorted a laugh. Obviously the drunkenness had not completely left him. "Of course it's not safe. You could drown." He made a face. "Man, this water looks like shit. Like its got live oatmeal in it."

I climbed into the rowboat behind him.

He gave me his lopsided look again. "By the way, where's Paul's body?"

I pointed at the end of the dock.

He stared at me. "If you're pulling my leg. I'll throw you overboard into this muck."

I said nothing, and suddenly he seemed to completely sober up a bit. "Look, I overstated how bad things are before. I know all of you, including Jane, think I'm an asshole lawyer, but I really do love her. I did and I still do. I've tried to fix things. I cheated on her a few times, and made a jerk of myself. But she's still it. And I do want to have kids. Soon. Not right away. This week was supposed to be my way of telling her that." He stared at me in the fading light. "Please tell me the girls are all right, that the whole thing's a joke."

I stared back, and he picked up one of the oars and began to row, stopping at the end of the dock and looking down.

"Oh, shit in heaven," he said.

I looked where he was looking, and saw the vague outline of a skeleton lying in the sand at the bottom of the silty shallow water.

///

Twilight seemed to hang on. The water was strangely dull and still. The sun looked as if it had stopped in the sky, just below the trees.

"How will we get back?" I asked.

"Look at the house," he said, his voice dull, as if he was in shock. "I turned every light in the place on before I lit the barbecue."

We each manned an oar, side by side, and made for the middle of the lake. Unconsciously, I think, I was aiming for the spot where we had heard the splashing noises earlier.

After twenty minutes or so, Jerry stopped rowing. He was staring over the side of the boat.

"*Jesus*," he said.

I looked over, and almost vomited.

His wife Jane's face was staring up at us from perhaps two feet of murky water. She wore a one-piece bathing suit and her eyes were wide open.

"Oh, God," I said, and then was too late as Jerry plunged his hand into the water up to his elbow.

"Maybe it's not too late," he said, gagging.

He gasped, and pulled his arm out. Only there was no arm anymore, only a hand and arm bones, covered with miniature moving hissing things, leading up to his still-fleshy elbow, which pumped blood over the side of the boat.

He moaned, and leaned over the side, then fell in before I could catch him.

I saw him entwine himself with Jane, and then the two of them slowly turned down and away, disappearing into the agitated water, even as his severed arm still pumped blood, his eyes were glazed with disbelief.

And then, as the boat drifted deeper into the lake, I saw my own wife Beth, and Paul's wife Mary, each wearing their bathing suits and staring wide-eyes up at me.

Beth seemed to motion lazily toward me, beckoning me down with her hand, her brown hair shimmering away from her head.

With a force of will I turned away, and grabbed the oars, and began to row.

Twilight had turned to deep dusk, almost night. Stars were appearing overhead, the sharp constellation Cassiopeia and, off the north star Polaris, the big dipper. I had spent other nights on other lakes in the Adirondacks, fishing and drinking beer and thinking how good life could be.

This night, I rowed madly to shore, towards the lights now-dead Jerry had left on.

I don't know how long it took me, or what effort I put into it, but abruptly I felt the hard thump of sand beneath the aluminum hull of the boat, and tumbled out, and vomited on the sand.

After a while I rose.

Behind me, the beach seemed thinner, the water closer. And then it seemed as if the whole lake, from shore to shore, rose a few inches.

I stumbled up the deck steps, threw open the sliding glass door and nearly fell into the house which I had seen only in pictures.

Behind me, the water continued to rise.

It rose, in humping increments, all at once across its entire surface, and came toward the house like a living thing. I had barely recovered when I saw that there was thick, viscous water pushing at the tires on Mary's SUV in the car park. There was no moon, but the stars were blotted out now with something like a fog, which hung above the lake like a low cloud.

And then I heard it, lapping like a dog drinking water from a bowl, slurping, coming closer.

It was up to the bottom step of the deck now.

Quickly, as if in a dream, I entered the house and bypassed the great room with its wood burning stove. I thought of trying to fight the water with fire but there was no time – lake water was already seeping over the sill of the sliding glass door. I briefly considered backtracking and slamming the door shut, but somehow knew it would be useless.

I ascended the stairs to the second floor and threw open the bedroom doors. They were all similar, with a single window and twin beds.

In the hallway I found a pull-down set of steps to a crawl space, and scrambled up it to find a tight little room with no windows.

Below, I heard water pushing, edging into the house with soft, moaning, hungry sounds.

I climbed down the steps from the crawlspace and entered one of the bedrooms facing the lake. Water nearly filled the window view. The eerie milky fog seemed to be moving in rhythm to the rising lake.

I looked down from the loft and saw water at the second step of the stairs.

It was coming through the open sliding glass door, rising inches with each little humping wave.

I ran back up to the crawlspace, and studied it again.

It was sealed tight, a death trap if the water rose into it.

I checked out each bedroom, throwing open the window in each.

In the second one, I discovered a roof over the carport, and another roof level above.

When I stepped back into the room there was water in the room, and I heard an eerie moan from the lake, as if something was very hungry. The fog pulsed.

The water rose, soaking the carpeting in the hallway.

I retreated into the second bedroom, and climbed out gingerly onto the roof.

I squinted and looked up; the fog was closer, following the water.

Water edged up over the sill of the window, opaque, cloudy, looking like suet.

A drop fell onto the roof inches from my foot, and then moved toward me.

I stepped around it and tried to pull myself up onto the roof above the crawlspace.

There was a gutter which momentarily held my weight, then pulled out of the facing. I fell, and rolled almost to the end of the roof before frantically stopping my progress.

Water was flowing at me.

I stepped around it. There was an odd look of depth and weight to the water. *Things* moved within it.

With effort, I pulled myself up over the broken gutter. I almost fell again, which would have landed me in the growing puddle on the roof, but managed to dig my fingers into the shingles above and yank myself up.

Gasping for breath, I turned around and looked at the lake.

It wasn't a lake anymore–it was an ocean, devouring the lower levels of the house and the woods around me. There were slow waves lapping at the top of the roof I had just left, and a frightening keening of something that sounded as if it was from another planet.

I lay back, my lungs still pumping, and looked at the sky.

Cassiopeia peeked down at me through a tiny break in the fog, and then disappeared.

I heard the hungry sound of water rising.

I fainted, or fell asleep, I don't know which.

When I awoke it was morning, and I heard birds singing.

At first I didn't know where I was, and almost sat up too fast, which would have thrown me from my little perch to certain death below.

I lay back and took a deep breath.

Slowly I rose, and looked around me.

The woods around the house were restored, the water had receded.

The lake was blue and fresh-looking, wave-free, content in the early morning sun which warmed behind me in the East.

I looked down.

There was no sign of water damage, no rising water, no sign that there had been a rising thick torrent threatening the house and me.

Carefully, I made my way down to the window into the second bedroom.

It was dry and as clean as it had looked the night before.

I took a deep breath, exhaled, and then began to weep.

I was safe, for the moment, but my wife, and my friends, were all dead.

I climbed down to the first floor, and went out onto the deck and then down to the carport.

The cars were there, the row boat where I had left it on the beach, nestled in the sand, its thick line restored.

But there was no driveway, no road leading to the house, nothing but a mass of trees surrounding the house.

And then I heard a sound, and turned to look at the lake.

The water was rising up again, like a living thing on its haunches.

I ran into the woods, and kept running. I remember the sounds of water behind me, becoming intense. I never looked back. I dodged brambles and bushes and rock walls and just kept running.

And then, suddenly, I was on Route 32, and was almost hit by a car. Another one picked me up, though I don't remember hitchhiking. I think I had collapsed on the side of the road. I vaguely remember an emergency room, and then they released me, and someone mentioned you, and here I am.

PART 4

Grant had long stopped making notes of any kind, but he still played with his pen. He put it down, and pulled the bourbon bottle, which was nearly empty, back towards himself, but did not fill his glass. Instead he capped the bottle, opened the bottom drawer of his desk and put it in. He pulled out a new bottle of Jim Beam but didn't open it.

He said, "That's a great horror story, kid. There's only one thing wrong with it."

"What's that?"

Grant leaned forward on his desk and said, "There isn't any Orange Lake. Not here, anyway. Not anywhere near here."

"I'll take you there," the kid said. He drew out a folded piece of paper. "I kept the directions."

"Figured you'd say that. And believe it or not I do have a plan." Grant stood and lifted the bottle of Jim Beam, cradling it. He motioned with his hand at the door. "Lead on, Macduff. You're driving my pickup. I'm too drunk to do it."

The kid said, "The quote is actually, 'Lay on, Macduff.'"

"Whatever. You're driving my pickup."

PART 5

They made two stops, at Grant's insistence. The first was the Orangefield police station, where Grant got out of the car and told the kid to stay put.

"Keep the engine running," Grant said, and then he walked to the front plate glass door and yanked it open. The kid could see a desk up on a platform with a fat cop studying a newspaper.

"Hey, Sarge!" Grant yelled, and when the fat cop looked up Grant said, "Fuck you!"

He turned, laughing, and let the door close behind him, while the fat Sergeant sputtered and tried to get out of his chair.

When Grant climbed back into the car and motioned the kid to move on he explained, "Little ritual of mine, every time I'm in town since they fired my ass."

They then stopped at a Hardware store on the main street named "Struck's," where Grant instructed the kid to park the car and come in with him. When they entered a man behind the counter with a pencil lodged behind one ear greeted Grant by name.

"What do you need?" the man asked.

"I need every bag of rock salt you have."

Struck's eyebrows went up. "Wow. I don't have a full supply yet for winter, especially since it's been so warm, but I do have maybe thirty or so twenty pound bags."

"I'll take them all." Grant produced a credit card and slapped it on the counter.

Struck shrugged and ran the card, then the three of them loaded the bed of Grant's truck with the bags of salt.

"Can I ask—" Struck started to ask when they were finished, but Grant said, "No," smiled and shook his hand.

They got back in the truck and the kid angled them off the main street, and, with Grant's urging, took a short cut to meet up with Route 32. On the way they saw why Orangefield was the self-proclaimed Pumpkin Capital of the World. Already pumpkins were out in front of every house and shop, or in windows, which were also decorated with black and orange crepe paper and cardboard cutouts of witches, jointed skeletons and pumpkin heads. Everything was orange and black, and Halloween was almost a month away.

"This is my world, kid," Grant said, and snorted a laugh.

They drove in silence for a while, until the kid whispered, almost as if in a trance:

"But when the Night had thrown her pall

"Upon that spot, as upon all,

"And the mystic wind went by

"Murmuring in melody—

"Then—ah then I would awake

"To the terror of the lone lake."

"What the hell was that?" Grant asked. He had twisted open the bourbon bottle and took a short sip.

"Edgar Allan Poe," the kid answered. "I used to try to teach it to my high school students around Halloween. They were more interested in using their cell phones while I lectured."

Grant took a long look at the kid.

"You know, you really do look like shit. Maybe you should be back in the hospital."

"I can handle this."

"I can go on myself if you like. I still only half believe this lake is there."

The kid's hands were trembling and white-knuckled on the steering wheel, and he pulled the truck abruptly off the road into the service lane and braked it.

"Look," he said, staring straight ahead, "I lost my wife and all of my best friends to that...*thing*. I'm not going anywhere but forward."

Grant softened his voice. "Okay, then."

The kid smiled crookedly. "And you said you have a plan, right?" He pulled the truck back onto the road.

"Of sorts. Let's just say I had a bit of coaching. I just don't know if I can fully trust the source."

The kid's crooked smile grew. "Fellow in a black cape named Samhain?"

Grant was in the middle of another sip of bourbon and nearly sputtered.

"He was the one who mentioned you to me," the kid continued. "I thought I was dreaming when he appeared."

"Where..."

The kid shrugged, and said nothing.

Grant took another, deeper sip of bourbon. "Is that why you didn't ask me any questions when I bought 600 pounds of rock salt?"

"He told me we would need salt, too."

Grant just shook his head.

They came into Warrensburg, and Grant told the kid to find the real estate agent who had rented them the property. After one wrong turn they found the dead end road, and the kid turned Grant's pickup down it. Grant studied the telephone pole where the kid had said the sign had been – the sign, was, indeed, gone.

The road was empty of houses, and when they came to the end the kid stopped the truck.

"That's where Richter Real Estate was," the kid said, pointing to a weed-grown lot with a dead sagging white birch tree nestled dead center in the middle of it. There was no sign that a structure of any kind had ever been there.

Somewhere distant a dog howled.

"All right, let's go," said Grant, and the kid turned the car around. As he did so Grant looked down at the road and saw a crumpled cardboard sign that read "Richter Real Estate."

He took a deep breath.

The kid stopped briefly at the head of the dead end to study his folded instructions, then made a right turn.

"It's maybe twenty minutes away," he said.

Grant said nothing.

They had the windows down, but the day had turned markedly colder, unlike the recent Indian Summer weather. Grant rolled his window half way up. The leaves had finally started to turn, the first hints of yellow and red making it suddenly autumnal. The sky through the tree tops was slate gray, and the wind had picked up markedly. Grant rolled his window up another turn, and waited for the kid to do the same, but he seemed preoccupied, staring intently through the windshield.

He abruptly slowed, making the car behind them, which had been following too close, brake and blow its horn.

"Fuck 'em," Grant said. "If I was still a cop I'd give 'em a ticket."

"This is the turn-off," the kid said, and eased the truck onto a road Grant had never seen.

When the pea gravel turned to hard dirt, Grant said, "Stop."

The kid braked, and Grant got out of the truck. He examined the dirt road, then walked back to where the pea gravel ended. When he got back in the truck he grunted.

"What is it?" the kid asked.

"I've never seen gravel like that around here." He reached into his jacket pocket and produced a few pieces.

"I told you, that road disappeared. It all disappeared."

Grant nodded, and the kid drove on.

And there was the lake.

They came upon it suddenly, just like the kid had described. Up a little crest, a little right turn, and there was a vast expanse of water, lit with cloud-laden sky, filling the windshield. The kid drove carefully, edging the car to the right, and the cabin appeared, just as he had described it. There were two cars, a sedan and an SUV, parked in the carport, and the kid stopped the truck behind the sedan and handed Grant the keys.

Grant waggled the quarter-empty bottle of bourbon and said, "Maybe you ought to keep them, and drive us home."

The kid pressed them into his hand, his face grim, and Grant took them and put them in his pocket.

"Do you want to see the house?" the kid asked. He sounded reluctant.

"Not really." They got out of the truck, Grant leaving the bourbon bottle behind. Grant studied the sky, which was getting thicker with gray clouds. The temperature had dropped even more, and the trees at the edge of the lake were swaying slightly with the wind.

"Actually," Grant said, "I'd just like to get this done. It looks like it might rain."

He studied the lake, the rowboat sitting on the beach, shook his head, and said, "Goddamn. It's actually here."

"Orange Lake," the kid said.

Grant was already heading for the back of the pickup. He lowered the tailgate and hauled out the first 20 pound bag of salt.

"How many do you think we can get in the boat?" the kid asked.

"As many as it can hold. But before we waste our time..."

He brought the first bag to the end of the dock, ripped it open, and poured in a handful.

The water coalesced, swirled a little, and then settled.

"Shit." He poured half the bag in, and this time there was a reaction: a funnel which formed and settled nearly to the bottom. It revealed what looked like part of a human skeleton.

"Is that...?" Grant asked.

The kid looked down. "Yes, my friend Paul."

"Shit again, it's gonna work," Grant said. He almost grinned. "I wonder if we could just dump it all here?"

"That's not what Samhain told me," the kid said, earnestly. "We've got to bring it out to where the…bodies are."

Grant looked down at the water, and saw that the funnel had filled in with water again. The skeleton was still there, visible through the chalky water, which was filled with tiny fish with huge gaping jaws, like horrid simulacrums of deep sea creatures.

He looked at the kid's face, which was white as a sheet. "Okay, we'll do as instructed. Let's push the boat into the water, tie it to the dock, and load it up."

When they looked at the boat, lake water was lapping at its bow, pushing it up.

"What happened to the beach?" Grant said.

"The water's rising."

"Shit. Well, let's get this done then."

When they had finished Grant was sure the rowboat would sink when they got into it, but it didn't happen. But it did ride a bit low in the water. He manned the oars himself, because the kid looked like he was going to be sick. Overhead, the skies darkened even more, though Grant noted by his watch that it was only 3:30 in the afternoon.

The kid guided them toward where he and his friend Jerry had discovered the bodies. As they neared the spot, the kid became even more sickly, and retched over the side of the boat.

"Is this where…?" Grant asked.

"This is where Jerry and the girls' bodies are," the kid said in a weak voice.

Grant felt the first spattering of raindrops, and looked up at the lowering sky. The wind had picked up, too, making the lake choppy. When the raindrops hit the lake they hissed, as if the lake was made of fire. He looked back at the house and could just barely see the top of it.

"The damn lake is still rising."

"Samhain told me that once the lake has what it owns, it will keep rising."

"How far?"

"It won't stop." The kids stared at him and said, "Ever."

Grant just stared back at him. "You mean—"

The kid nodded. "You can start dumping the salt," he said, in a bare whisper.

Grant stopped rowing, reached for the nearest bag of salt, and ripped the top off it. He looked up at the kid, who was halfway out of the boat.

"Hey—!" Grant shouted.

The kid had lowered himself over the side, and was barely hanging on.

Weakly, he said, "This is where I belong."

"What—"

"That was the only part of my story that was a lie," he answered in a fainter whisper. It sounded as though he was fading away. "After I spent the night on the roof, I never made it out of the woods onto the main road. The lake overcame me there. That's where I met Samhain. He told me to tell you that. He said it would make my story more believable. He…helped me come back. But he could only do it for a short time. The lake will have what it owns, now." His eyes were hooded black holes in his face, and his hands slipped off the boat and he was gone.

Grant went to where the kid had disappeared, and saw the kid staring up at him from a shallow depth. Around him the water was churning with the tiny sea creatures he had seen at the end of the dock.

"You never told me your name, kid," Grant whispered.

The dead body motioned at him, one finger beckoning.

"No damned way, kid."

Grant took a quick look back at the shore; the top of the house was no longer visible.

The rowboat began to rock, and Grant could feel the water rise beneath him, as if he was being pushed up from below by a giant hand.

There was a clap of thunder.

Grant looked up.

And now the skies above opened, and rain and sleet fell in torrents. There were clouds that seemed to be lowering, like fog.

Grant cursed, and ripped at the bags of salt in the boat, climbing from one end to the other and, once, almost falling into the lake. He gouged at the plastic bags, ripping them in the middle, along their seams, tearing his fingernails, screaming curses, as the storm intensified and the wind came up and rocked the boat like a cork in a bathtub. The lake was trying to make him fall from the boat.

The wind began to moan, a loud inhuman sound, and in the distance, through the sheets of water, Grant saw a water spout as high as the fog roaring toward him over the surface.

"*Shit!*"

Grant tore at bags, pulling them open in the middle, throwing salt into the water.

The spout grew closer, towering over him. Grant felt the wind turn sideways as the first tendrils of the monster reached out for him—

And then, with an exhausted push, Grant emptied the last bag of salt into Orange Lake.

A sudden eerie calm came over the sky and water, as if a switch had been thrown.

The water spout evaporated.

The keening roar ceased.

The rowboat beneath Grant disappeared, dropping him onto something solid.

Grant lay back, exhausted, panting for breath for minutes that seemed like hours, and then he pulled himself up and looked about him.

The water was gone.

All of it.

He stood in the middle of a huge valley bordered by rolling Autumn hills.

A scant four feet away were five lines of bones, laid out in neat skeletons on still-green, Indian Summer grass.

Grant looked up at the sky, which was clearing with the new absence of wind. The sun was coming out, and it felt warmer.

He looked toward what had been the shore, and saw three automobiles stranded in a thicket of brambles and weeds.

There was nothing else – no house, no carport, no driveway, no dock, no road. Searching his pocket, he found that the gravel he had retrieved from the road as evidence was gone.

He staggered toward home, passing a full human skeleton reclining on the grass where the end of the dock had been. He stopped to retrieve the bottle of Jim Beam from his truck, noting a pile of empty Corona beer bottles laying in the tangled grass nearby.

PART 6

Samhain came to visit on Halloween, late in the afternoon. Grant knew he would. Grant had been very drunk for almost three weeks, turned down two adultery cases, an offer from the jeweler downstairs to investigate his nephew, who the jeweler was sure was embezzling him, and even a surprise from the Orangefield police department, to consult on a sensitive case involving their accountant.

He figured at this point his savings account would be empty by the end of the year.

But Samhain did come. Grant offered him a drink, and the black cape flapped ever so slightly and the thin red lips almost turned up in a smile.

"Just tell me you took care of that kid," Grant said.

"His name was Jeffrey. And yes, he has already moved on from my place. As have the others."

"Your place. You didn't bother to tell me Jeffrey was already dead."

"As he told you, it made his story more...urgent."

"How did you...?"

The cape fluttered. "Being who I am, I have certain gifts and abilities, as you know. In old times, and even now, I would be able to...accommodate a human from my place to here for one night. That night is usually Halloween. But in special circumstances..."

Again the cape fluttered, the horrid red slash of his lips lifted lightly.

"You never cease to horrify me," Grant said, reaching for the bottle.

To his surprise, Samhain's spectral hand stayed his own. "Mind, Mr. Grant. Or you may see me sooner than you wish."

"And...?"

"We would have lost a...valuable partnership."

"I see..."

Grant closed his eyes for just a moment, but when he opened them Samhain was gone. There was a slowly dissipating chill in the room.

Grant put away the bottle, got out of his chair and closed the window.

"Happy effing Halloween," he said, to no one in particular.

Nathan

SELINA ROSEN

No one believes me now.

Why am I saying now? The truth is no one has ever really believed me. Sometimes... Sometimes if I cover my ears and close my eyes real tight even I can begin to think it was all just some horrible nightmare. But eventually I have to open my eyes and my ears because if I don't he will poke me, and when he does and I open my eyes...Well there he is right there. He's here now, even now, watching me and running his stupid mouth. He's as real to me as this pen in my hand, this bunk, that toilet, the bars that protect the rest of the world from me, and from him.

He has to be real because if he's not...if he's not then I really have done all the things I stand accused of doing. If he's not real then I'm the monster everyone thinks I am.

I wish he would shut up. I wish he would *ever* just shut up, but he never does. He's always talking, never saying anything worth listening to; certainly nothing I want to hear. Slurs and innuendoes are his pallet and deceit of the highest order his art form. He rationalizes, blaming everyone for what is wrong with his life. He never takes responsibility for his own actions. *Others* always force him to do the things he does and I always pay for his crimes.

I hate him. I *loathe* him, and because of him and the things he has done he is my only companion.

Even now as I sit trying to ignore him, trying to write, he is talking making it hard for me to have my own thoughts. He never shuts up! I am writing this to tell you of the living hell which I have endured, so that maybe someone, someday, might read my words and realize that what I am saying, what I have always been saying, is true. That I am not the reprobate that everyone thinks I am. I am as much one of his victims as anyone else maybe more so than all the others.

I'm not lying, I'm not making it all up, and I'm not deluded. He's real! He's right there; he's always been there. My own personal antagonist putting me through the worst kind of hell.

Often in these last few months I have cried out, "Shut up, Nathan!" when I couldn't stand his hateful ramblings any longer and always from down the cell-block someone would scream back.

"Shut up ya fuckin' nut job!"

And Nathan would just laugh louder and then blame me for us being in jail. He did the crimes yet he blames me for our incarceration. He is a passive-aggressive bastard! A fat, ugly dwarf-looking man, who in reality hates everyone and everything. No one but me sees him, no one but me can hear him, yet he makes everyone around me miserable through his actions.

At first my parents and everyone else called Nathan my invisible friend, but Nathan has NEVER been my friend. Even for the brief time I thought he was he really wasn't.

I don't even know exactly what he is; over the years I have changed my mind a hundred times. He's not a ghost. I don't think he ever lived, at least not in the way we understand life. He's too evil and too physically strong to be a spirit of any sort. Whenever I have touched him or him me, he is as solid as any man. His thoughts are twisted, but twisted in the way a psychopath's are, not in the way a demon's would be. He has no super-human powers. In every way except his invisibility he is only a man, but unfortunately a man much stronger than I am and one that never sleeps.

He is the most vile and evil of creatures, something so black and horrible that the rest of you simply blot him out.

I think he is that thing, that—what is it?—when you hear a noise and no one's there. That shadow that people see out of the corner of their eyes that they quickly dismiss. That horrible, unclean thing you imagine is in your house when you are the only one at home and you don't dare turn around to look at—for fear you'll find it.

He's the reason why people draw their curtains at night and make an effort not to look out their windows as they do so. He's that thing that's in the closet and under the bed. That odd, dark shape you occasionally see in your mirror that's gone before you can identify it. The thing you think will grab your ankles and pull you down and devour you if you uncover yourself and step on the floor after you've had a nightmare.

The real problem for me is that unlike the rest of you I *do* see him, and that makes him completely real.

I was just four when Nathan stepped into my life. My little sister had just been born, and I was lonely. I felt like no one loved me any more, like no one had time for me. One night I looked up and there he was sitting not in but on my little chair in the corner of my room. It was a ridiculous pose yet in that first instant upon seeing him I knew he was evil. I was terrified. I screamed and yelled till my parents came. Nathan laughed at me, pointed and just laughed, which only scared me more. He called me a sissy baby, a bed wetter. My parents didn't see him, didn't hear him, and the more I insisted he was there the madder they got.

I didn't get it then, didn't understand it. I could see him, why couldn't they? I just thought they were being mean when they scolded me and kept insisting there was nothing there. When they left, leaving him in my room and even turned the lights off, I thought they were the worst parents in the world. I started to cry and then I felt him sit on my bed. I screamed again. My father came alone this time and he had no patience for me at all. There was nothing there and it was stupid to insist that there was. Further he told me, "Scream as much as you like, no one will come. Remember the story about the little boy who cried wolf."

I get it now, how it must have looked to them. They couldn't see or hear him. It must have seemed that I was just acting up to get attention.

Nathan laughed and laughed and laughed. He said he was my friend, that I shouldn't be afraid.

He didn't go away and I couldn't make anyone believe me so I got used to him. In fact after I got over being so scared it was great for a while. He would talk to me and play games with me. He was never really mean or hateful. He was always mad, I knew he was, but most of the time I had no idea what he was talking about so it didn't really bother me. He was a grown up and I was just a little boy. He said bad words and called people awful names, but as long as he wasn't mad at me it didn't really bother me.

I'll admit it. There was a time when I truly thought he was the only person in the world that I could trust. The only person who cared about me, my only friend—and he never left. He would stay there in my room with me and for a while he made me feel safe.

I told Nathan how much I hated my sister. How my parents had loved me until she came along and now they never had any time for me unless they were chewing me out. Everything had been better before she got there.

One afternoon when mother was giving her a bath Nathan said it would be really fun if I hid in the pantry downstairs and screamed real loud, so that mother would get scared and come and check on me. I hid in the pantry and yelled like someone was ripping me to pieces. When my mother wasn't there in a few minutes I screamed again. After a few minutes I came out of hiding to see why our trick wasn't having its desired effect. Mother lay at the bottom of the stairs, hurt. I shook her, but she didn't move. Her leg was twisted all funny, there was a gash on her head, and blood was running all over the floor. The baby was quiet, and I knew that wasn't right, either.

Nathan sat on the banister at the top of the stairs, laughing, and my blood ran cold. I knew then that my first impression of him had been right, that he was truly and unredeemably evil. I asked him to help, but he said he already had. I sat on the bottom step and started to cry.

The doorbell rang and I answered it. It was the next-door neighbor bringing mother's good pan back. She saw that I had been crying and asked me what was wrong. I pointed at mother. She called the ambulance.

Then she asked me, "Honey, where is the baby?"

I shrugged. She screamed at me, "Where is the baby!"

I just pointed upstairs. She came back down a few minutes later, crying and holding my sister in a wet towel, try to breathe life back into her.

They saved my mother, but Bethany was dead. At the funeral my mother cried and cried. Her leg was in a cast and her head was all bandaged up. When they threw dirt on the coffin she started sobbing and she didn't really stop for two years. The light never came back to her eyes. She never really looked at me again and truthfully I didn't blame her.

I had thought I hated my sister, but I didn't, not at all. I missed her, I wanted her and because of the way she had died no one cared at all about my grief. I never really felt alive after that. It wasn't really my fault, but it wasn't *not* my fault either because I felt like Nathan was my fault and he kept telling me he did it for me.

They knew it was my scream that had caused my mother to leave my sister in a tub alone, and they knew now that scream was just a hoax. They all blamed me. I tried to tell them that it was Nathan. No one believed me. In fact, this made them even angrier. On good days they thought my prank had caused my mother's accident and my sister's death. On bad days they thought I tripped my mother and held my sister's head under the water.

My family, hell even everyone in town stopped talking to me. You know that meaningless banter that adults address children with when they see them, mess their hair and say things like, "Hey sport how's it going?" That never happened to me after my sister died. People looked away. They acted like I was as invisible to them as Nathan was, and I started to feel that way, started to wish I could just vanish.

My own guilt and deep grief over Bethany's death only fueled the growing chasm that was developing between me and my parents. They didn't really care what happened to me and it was hard for them to pretend that they did. It was especially hard for my mother because I think she knew she'd been tripped and she thought I was the only person in the house, the only one who could have done it.

At the urging of the pastor they sent me to a shrink. He didn't make things better. He couldn't make Nathan go away and neither did all the drugs they gave me for everything from manic depression to full-blown schizophrenia. Nothing got rid of Nathan. The bastard was always there. He'd say he was my friend, but I knew that was a lie.

The shrink said having a pet, something living to bond with, might help. So dad kept bringing animals home. The minute I would even start to get attached to them, Nathan would start teasing and taunting the animals, and then he would... Well, he'd sodomize them until they died, with me crying the whole time and him laughing like it was some big joke. I knew if my parents saw the dead animals I'd be blamed, so I would take them and bury them in the woods behind the house. As far as I know, no one ever found my animal grave yard.

Time and time again I told Nathan to go away, but he wouldn't go. I now believe that in reality he can't leave me. Somehow he needs me to be here. He always says he's my only friend. He isn't my friend but he's all I have because he's made damn sure that no one wants to get close to me.

My parents secretly, and sometimes not so secretly, hated me.

He made sure everyone else hated me, too. Nathan once stuck my little cousin Rena's hand on the radiator till she was burnt really badly. I was trying to pull her away from Nathan, but I guess it looked to everyone else like I was the one burning her.

They changed my medication again and after that none of our extended family ever came to the house and we never went to family gatherings.

At school I finally made a friend. Peter was a nice boy with a bad lisp. The other kids made fun of him but I didn't so he liked me. He was a really good friend he even pretended to believe me that Nathan was real and that he did all of the terrible things that he did. He and I would whisper ideas about how to get rid of Nathan. Nathan warned me. He told me to quit hanging out with Peter or I'd be sorry. I told Nathan to go away, that I hated him.

He didn't go away.

One day as Peter and I were walking home from school he shoved Peter in front of a big truck. I tried to stop him, but I couldn't. The truck hit Peter, splattering him everywhere. That night as I was crying Nathan picked me up off the bed and beat my head into the wall over and over again. My parents thought I did it to myself.

I was sent back to the shrink. They changed my medication again.

I could see the way people looked at me, the way they pulled their children to them whenever they saw me. The other kids stayed clear of me, too, so I couldn't have made another friend even if I had wanted to. But I didn't want to. I knew that Nathan would kill anyone I liked.

Nathan would never shut up, whether I was working in class or at home, so I barely made passing grades. Neither my teachers nor my parents seemed to care about my lack of academic prowess. They were all just happy if I wasn't killing or maiming anyone. Every once in awhile a new bully would come to town and he'd "prove" himself by pounding on me and calling me names. Nathan would laugh and say I deserved it because I would never do what needed to be done, that I always left that to him.

Schoolyard bullies were always surprised when even after a good ass whipping I wasn't afraid of them. Let's face it; a minor beating was nothing compared to the physical and mental abuse Nathan had showered me with most of my life.

When I was a sophomore, right after a football game—the only one I had ever dared to attend—Keith Philips, one of the fullbacks and a guy destined for a full college scholarship, grabs me and slings me up against the side of the bleachers.

"Hey spooky!" That's what they called me. "Here's a clue. Keep your baby-killin', pushin'-people-out-in-front-of-cars, weirdo ass at home."

I didn't say anything. I never did. Why would I? All explaining myself had ever done was get me in more trouble.

Nathan started yelling at me to punch Keith, but I wouldn't. Nathan shoved me so that Keith thought I was coming at him. Keith beat the shit out of me, and then Nathan hit me a couple of more times on the way home for "Bein' a pussy."

Nathan picked up a big rock on our way home, and when he saw Keith coming he shoved me into the bushes. Then he ran out in the road and slung the rock right at the windshield in front of Keith.

Keith had been driving so fast the windshield exploded. The rock plowed through the breaking glass and struck Keith in the head. The car rolled a half a dozen times and burst into flames.

I ran through people's yards and over their fences knowing I would be blamed once again. I got upstairs without my parents seeing me, stripped off my clothes and started showering.

Keith wasn't the only person killed in that wreck. There had been a girl in the car with him. A nice girl, Jamie Hyatt, was killed, too. That time, though, no one thought it was me. It was written off as a traffic accident caused by a teen's reckless driving. So for the record, if you're reading this, Keith and Jamie's deaths weren't an accident. Nathan killed them, too.

When I turned eighteen I started working at a fast food restaurant. There was a girl who worked with me named Alice and I let myself do something really stupid. I fell in love with her. I really tried not to but then it became obvious that she had feelings for me, too, and it seemed like Nathan was going to leave me alone about it so I made a date to go out with her. No sooner had I gotten her into my car than Nathan beat me senseless and tied her up. He laughed at her screams as he drove out to the middle of nowhere. He beat me up again then tied me up and then he went after her. I pleaded with him, I begged him, but now I know that only made him more determined than ever to do his evil best.

The sick bastard did things to her that a man shouldn't do to a woman, and when her screaming had become only a sad, lost sob he started cutting her apart, piece by piece, till she was completely silent. I begged him to kill me, too, but he wouldn't. He just laughed and laughed and laughed.

That laughing is sometimes all I hear, even when he's not laughing at all.

See, every sick and depraved thing we abhor he thinks is funny. He thinks if he laughs, he can say and do anything he likes and that we should just accept it as the joke he thinks it is. He doesn't think he's evil. That's perhaps what makes him the most perverse. He actually thinks everything he does is justified.

When Nathan had untied me and I'd got over the beating I'd taken I looked around at the carnage and realized that everyone would think I had killed Alice. So I dug a hole and buried all her pieces. Then I drove to a nearby creek and cleaned up myself and the car as best I could.

The fat bastard thought this was really funny. He giggled at me all the way home, called me a faggot and such things like that. When I told him I hated him and that I wished he would die, he just laughed louder.

I knew I was never going to get away from Nathan, that I was never going to get the images of Alice's rape and murder out of my head. I thought about killing myself for the thousandth time in my short life. But the truth is if I had really thought that would set me and the world free of him I'd have done it long ago.

The next morning the cops came to question me. Alice had last been seen with me. Was it true that I had taken her someplace? Where had I taken her? Why was I all beat up? Did I know where she was? I answered as best I could knowing they'd be back with a search warrant in a few hours at the most.

When they left I told Mom and Dad what Nathan had done.

They just cried and screamed. What could they do? They didn't believe me. They couldn't see him, and in that moment whatever shred of doubt they'd held that it wasn't really me who killed Bethany must have vanished.

I don't blame them for any of the things they said. They didn't know how could they? In their place I would have thought that I was the devil, too.

My mother just cried loud, wracking sobs.

My father called me awful things, all the things anyone would call someone who had done the things he thought I had done.

That's when Nathan got really mad. See, Nathan had done all the things Dad was saying were so sick, and Nathan thinks he ought to be able to do whatever he likes, and no one has the right to get too upset about it. They surely don't have the right to think there is anything *wrong* with him.

One minute my dad is screaming at me that I'm a sick, twisted bastard, and they should have killed me years ago, and the next Nathan slings an axe into the back of his head with such force that it comes out his face. His blood and brain matter cover me and the wall behind me.

My mother was screaming and she looked at me and cried, "God, Willie I'm so sorry," and I knew that she finally knew I wasn't crazy or lying. I tried to stop Nathan, but I'd never been able to beat him and as he hit me in the face and sent me skidding across the floor on a piece of Daddy's brain he slung that axe right into my mother's face.

I got up from the floor and sat down in one of the kitchen chairs. What else could I do?

I just sat there while that bastard kept laughing and chopping my parents into a thousand pieces. The blood splattered all around and over me, and I just sat there.

When he'd finished he looked at me and screamed for me to get moving. We had to get out of there before the cops got back. But I wouldn't budge; this is no doubt why he blames me for being in jail. He yanked on my arm and even beat me up some more, screaming for me to get up and go.

I just sat there and told him. "I'm not going anywhere. You go if you want to go."

When the cops got back with their warrant I was still sitting in the middle of what was left of my parents. I told them I'd killed Alice and where to find her and that I'd killed my parents. I told this to them as they were cuffing me.

I didn't tell them about Nathan. I didn't want to plead insanity. I wanted to go to jail. I figured if I was in jail Nathan'd be in jail, and then he couldn't hurt anybody.

They had given me two consecutive life sentences. I figured that in jail people would be safe from Nathan, but I had forgotten there were other people in prison.

I asked them not to give me a cellmate, but when you're a convicted mass murderer you don't have a whole lot of say in what goes on in your life.

My cellmate seemed like a nice guy. He tried to talk to me a half dozen times, and when he heard me talk to Nathan he even tried talking to him. Finally he just gave up.

I figured if I didn't talk to him Nathan would leave him alone. Of course he didn't. One night when Nathan was more bored than usual, he slammed me around until I was so damn punchy I couldn't think straight, no doubt from the look on his face my cellmate thought I was doing it to myself but by the time he realized I wasn't it was too late for him. Nathan tied that poor guy up and gagged him with the sheets. He did unthinkable things to him until the guy was almost unconscious. Every time I would ask him to stop he'd hit me again. Finally he knocked me out. I woke in the morning to the guards' screaming. My dead cellmate was in bed with me. His head had been turned entirely to mush—there wasn't one piece of skull larger than a dime. It was a puddle of gore.

I screamed, too.

They gave me the death penalty. Sort of odd, when you think about it. When I'd been convicted of killing my girlfriend and my parents they'd just given me life. But when they think I killed a convicted meth dealer they gave me the death penalty.

I have waived all appeals and asked them to get on with it. Death now seems to me like my only shot of getting rid of Nathan, of maybe taking him someplace where he can't hurt anyone any more. Maybe if there is no one to see him, he won't exist. I hope I can finally be clear of him. This is my last chance, the only thing I haven't tried before.

If you are reading this, then I am already dead, and I guess it's up to you to figure out whether I was just a deranged sociopathic killer, or if Nathan was real. Then if you think he might have been real, did he die with me, or when you walk by your child's room at night can you hear them talking to someone who isn't there?

Blood Moccasins

BRADLEY DENTON

Carl returned to the musty waiting room, shuffling like a man fresh out of a coma. It wasn't easy to put one foot in front of the other when he couldn't stop thinking about the things in the exam-room sink.

He stopped and peered through the slow swarms of dustmotes in the waiting room. The blinds were shut tight over the front windows and the door, so only thin strips of sunlight made it inside. Carl's eyes had trouble with it after the cold fluorescent glare of the exam room. But he was able to spot his daughter Mary in one of the sagging chairs on the far side of the room. She was holding his year-old grandson Aaron in her lap. They were the only other people there. Even Billy Doc's receptionist had vanished.

Carl stared at the baby. He hoped Billy Doc was right, and that Aaron wouldn't get the family disease.

But even if Billy Doc was wrong, Aaron ought to have six or seven good decades before it hit him. It had taken seventy-two years for Carl. So maybe Aaron had a good long life ahead of him, regardless of genetics. Maybe.

Mary shifted Aaron to her shoulder and stood. She was a slender young woman with wavy auburn hair that wasn't from Carl's side of the family. He took some comfort in that.

She met him at the exit. "What did Billy Doc say?" she asked.

Carl put his hand on Aaron's back. The child was like a warm bundle of fresh biscuits. He smelled so good that it was almost a taste.

"Not much," Carl replied. He took his hand away from the baby and pushed open the heavy glass door.

As he stepped outside, the Central Texas summer hit him in the face like hot sand. But he didn't mind. It felt pretty good.

He had been craving heat lately.

Carl had thought that going to his cousin right here in Kingman would be better than being examined by some punk in Austin or Houston. But as he sat alone in the windowless little exam room, listening to the buzzing of the fly-specked fluorescent ceiling light, he thought again. Maybe doctors were all the same, whether they were your own blood or not. It was inhuman to make a man wait like this.

He didn't really know Billy Doc anymore, so he had no idea whether the old fart was any good at his job. They hadn't exchanged two words in thirty years. Billy Doc had dropped off a basket of sausage and cheese when Mary had been born, but all he'd said then was "Congratulations."

Before that, their last conversation had been an argument, at age twelve, over how many inches of intestines were stuffed into your average tadpole. Carl had maintained that it couldn't be more than three or four, but Billy Doc had insisted that despite a tadpole's small size, it was at least seven.

Twenty minutes before the argument, they had stood around a puddle shooting the little critters with their BB guns, marveling at the spirals of guts. But they hadn't measured them, and that had led to the trouble.

Now Billy Doc was making Carl wait on his test results. Just to get back at him.

Carl and Mary stepped onto the sunbaked brick sidewalk of what passed for downtown Kingman, and baby Aaron winced and whined. Mary shushed him and shaded his blond head with her free hand. Something about the way she did that reminded Carl of her mother. His wife, Louise. Long dead now.

Lucky woman.

"Billy Doc must've told you *something*," Mary said. "You've been so rundown."

Carl shrugged, and a twinge of pain shot through his shoulders. "Well, he did say I'm getting old."

He started up the block, shuffling past a few battered pickup trucks. He shouldn't have let Mary bring him. He should have driven himself. His old Ford still ran. And it wasn't as if this one-horse town, with its three-block business district, was tough to navigate. Besides, if he had come alone, he wouldn't have had to put up with any questions. Not until he got home. And by then he might have thought up a decent lie.

"'Getting old' isn't much of a diagnosis," Mary said. "I wish you'd let me take you to someone in Austin or College Station. I mean, Billy Doc isn't exactly in his prime. Alex went to him for those stitches last fall, and now he's got that big scar on his face. He thinks Billy Doc is a quack."

Carl didn't give a damn what Alex thought. "Billy Doc suits me," he said. "And he's family."

Which was something that couldn't be said for Alex. Not now that he and Mary were separated. Not ever, as far as Carl was concerned. He actually hoped Mary had been screwing around on the useless son of a bitch when she'd gotten pregnant. It was an awful thing to hope about your own daughter. But there it was.

"Family?" Mary said. "Then how come you didn't mention Billy Doc the whole time I was growing up? Here he was, twenty miles from the house, me and my friends going to him for school shots, and the only way I knew he was a relative was because his last name was Morgan, too."

They had reached Mary's little Toyota sedan. Carl stopped, looked at his daughter and her baby, and shrugged again.

"Billy Doc and I didn't have much reason to see each other after we grew up," he said. "I guess he never needed a carpenter. And until now, I didn't need a doctor." He glanced back down the block. "Besides, we once had a serious disagreement about tadpoles."

The exam room door opened, and Billy Doc came in with a manila folder. He was paunchy and bald with eyeglasses the size of skeet, and his red-and-white checkered shirt was hanging out of baggy black pants. He didn't look like much of a medical man. He looked like a retired geezer at the 4:00 PM Luby's buffet.

Carl wondered whether he looked that bad himself. After all, he and Billy Doc were the same age. But Carl was taller and skinnier. Maybe that gave him the edge. Or maybe it only made him look more like a cadaver.

Billy Doc closed the door, sat down on a wheeled stool, and tapped his knee with the manila folder. He looked at Carl, who was parked in a wooden chair against the wall. Carl had gotten off the exam table and put on his denim shirt again as soon as Billy Doc had finished taking his blood.

"I was just thinking," Billy Doc said, his voice thick and low, "about that fight we had over the tadpoles."

"I was just thinking about that, too." Carl's voice wasn't as low as Billy Doc's, but it had an old man's crackle. It was as if he had a piece of cellophane caught in his throat. He wasn't happy about that, and he wasn't sure when it had happened. "But it wasn't really a fight. We just disagreed about the length of the guts."

Billy Doc gave a brief grin, and Carl noticed that his teeth were still pretty good. That was a Morgan family trait. "Carl, we didn't just disagree. We beat the hell out of each other. But I'm not surprised you don't remember, since you were just about out of your mind. I made the mistake of laughing at you, and that sent you over the edge."

Carl remembered being pissed-off, but he didn't remember a knock-down fight. "You must be thinking of some other kid. I don't think I could get that worked up over tadpole guts."

Billy Doc reached out and put the folder on the exam table. "Well, that's what happened. And that's why our mothers wouldn't let us spend any more time together. Since they'd both married Morgan boys, they knew what the males in our line were capable of." Billy scratched under his jaw. "You know, I never could figure why two smart women like them both married such assholes."

Carl took no offense at the insult to his father, since he couldn't argue with it. "I suppose assholes were all that was available," he said. "And at least the Morgan boys were better looking than most of the others." He pointed at the manila folder. "But I also suppose you've got some bad news there. So let's just get it over with."

Billy Doc took off his enormous eyeglasses. He breathed on each lens, then wiped away the fog with his shirttail.

"The bad news ain't in the folder," he said. His voice was even lower now. "All it says there is that your blood pressure is on the high side. But not bad for a man who's seventy-two and hasn't seen a doctor since he was in the service."

Carl didn't have the energy to get mad, but he leaned forward and tried to glare. "So what is it? I know it ain't VD, because I've been celibate since the Reagan administration. But I feel like crap most of the time, and worse than that the rest of the time. I was thinking maybe leukemia. But you'd put that in the folder, wouldn't you?"

Billy Doc looked at the floor for a moment, then put on his glasses and stood. "You won't get it unless I show you. Come here."

He went around the exam table to a small counter with a wash basin. Carl stood up, grimacing as his joints creaked, and followed.

Billy Doc opened a drawer and brought out a small scalpel. He pulled off the plastic blade guard and let it fall. Then he raised the scalpel and looked at Carl.

"Showtime," he said.

Once Aaron was strapped into the baby seat in back and Mary was at the wheel, Carl studied his daughter's face. He'd had a suspicion for a long time, but had stopped worrying about it when Mary and Alex had separated. And he had gotten too wrapped up in his own personal shit. But now that his personal shit wouldn't last much longer, maybe he ought to pay some attention while he still could.

And as Mary brushed back her hair to put on her sunglasses, there it was. She had tried to hide it under makeup, but with the bright sun glaring through the windshield, Carl could see the faint bruise around her right eye. Yet none of the Morgans had ever bruised easily. It took some doing to get even a faint one.

Carl had never hit Louise, despite the fact that such behavior was common among the males of his family. And since he and Louise had just had one girl and no sons, that should have been the end of it. In his branch, anyway.

But maybe there were some flaws in the Morgan women's chromosomes, too. Once Aaron was born, Mary had been smart enough to leave Alex, move back home, and get the separation. But she hadn't been smart enough to follow up and file for divorce. Or to cut Alex out of her life altogether.

And Carl hadn't been strong enough to say "No" when Mary had come to him with a request a week ago. So Alex, who had defaulted on the payments for his double-wide in Kingman, was now living in Carl's basement.

"Is he still gonna be there when we get home?" Carl asked.

Mary started the car and checked her mirrors. "He's got nowhere else to go yet, Daddy."

For once, Carl couldn't help saying it out loud. "It's my house. I built it. And he ain't family. Why doesn't he go stay with his own blood?"

Mary backed the car into the street. "He's Aaron's father, so yes, he is family. And he's a good provider for his child. Or he was, until he got laid off. And that wasn't his fault. It's the bad economy."

Carl had a suspicion about that, too. The concrete company Alex had worked for seemed to be doing fine. Alex had been the only employee they'd "laid off" a month ago, and Carl knew for a fact that they'd hired three men since then.

"He says it'll just be two more weeks at most," Mary said. "So I'd be grateful if you could tolerate the situation a little longer. I promise it's only temporary."

Carl glanced back at Aaron. The child was already asleep.

"Everything is," Carl said.

It was hot in the car, which felt fine to Carl. But he doubted it was good for the baby. So he faced forward and cranked up the air conditioner. As he did, he saw one of the veins in his hand throb.

He had been seeing that for two months now.

But it was only today that he knew why.

Carl stared at the scalpel in Billy Doc's hand and took a step back. "I don't know what you've got in mind, Cuz. But I've been poked enough today. I'm done."

Billy Doc gave a snort. It was the kind of forced chuckle a man makes when nothing's funny at all.

"It's not for you," Billy Doc said.

Then he pressed the tip of the scalpel against the end of his left middle finger and sliced downward, opening a cut about a third of an inch long. Blood welled out immediately.

Carl flinched. "What the hell?"

Billy Doc set the scalpel on the counter and held his hand over the sink. "Don't be a sissy, Carl." Drops of blood began to fall. "Come look. It just takes a minute or two."

Carl stepped closer and looked into the stainless steel basin, where three droplets of Billy Doc's blood were quivering.

As Carl watched, the droplets stretched toward the drain. But instead of sliding down into it, they convulsed and swelled into three tiny red cylinders.

The skinny tails of the cylinders began whipping back and forth.

An instant later, Carl was staring at three little dark-red snakes twisting and squirming atop a thin film of blood.

Carl couldn't move. For a long moment, he couldn't even blink.

Then one of the snakes coiled, turned its head upward, and opened its mouth. The white flesh inside glistened, and the tiny fangs gleamed.

Billy Doc pulled a tissue from a box beside the sink and wrapped it around his finger.

"I started feeling pretty lousy a few months ago," he said. "So I ran some tests on myself. Didn't find much wrong, until I happened to spill one of my blood samples. And then this happened."

"Snakes," Carl said. His voice was a rasp.

Billy Doc reached out and turned on the hot water.

"Yup," he said. "In our blood."

////

As the Toyota pulled into the live-oak grove where Carl's house stood, Carl saw his twenty-year-old Ford F-150 pickup in the carport with its hood up.

Alex's much newer Ford was parked in the gravel driveway behind Carl's truck, and its hood was up, too. Alex was just emerging from its cab. He scowled as Mary parked her Toyota beside him, then wiped his hands on his jeans. His scowl became a forced smile.

Carl knew that smile. Oh, Alex was a good-looking guy—sandy hair, sunburned face, blue eyes, straight nose, strapping physique, all that crap—but that half-smile, half-sneer had put Carl off from the beginning. It had gotten worse since the separation, and worse still since Alex had acquired the three-inch purple scar that trailed down from his left cheekbone. The one he'd said had happened while cutting firewood.

Mary stepped out of the car. "Something wrong with both trucks?" she asked.

Alexshook his head. "Not anymore. Mine had a bad starter relay, but I fixed it."

Carl opened the Toyota's passenger door and emerged slowly. Every part of his body hurt now. Joints, muscles, head, heart. Everything.

"I guess you borrowed the relay from mine?" Carl asked. His voice came out even hoarser than usual.

Alex kept smiling. "I've got a job interview tomorrow. And I figured you wouldn't mind, since Mary's been driving you places anyway."

Carl almost smiled himself. The funny thing was that Alex was right, in a way. He didn't mind. Not really. He only had so much strength left, and this wasn't worth the effort.

Besides, his real problem with Alex was a whole lot more serious than a starter relay.

He looked past Alex at the two-story frame house he had built the year before Mary was born. It was the home she had known all her life, and when Carl died it would go to her along with its five acres and everything else he owned. He had to be sure she would keep it for herself and Aaron.

"It's all right," Carl said. "You're welcome to the starter relay and anything else on that old truck. I'm done with it."

Alex's smile faltered. He'd probably expected Carl to protest, and no doubt had a line of bullshit all ready for it. But Carl had confounded his expectations.

"Well, I appreciate that," Alex said.

Carl glanced back into the car as Mary unbuckled Aaron from the child seat. Mary had become a fine woman. And Aaron would become a fine man, if he had the chance. But at the moment, neither of them was capable of self-protection.

"Where's your job interview?" Carl asked without looking at Alex.

"Uh, it's another concrete-mixer driving job," Alex said. "Little company down near Conroe."

Conroe was about forty-five miles southeast. "That sounds promising," Carl said. But he knew there was no point in asking the name of the company.

He shuffled around the back end of the Toyota and held out his arms for his grandson. That child sure did smell good.

"Thanks, Daddy," Mary said, handing over the baby. "Now I think I'll get you boys fed and then go to bed early. I have the morning shift, so I'll have to be out the door by 6:00 AM to get Aaron to daycare before work."

Carl and Mary started toward the house, and Carl could hear Alex following them. He could hear every piece of gravel that crunched under those black boots. Or maybe he felt it.

It occurred to Carl that even as everything else on his body had started hurting and failing these past few months, his senses of smell and hearing had actually improved. Sort of. His nose and ears didn't seem to be working any better. But if he opened his mouth a little, and paid attention to the painful vibrations in his bones, everything was sharp.

He supposed that made sense.

Carl watched the three tiny snakes squirm and thrash as the hot water washed them down the exam-room drain. He kept watching long after they were gone, until Billy Doc shut off the water and the last of it swirled away.

"Snakes," Carl repeated.

"Look like little water moccasins, don't they?" Billy Doc said. "They got the same fat red bodies and skinny tails, and those nasty white mouths. Except instead of living in the river, they're in our veins. So I reckon that makes them blood moccasins. And I reckon they're probably poisonous, too."

Carl looked up from the sink, and it made him dizzy. He stumbled backward and bumped against the exam table. It kept him upright.

"So," Carl managed to say. "What's the treatment?"

Billy Doc snorted again, louder this time. "This ain't exactly been written up in the goddamn Journal of the AMA. *It might even be unique to our Morgan family chromosomes. So I doubt any treatment is possible. And even if there's something that might help, we won't have time to figure out what it is."*

Carl's mouth was dry. "How do you know?"

Billy Doc took off his glasses and wiped them again. "Ten days ago, I hand-delivered some of my own blood to a lab in Austin. I wanted to make sure none of it got spilled, since it's exposure to open air that seems to bring out the snakes. Anyway, the tests said my kidneys and liver are going bad. Just to be sure, I took them another sample four days ago, and things were even worse. So the progression is on a pretty steep slope. Now, I admit that I wasn't able to do all of those same tests for you today. But I've seen enough to know you're in the same shape. I even exposed your blood to the air back in the lavatory and produced a couple of snakes." He started to put on his glasses, then seemed to change his mind. "The good news is that I have access to morphine. So the pain won't drive us crazy, the way it did our fathers. We can go out peaceful when the time comes—which I don't think is more than a month away. But we won't die as ugly as our daddies did."

Carl was getting confused. "What are you talking about? My old man got drunk, drove off a bridge, and drowned in the Brazos. And yours had a heart attack."

Now Billy Doc put his glasses back on, returned to his wheeled stool, and sat down again with a groan. "Those were the stories our mothers told the neighbors here in Kingman. Gotta keep up appearances in a small town. But I believe our fathers both killed themselves. Hell, I know for a fact that mine did. I found him in his garden shed with his throat cut. So I just assumed your old man drove off that bridge on purpose, too."

"Uncle Bill cut his own throat?" Carl said.

Billy Doc raised an eyebrow. "Well, if you want to get technical, he stabbed himself in the jugular. The hedge clippers were still in his hand, and the pointy ends were in his neck. But there was only about half as much blood as you might've expected. And what was there instead of the rest was a seven-foot cottonmouth. Coiled next to the corpse, its head tilted up with its mouth open. And don't argue with me about its length, the way you did about the tadpole guts. I measured that sucker after I chopped off its head with Pappy's garden hoe. But I guess I don't have proof, since it liquefied after that."

Carl closed his eyes and took a shuddering breath. "Jesus."

"No, there was no room for him," Billy Doc said. "It wasn't a very big shed."

The next morning, Carl rose at 4:00 AM, shaved carefully, and put on a clean blue short-sleeved work shirt and some old Dickies work trousers. He tucked his favorite Barlow knife in a back pocket. Then he was in his big, airy kitchen by 5:00 AM, making coffee and scrambling eggs. He had been feeling worse every day, and today was no different. His joints hurt, his muscles ached, and his veins throbbed. So his body would have preferred to stay in bed. But Carl wanted to be sure to see his daughter and grandson before they left for the day. And he hadn't been able to sleep anyway.

Mary came downstairs with the baby at 5:15, and the three of them had a quiet breakfast at the kitchen table. Neither Carl nor Mary said much, and the baby was groggy and fussy. But Carl didn't mind. If he didn't have to talk, he didn't have to let on how bad he felt. And the baby required enough of Mary's attention that she didn't ask Carl any questions. So he didn't have to lie.

Best of all, Alex was still asleep in the basement. So for a little while, Carl could pretend he wasn't there. For a little while, there at the table, it was just Carl and his own blood.

But before he knew it, it was 6:00 AM, and Mary was out the front door with the baby. She had to drop Aaron at daycare in Kingman, then hurry out to the Wal-Mart on Highway 30 by 7:00. She'd be standing at a checkout register for most of the next nine hours. But she was sure she'd be a manager soon.

Carl wanted to hug them both as they left. But that wasn't his habit, and Mary would have worried if he'd done it. So the best he could do was walk them to the front door and put his hand on Aaron's back for a moment, as he had at Billy Doc's office. And then he closed the door behind them.

He remembered to leave it unlocked.

Carl watched from a living-room window as the taillights of Mary's Toyota wound through the live oaks to the road. He watched until they were gone.

Then he heard a thump down in the basement.

Every morning for the past week, Carl had been going out to his wood shop in the back yard and spending several hours there, just to avoid dealing with Alex. But today, he shuffled back into the kitchen.

He picked up the cordless telephone from its cradle beside the stove and called Billy Doc, as he'd promised he would. And when that was done, he poured himself another cup of coffee, sat down at the table again, and waited for Alex.

It was only when Carl saw the blood moccasin from the cut on his own finger that he was able to make peace with the situation. He had given himself a quick stab with the scalpel, producing a drop of blood that was less than half of what Billy Doc had drawn from himself. But even that tiny drop had transformed into a writhing, snapping little snake in the exam-room sink.

Carl washed it down the drain. Then he wrapped his finger and turned to his cousin. "So now we just wait to die?"

"I reckon so, unless we choose to accelerate the process," Billy Doc said. "I don't know what'll happen if we don't. Maybe they'll solidify right there in our veins instead of waiting to hit the air. Or maybe our organs will fail before that happens, and we'll appear to die of natural causes. Which, when you come right down to it, is what this is. For us."

Carl felt a chill run up the back of his neck.

"My grandson," he said. "Is he going to get this too?"

Billy Doc frowned. "You and I had Morgan daddies, and our mutual grandpa had one, too. May their foul souls burn in hell." He raised his tissue-wrapped finger. "Your little Aaron, however, has a Morgan mama instead. And my educated guess is that the moccasins are only passed from fathers to sons. So if I'm right, it ends with you and me. If I'm wrong, there's not much we can do about it. But I'll leave my notes for the boy to read when he's older. He's welcome to them, since neither of my marriages produced any children. Which used to trouble me. But not anymore."

Carl squeezed the tissue around his own finger. "That's it? That's the best we can do?"

"Well, I've left autopsy instructions for myself," Billy Doc said. "I can do the same for you, if you like. But I suspect that once we die, the snakes inside die too. Most likely leaving no trace a post-mortem would find, unless they've solidified."

Now Carl was squeezing his finger so tightly that both of his hands trembled. "It would sure be nice if certain human beings could die and disappear like that."

Billy Doc nodded. "I feel the same way, if you're referring to a certain knife-fighting, bathtub-grade methamphetamine producer named Alex Elroy. The knife-fighting I'm sure about, since I stitched him up. And he mentioned that next time, he'd be using a gun. As for the meth, I confess that's hearsay. But last Christmas I had a couple of young patients, one just fourteen, who most definitely got hold of some bad poison. And I don't know why they'd lie to me about the source, since I didn't even ask."

Carl took a deep breath. "I thought it might be something like that. But I was hoping otherwise, for Mary's sake. They're separated, but he's working his way back in, like a weasel. He's in my house right now." He shook his head. "And I'll probably be dead before I can do anything about it. Not that Mary would listen to me anyway. But that's my fault for not establishing a better relationship a long time ago. I always let Louise handle the talking. I just didn't think I'd be any good at it."

Billy Doc got up from his stool and winced. Then he put a hand on Carl's shoulder.

"You can still get rid of a weasel," Billy Doc said. "It's just a varmint." His voice was a dark growl. "And every varmint has its natural enemies."

////

Just after 8:00 AM, Carl smelled Alex behind him. It was a thick, moist odor not unlike that of a wet muskrat. Carl wasn't sure how he knew that. But he did.

"Come sit," Carl said in his crackling-cellophane voice. "There's coffee."

Alex went around to the other side of the table, but he didn't sit. He was wearing the same clothes he'd worn the evening before, when he'd stolen Carl's starter relay.

"I figured you'd be out in your workshop by now," he said. "Making a new end table or something."

Carl glanced over his shoulder, through the arched passage that led to the living room. He had made every stick of furniture in there, plus the floor it all sat on. Not to mention the white oak table he was sitting at right now, and the matching chairs. Most of it was pretty good, too. And so was the house. It was a decent legacy.

He looked back at Alex. "I wanted to speak with you before you left for your interview."

Alex's forehead pinched. "My what?"

Carl gave a little smile. He couldn't help it.

"Oh," Alex said. "That's not until this afternoon."

"Good. Then we have some time to talk."

Alex's eyes shifted left and then right, as if he were trying to decide which route he would use to escape from the kitchen. The living room, or the front hallway. "Actually, Carl, there are some things I have to do."

"This won't take but a minute." Carl reached into his shirt pocket, brought out the check he had written in the middle of the night, and put it on the table. "Here's five thousand dollars. That's most of what I have in ready cash. All you have to do is pick it up, get your personal stuff from the basement, and go do all those things you have to do. And never come back."

Alex's eyes stopped shifting. They focused on the check.

"I don't get it," Alex said. But he didn't sound confused.

Carl chuckled. It came out as a short, sharp hiss. "Let's not bullshit. Just take it and go."

Alex's eyes met Carl's now, and he grinned. His scar almost glowed. "But Mary and I have been talking about getting back together. I can't mess that up." He put a finger on the check and pushed it toward Carl. "She says you're not doing too well. And this should go to her family when you die. Don't you think? Along with the house and whatnot."

So far, this had gone about the way Carl had expected. But at least his conscience was clear now.

He reached into his back pocket, brought out the Barlow knife, and snapped it open.

Alex laughed. "A pocket knife?" He pointed at his cheek. "I'll tell you a secret, old man. This wasn't from cutting firewood. I just said that so Mary wouldn't freak out. And like the old saying goes, you should see the other guy."

Carl didn't respond. Instead, he drew the knife across his left palm. The blade was sharp, so there wasn't much pain at first. And for a moment, he was afraid there wouldn't be enough blood. But then it welled up over the edges of the wound like a river flooding its banks.

He glanced up at Alex and saw that the punk's eyes had widened.

"Shit, you aren't just old and sick," Alex said. "You've lost your mind, too."

Carl put down the knife, then held up his left fist and squeezed. Blood dripped down and pooled on the polished oak beside the check. And now the wound began to sting. But Carl didn't mind. It was temporary.

There were four or five tablespoons of blood on the table when the quivering red blob began to elongate. Then it all happened more quickly than it had happened the day before, and Carl almost didn't look up in time to see Alex's reaction.

Alex's mouth opened wide, and his scar seemed to twist. He stumbled backward and collided with the maple china cabinet Carl had built for Louise. The glass cracked, and the dishes inside tumbled and clattered.

Carl frowned. "That should come out of the five thousand," he said.

Then he looked back down and saw a foot-long blood-red snake thrashing its way toward Alex. Its jaws were open wide.

"You can see why some folks call them cottonmouths," Carl said. "It looks so white and clean in there. But of course it ain't."

More drops of blood had fallen from his hand, and now four of them transformed into little five-inch serpents. Meanwhile, the larger snake had reached the edge of the table and was about to drop to the floor at Alex's feet.

"If you came around the end of the table to your left," Carl said, "you could grab the check, run behind me into the living room, and then head for the door."

Instead, Alex bolted to his right through the kitchen, turned when he reached the hallway, and disappeared toward the center of the house. A few seconds later, Carl heard the basement door slam against the wall.

Carl looked down at the blood moccasins on the table. "That's fine," he said. "I imagine he has some things to take with him."

The foot-long snake turned and slithered back toward him. Its mouth had closed.

Carl lowered both of his hands to the table, and the smaller snakes began coiling around his right-hand fingers. When the larger one reached him, it wrapped itself around his left wrist.

They were his own blood, after all.

When he smelled Alex re-entering the kitchen, he said, "You can still take the check. I won't let them get you."

Then he heard a click, and he turned in time to see Alex pull the trigger on a nine-millimeter pistol in his right hand.

Carl's left arm jerked, and he looked down and saw that the shot had blown off the head of the larger snake. The body convulsed, then collapsed and dissolved into a pool of blood under Carl's hand.

The four smaller snakes uncoiled from Carl's right-hand fingers, slithered over his left arm in a flash, and plunged off the edge of the table. As they hit the floor, they started toward Alex, hissing, their fangs bared.

Alex fired at the snake in the lead, and splinters of red oak flew up from the floor beside it. The next shot turned the snake into a bloody smear, and the shot after that did the same to the next one.

It took five more shots to dispatch the last two. Then Carl stared down at the smears of blood, at the nine shell casings around Alex's scuffed black boots, and at the splintered sections of the kitchen floor. It looked as if six different boards would have to be replaced. Carl had matching spares in the basement, but he wasn't sure Mary knew they were there. He hoped she would find them.

"What the fuck," Alex said. He was staring down at the floor as well. "What the fuck. What the fuck." He couldn't seem to stop saying it.

Carl's ears were ringing from the gunshots, and his nostrils and tongue were burning from the stink. But he could still hear the tremor in Alex's voice, and he could still smell the fear in Alex's sweat.

He held up his left hand again. Blood was beginning to run down his forearm from a new wound at the edge of his palm. Carl couldn't feel it, but he was beginning to see a checkerboard pattern at the edges of his vision. He might pass out soon.

"You nicked me," he said. "So you'd better take your money and get out fast. This next one's gonna be bigger."

The blood was dripping from Carl's elbow onto the table. There was a lot. And it was already starting to quiver and stretch.

Alex's face glistened. He blinked, and his scar twitched.

"All right," he said. "All right, all right." Then he lowered the pistol, took three quick steps to the table, and reached past Carl's upraised arm with his free hand.

His fingers closed on the five-thousand-dollar check.

But at that moment, the blood on the table solidified into a two-foot cottonmouth, and it whipped around and sank its fangs into Alex's left wrist.

Alex screamed, and the pistol in his right hand fired again.

This time, Carl felt it. It was as if his entire left side, from his armpit to his pelvis, had been doused in gasoline and set ablaze.

Everything washed red and black, and then Carl was lying on the floor with a sideways view of Alex staggering backward through the kitchen. Alex was still screaming, and the snake still had its fangs buried in his wrist. And seven new little snakes were now slithering after him as well.

Carl could feel still more blood pumping out from the hole in his side. And he could feel it stretching and quivering on the floor next to him.

Then he saw Alex stop backpedaling, place the muzzle of the pistol against the body of the snake below his wrist, and fire. The snake's body blew away, liquefied, and splattered against the refrigerator. The head and neck fell from Alex's arm and became a red blob on the floor.

Now Alex aimed the pistol at the seven little snakes advancing on him. But when he pulled the trigger, there was only a hollow click. So he threw the pistol, and the first two snakes were knocked back into the others. For a few moments, they all squirmed around each other in apparent confusion.

Alex looked back toward Carl and held up the check.

"It's okay!" Alex shouted. His voice was wild. "One bite won't kill me! I'll go to a doctor! Then I'll come back and shoot the rest of these things, and they'll all melt into blood again! And the cops'll think somebody broke in and murdered you while I was down at the river getting snakebit!"

Alex began to backpedal toward the hallway again.

Carl tried to crawl after him, but he couldn't move. He was done. He could feel the big snake beside him taking shape, and he could see the little ones starting after Alex again. But Alex would reach the hallway, turn the corner, and be out the front door before any of them could reach him.

Then, with Alex still in sight, Carl heard the front door open. It felt like a small earthquake in his bones.

A moment later, Billy Doc appeared in the doorway between the kitchen and the hall. He was grizzled and rumpled, and Carl knew he hadn't slept, either.

"Somebody need a doctor?" Billy Doc said in his low growl.

Alex spun around and screamed at him. "Get out the way, you quack!"

Billy Doc shook his head and held up a scalpel three times the size of the one he'd used the day before. He pulled off the plastic sheath, then took a step toward Alex.

Alex jumped back into the kitchen and almost stepped on one of the small snakes. Then he was in the middle of them, and they all began striking. Alex shrieked and leaped up to the counter beside the stove, knocking the cordless telephone to the floor. Two of the snakes were hanging from his boots, and he kicked them loose as he hauled himself up to crouch on the counter, his back crammed against the cabinets.

"What the fuck," Alex said yet again, staring down at the seven little snakes hissing and straining toward him. "What the *fuck*."

Carl reached toward the phone on the floor. But it was too far away.

"It's all right, Cuz," Billy Doc said. "I called the sheriff from my cell phone. He won't let your daughter see any of this. I'm just sorry I didn't get here as soon as I meant to."

Carl tried to grin. "Didn't have to come at all."

Billy Doc snorted.

"Course I did," he said. "We're blood."

Billy Doc raised the scalpel to his throat.

The big snake from Carl's side was complete. It slithered over Carl's outstretched arm and headed straight for the spot where Alex was crouched on the counter. Five feet long if it was an inch. Carl couldn't help feeling proud.

It coiled on the floor, its head raised and mouth open, hissing up at Alex. But instead of making its move right away, it waited for its cousin to join it from the far end of the kitchen. And this new one was even larger—seven feet, at least.

"Figures," Carl whispered.

He watched long enough to see the two big snakes rise up together, sink their fangs into Alex's legs, and drag him back down to the other seven.

Then Carl closed his eyes, enjoying the smooth grain of the floorboards against his cheek. These right here hadn't been shot up, and they were nice. He had planed and sanded them himself, years ago, and he had done a good job.

Someday, his great-grandchildren would stand on this very spot. And like his daughter and grandson, they would be fine people.

The Case of the Angry Traveler
A Dana Roberts Adventure

JOE R. LANSDALE

When Dana Roberts arrived she went straight away to the storyteller chair and sat down and took the drink offered her. She was certainly her usual attractive self, but there was about her an air of exhaustion. Without any fanfare, she launched straight away into her story.

As was the custom, I recorded it and then typed up the transcript. I call it the Case of the Angry Traveler. Melodramatic, I admit, but, there you have it.

This is what Dana told us.

I received a call from a friend of mine—we'll call him Frank—who works as an exterminator in a large city. I won't name the city, since this tale will be published, and I won't name my friend or any of his associates by their real names. I will provide names, but understand, they are contrived so that those involved shall remain nameless. The exception to that will be the names of my assistants, which are correct. All of you here, of course know who they are from at least one of my previous narratives.

On a blustery fall day when I was at home with a mild case of the common cold, sitting up in bed with a lap tray, sipping coffee, the phone rang. It was my friend the exterminator.

Perhaps I should also explain that big city exterminators are not at all what you might think. They certainly do not fit the stereotype of a greasy man in overalls with a rat trap slung over one shoulder, a string of dead rodents being dragged behind him on a chain.

It is actually, at least in the city I'm talking about, a respected business. Someone has to take care of the vermin, and my friend is a specialist, well trained in the science of insects and rodents, all manner of animals, reptiles, etc., that might pose a problem to residents of the city. In many cases, a simple trapping is all that's necessary. He has told me numerous accounts of removing large reptiles, pythons in particular, from numerous homes and apartment complexes in the city. Often he removes them from toilets, as from time to time they arrive there from the sewers below, as do rats. It sounds like an urban myth, but I assure you it has happened, and will happen again. He kills the rats, the snakes he often gives to zoos or research centers. But, that is neither here nor there, other than to let you know that Frank is a professional. So, when I got a phone call from him asking for my help, I was surprised.

"I believe I've come across something new," he said. "And I was wondering if you might be willing to lend me a hand."

"To chase rats?"

"No. It isn't a rat. As I said, it's something new. Something most peculiar and it might lend itself to your particular talents."

"My talents?"

"Yes."

"You mean you are dealing with the supernormal? Your pest is supernormal?"

"To be honest, I don't know, but I suspect that could be the case. Perhaps, in the long run, it will turn out to be quite normal, but so far the common methods of removing pests have failed, and this particular pest seems to be more than a little vicious."

He had peaked my curiosity, I must say. I sat up straighter in bed with the phone in one hand, my cup of coffee in the other. I sipped the coffee and put it on the tray and leaned back into my pillows.

"Tell me about it," I said.

"Three days ago I was asked to check out an apartment on the Upper East side. I was directed to the toilet of a small, but well cared for home, and in the toilet I found a large rat. He had come up through the drains. They can swim well and are fantastic survivors, so this unto itself isn't unique.

"Anyway, I dispatched the bugger and took him away. There was something odd about the critter though. He was nine inches long, not counting tail. That is a big rat. A uniquely large rat. I was curious enough to take photos of it and carried it back to the laboratory. I decided to perform a rodent autopsy. When I cut it open, I was surprised to find a small piece of a human finger. The finger tip and the nail to be exact."

"My goodness."

"Not exactly what I said in the moment of discovery, Dana, but the sentiment is there. I immediately contacted the police. They came and took it away, and the police lab technician, who is a friend of mine, called me the next day to tell me that the finger was fresh, meaning that it hadn't been taken by the rat too long ago, and that it had come from an elderly man, most likely malnourished and dead when the rat had its lunch."

"A homeless person, perhaps," I said, and as soon as I did, I somehow felt snobby.

"A strong possibility," Frank said. "Perhaps he crawled down in the sewer, as many do, to find a place to sleep, or rest, died, and a rat came along and bit off a portion of his finger."

"It's intriguing," I said, "but I don't see how this has anything to do with me. It sounds like you have a dead body to find. Or the police do."

"I'm coming to that, Dana. Bear with me. So, we try and trace the possible path of the rat, and since it came up through a sewer pipe, and found its way into a home, that isn't easy. That small piece of human flesh had set something uncommon in motion.

"Soon, I was aiding the police, and we were searching the sewers. They are quite deep and very complex, and many of the routes below were constructed at an earlier time. And there are areas beneath where the old city was. Large areas. This means there are buildings down there."

"Buildings?"

"Exactly," Frank said. "There are shops and alleys and even houses of a far earlier time. Recently, ruins below those known ruins were found. The ruins I knew about were from the eighteen hundreds, with some remnants of the seventeen hundreds, but these were earlier yet. Much earlier. Quite crude. Mud buildings. Narrow cobblestone streets, damp with dripping moisture from above. Archeological layers of civilized development.

"The upper sewer paths have lights. Limited, but there are lights for construction, and for me to be about my job, and for archaeologists to noodle about. But the lower cities, the recently discovered ones, are not lit. I saw them first by flash and headlamp."

"And this all has to do with the finding of a piece of human finger inside a slightly oversized rat?"

"It does," he said. "I determined from my own investigation the likely area in the sewer where the rat had come from. An area where the above locations provide sufficient waste from restaurants and homes to allow the sort of diet that might lend itself to such a large sized rodent. A rat that would be willing to come topside for that kind of nourishment. It could easily have gotten into a pipe, looking for a short cut, and ended up in a toilet.

"It also struck me, that if I were a homeless man, and I were struggling to survive, that like the rats, I would visit this area as well. Meaning the spot that provided the better hand outs, and the superior toss outs in the dumpsters."

"But didn't you say the finger indicated that he was undernourished," I said.

"Better nourished than he might have been, is my guess," Frank said. "Not as well nourished as the rat, but better than he would have been without access to those dumpsters. And maybe he hadn't been visiting the area long. It was all a guess, Dana. Anyway, I went there and looked around.

"The weather was cold, and it occurred to me without too much use of the brain cells, that a homeless person might be desperate to find a warm place to sleep. Of course, our missing man could have died anywhere, but I was just following hunches, aided by a bit of logic, so the truth is, I wasn't expecting to actually find the remains of our missing man.

"Just as I was about to leave, I spied a grate in the alley wall, about three feet behind a large dumpster. I removed the grate and looked into the darkness. I chose this spot, because the grate came loose easily, and I could tell without too intensive an examination, that someone had been removing it and replacing it; the wall was scraped considerably from this action, and the screws that should have held it in place had been removed. The only thing that contained it was its snug fit.

"I had my headlamp, and I fastened it on, and before entering, examined the blueprints I have of below. When I had put them to memory, I folded them up and placed them in my fanny pack, and entered the opening on hands and knees.

"Inside there were a number of rags, and I deduced these had been placed there as a kind of mat for the knees. The way the opening was, you had to crawl along for about ten feet before it widened, and there was a manhole without a lid that led down into the sewer. It was dark there, and unless whoever was crawling along had a light, or they knew the way by experience, it could easily turn out to be a death trap. It was quite a fall without service of the ladder.

"I carefully took hold of the damp metal ladder and went down. The smell was foul, not only from the sewer, but from the odor of unwashed human bodies. When I was down there, I saw a number of people get up and move away. They had been sleeping along the edge of the sewer, on the concrete on flattened cardboard boxes, and I could only imagine what foul diseases they might contract from doing so. But, on the other hand, up above it was cold. Here, at least, along the concrete runs on either side of the sewer there were places to lay and there was a roof overhead and it was reasonably warm. None of them carried lights, but they moved easily and swiftly through experience and an acquired ability to see better in the dark than someone like me, fresh from the sunlight of above. Of course, there were a few lights in the ceiling of the sewer, the ones I told you about. But they were pretty dim. I was glad I had my headlamp.

"The people said nothing to me, and I said nothing to them. I was just some government worker, and they had no trust of me, and considering how they were often treated, I didn't blame them. I know there are some who would rather not work, and would suffer the greatest of indignities to avoid such, but for the most part I doubt this is true. It's hard to imagine that there are that many people eager to be homeless. It's hard to imagine anyone looking forward to each day being one of hunger and hardship and disappointment. Being homeless has a poor career arc.

"I hadn't intended to go deep, so I hadn't brought with me my protective mask with breathing device, but I was now certain that my rat had found his dead victim in this vicinity. I knew too that this was not far from where there was an opening to the older cities, and finally to the oldest city below; the one I had recently discovered and documented. That said, it was not an area that had been explored with any enthusiasm. Archaeologists might have it on their list, but due to finances, there was little provided for them to accomplish much. Nothing more than to visit what I had found and take a few photographs, some notes, and move on.

"Anyway, more on a hunch, than for any good reason, I started along the concrete landing, and finally I came to where the wall was split by an old alleyway that had not been covered up completely. Workers had tried, but the earth there was weak, and it wouldn't hold the concrete. It kept breaking open.

"I took to the alleyway, and went along it, looking at the old city, the one built in the eighteen hundreds. I entered one of the houses, and realized I had been there before, but had arrived this time by a different route. I removed the blueprint and studied it in my head beam to make sure, and within moments I was certain I was correct. I was near the other gap that led down to the older city. Village, actually.

"I searched for perhaps three hours, and was about to give up, when I saw something familiar. It was the way two old shops came together. It was what I was looking for. I entered one, and at the back, through a break in the wall—a break caused by time and the pressure of above—found the opening I was looking for. The trail down sloped even more dramatically than the other that led from the eighteen hundreds to the seventeen hundreds. I followed the path and it went down and turned and twisted, and became quite steep. I should add that though I have called it a trail, it was merely an accidental rip in the earth.

"I suppose there was more in my mind than the rat and the finger. I felt the need to explore. It was my thought that in a short time no one would be allowed down here, and that these older versions of the city would be off limits, though how that would be regulated was beyond me. I had a hard time envisioning the police force patrolling the area, or there being hired guards willing to stay down here in the dank with the homeless and the rats and the stink. Still, I wanted to see what I had discovered again before it was closed off for safety reasons, or archaeologists did in fact find the money they needed and occupied it on a daily basis.

"But, to come to why I am calling you. I went down there to the lower location, the oldest one, and looked around. There was peculiar writing on the walls and on the old mud buildings. It was nothing like anything I have ever seen. I found something else, as well. Bones and bodies."

"Of humans?"

"Yes," Frank said. "There were also some very large and peculiar tracks. I reported it and took the police there. Some of the remains I found were old. But there were fresh corpses as well. One that was somewhere between flesh and bones was missing the tip of its finger."

"Your rat's lunch," I said.

"Correct. But I should add that besides a finger, it was also missing a head and leg. The other bodies and bones were of a similar nature. Ravaged."

"Jesus," I said. "So what did the police do?"

"Not much they could do. Like I said, they came and looked and found that there were bites and claw marks on the bodies and the bones, and I assured them the bites and claw marks were too large for rats. They altered the idea from rats to dogs. This seemed equally unlikely, but I couldn't change their minds.

"I showed them the strange marks on the walls and buildings, the odd tracks. They dismissed the marks as graffiti by homeless people, and the tracks they said were not tracks at all, as they didn't match anything they could identify. Bottom line was the police department felt they had more important matters to attend to than the deaths of homeless people, and the whole matter was quickly dropped. And that is why I need you. I'm certain that what killed them isn't any known animal, or anything human."

I arrived in the city early the next morning. Frank met me at the airport. He looked as sleek and energetic as always. He drove me to the hotel he had arranged. I quickly checked in and put my luggage in the room. Then I went downstairs and he drove me to his office where he showed me photos he had taken underground.

They had been taken in poor light, but they were intriguing. There were several of the bone and body heaps they had found. Some of the remains were nothing but gnawed bones, while others held strips of withered flesh, all of this piled among ragged clothes. Some were missing heads and limbs. Looking at some of the closer shots of the bones, the skulls, it was obvious to me that what had chewed and clawed them was neither rats nor dogs.

The tracks were long and flat. There were holes at the tips of the tracks that looked like claw marks, or some rather large and nasty, bony toes. The heels of the tracks were perfectly round and deep.

Frank showed me where he had consulted numerous wildlife books, and websites, and explained to me he had even talked to experts on tracks, sent them the photos. None could identify them. All they could determine from the impressions in the photos was that whatever had made them was large enough to cause a severe indention, and was bipedal.

I immediately decided we would need certain equipment. Lights, motion cameras, some basic supplies. I went around renting certain items, buying others. This took Frank and I a full day. During this time, I called my assistants and had them prepare to fly in.

Nora Sweep and Gary Martin had been with me for some time. They had recently married, though Nora had kept her maiden name. They were experienced and reliable. I had a feeling right from the start that this was a situation that would call for considerable assistance, and along with Frank, they were just the ones to supply it.

It was with considerable anticipation that I went to bed that night, and I arrived at Frank's office fifteen minutes early. I had to stand at the doorway for ten minutes before he arrived five minutes early. He had required help with the equipment and supplies, and had hired two huge men to help carry the items down below.

Everything we had brought, for the most part, was either easily folded or easily bagged, and with all four of us carrying our share, we managed to work our way through the narrow passages, down to the crack in the old walls to the more ancient structure below. It was odd to descend into history like that, and to think that different civilizations, or different phases of it, were laid out in that manner. It was exciting, to say the least.

We wore construction style helmets with lights, and we carried flashlights as back ups. Of course, we had serious lighting equipment with us as well, but it was packed away and of little use while in progress.

When we finally arrived, the first thing we did was set up one of the lights with its small but powerful battery. We used this to work by while we laid out our camp.

We chose an adobe style hut without a roof and worked our way through the tight round opening that served as a doorway, and put our supplies in the center of the room. It was cool down there, but I will admit to you that I had a feeling of unease. Perhaps this was the nature of the situation. The isolated dark. But I have been at my work for sometime, so I think I am authentically sensitive to feelings of supernormal dread. I use the word supernormal as opposed to supernatural for the simple reason that I believe that the supernormal indicates that things we call supernatural have some natural explanation that is only unnatural to us because we have yet to learn the true nature of its cause. That has always been true in my experience. But, that is neither here nor there. Simply let me say that I was immediately struck by an air of oppression. I asked Frank if he felt the same, and he agreed that it had been that way each visit before, and if the mystery had not been so great, so tantalizing, he felt he might not have returned. Even our two burly assistants admitted to feelings of unease.

While Frank worked on establishing positions for the cameras, I went outside the hut and looked at the tracks with a flashlight and my head beams. There were a lot of them. So many, in fact, you couldn't help but step on some of them. Many appeared fresh in the dried dirt, while others were older and had been made when the ground was damp. That was something I noted. That from time to time the ground was damp. I wouldn't have liked to have been trapped there if some conduit from above was going to drop tons of sewer water on our heads, or some stream from below were to rise and wash us away.

Examining the tracks in person made me even more uneasy. It was one thing to see digital photos of them, but to be able to kneel down and put my hand inside of them was another matter.

That afternoon Nora and Gary arrived and were ushered down by an assistant of Frank's, Raymond we'll call him, who after delivering them to us, along with another decent sized battery for our equipment, went topside with the two men who had helped carry the lights. They were in quite a hurry. I think they felt what I felt, a kind of oppression and a sensation of being watched, or at least a feeling that something by some method or another, was aware of our presence.

I introduced Frank to Nora and Gary. Frank didn't say it, but I got the impression he was surprised they were so young looking, like magazine models who had given up on fashion. I knew that any misgivings he might have about their age and experience would disappear once we set to work.

The amount of markings on the walls were astonishing. They were not all clearly visible, however, and even those that were baffled me. I am fairly well versed in a number of older writings, hieroglyphics and such, but these markings, though somehow familiar, I couldn't decipher. Nora, who specializes in just that sort of thing, was also unable to deduce their meaning. These inhabitants most likely disappeared long before ships from Europe gave rise to the people who built the cities above us, old and new. We went about our research, and I was surprised to check my wristwatch and find that hours had passed, when it had only seemed like a few minutes. By saying this, I'm not trying to assign anything amazing or mystical to that fact. I'm merely demonstrating to you that we were well absorbed in our research. What we were doing was taking more photos, and even rubbings of the markings on the wall. We filed these away in a satchel, and then walked among the ruins.

It was not a large place, this village. All the roofs, which I presume had been thatch, or animal hides, were long gone now, but the walls stood thick and sturdy. Extremely thick.

We walked along narrow streets, nothing more than worn paths actually, using flashlight and head light beams to guide our way. We walked and stared in awe at all that was there. Eventually, we came to the largest structure we had encountered, and were shocked to discover that it had a roof, and that it was made of ancient timbers that had petrified. Our thoughts were that they had not petrified here, but had been relocated here already in that condition. The timbers were covered by large slates of clay. One slate on top of another so that the roof was about two feet thick and solid as rock. The walls to the house were even thicker and more solid than the others. There was one doorway; a kind of mouse hole. To enter, you had to get down on your knees and crawl through.

I volunteered, but Frank made the point that it was he who brought us here, and though he had no problem with me having the first discovery, he did have a problem with me entering into a strange, perhaps dangerous place first. That being the case, Frank was the first one through the mouse hole.

After a tense moment the beam of his light poked out through the hole and he waved us inside.

Although it was some trouble, we moved our entire camp from its previous place to this hut. I liked the idea that it had a roof. It gave me a greater feeling of security, even if that feeling might be false. We set up lights on the outside of the hut, and on the inside. Frank had placed our cameras at the rear corners of the hut, and near the opening. There were both night vision, and common digital cameras that would record in low light. Then we set out to explore.

Our decision was to follow the narrow path that wound amongst the hard mud buildings. We did this, and finally we came upon a split in the old clay walls, a split that was an avenue of sorts. Narrow, and shiny as if polished by something, it went deep and far, slanting gradually. The air was dense with an aroma of decay.

I'm uncertain how far we went before the tunnel narrowed to the point where we could no longer move four abreast, but instead had to go one at a time; it continued to slope downward and the stink in the air increased. I decided it was gas from the sewers.

We came to what was nothing more than a large hole in the wall. I peeked in, dipped my head. The light on my helmet revealed a tremendous drop off. I thought I could hear water below, but after a moment, whatever sound I heard stopped. I decided that what I had actually heard had not been water at all, but a kind of rustling. Bats, perhaps. Beyond the beam on my helmet there seemed nothing but a wall of darkness.

"The end of our path," I said.

We worked our way back the way we had come, moving slower as our ascent was obviously more tiring than our descent had been. It was not a horrid climb, but after our long journey to arrive at the drop off, and with the air being thin and foul, it took its toll. When we were back at what I now thought of as base camp, I was somewhat relieved. The air still stank, but something had gone out of it, a kind of skin-crawling rottenness.

Inside the large, roofed hut we sat in its center with a battery powered heater to warm us. Before it was comfortable as far as temperature went, but now I found myself not only pulling on a light jumper from my pack, but feeling quite grateful for the heater Frank had brought.

"It's like a cold wind," Gary said, "only there's no actual wind. It's just colder?"

I nodded. I didn't say it, but I knew what he was thinking, and for that matter, what Nora was thinking. It's often a phenomenon from beyond our dimension. What some call the spirit world, and what I frequently call the unknown or the supernormal.

"I think," I said, "I should lay out some of our protection."

I was referring to what some would brand witchcraft, but what I thought of as items in tune with the supernormal. I have found that crosses and swastika shapes—turned in the opposite direction of that the Nazis used—certain powders and minerals, etc., contain powers that can hold dimensional and astral visitors at bay. I'm uncertain why this is, but I've found that religious reasons have nothing to do with it. A cross for example has no effect on vampires. Yes, I have encountered one, and perhaps some day I will tell you about that case, but to stay on course, what I am trying to say is there are powers in certain objects and concoctions. Humans often assign religious reasons to their power, but I don't believe this to be correct. It's the object itself, something about the shape, or its source. Prayers from any dedicated religious leader have power, but it is not the power of god; it's the power of conviction.

Still, powerful as many of these symbols and concoctions can be, they are not universal. What may work against a so-called ghost, may not work against a bloodsucker or a lycanthrope, and so on. Not all denizens of dimensional netherworlds are affected by the same methods. It's always something of a crap shoot. That being the case, I put at the door of the hut a row of black candles, made from the fat of corpses. I assure you, I came by these by quite legal means, but this is not the time and place to dwell on that explanation. They were thick, black candles, mixed not only with corpse fat, but with a number of herbs and chemical sprinklings. Each wick was a spell wrapped in paper and then waxed to burn slowly. The candles were designed to last for hours, days even. I waited to light them.

After placing those at the door, unlit, I took a willow branch from my pack. It too was coated with corpse fat, except for the portion that I allowed as a kind of handle; it was wrapped in cord made from corpse hair. Again, I assure you, I came by all these devices legally. I waved it about and over our heads and recited spells from a number of cultures, hoping this would in fact give us protection. I wrote a few spells in Arabic on paper and placed them in small bottles and set them at the four corners of the hut. They too were designed to seal us off from anything supernormal that might want in.

When I was finished, I lit the candles, and then sprinkled around us a concoction of herbs and ash from paper on which spells of the strongest kind had been written out by means of a goose feather quill and ink made of human blood and urine. I know, it sounds unpleasant, and is, but it's a necessary and powerful deterrent to angry things from beyond.

Oddly enough they have to be angry. A comfortable and pleasant traveler from the dimensional worlds that borders ours is totally unaffected. Why? I can't say. Only those that would do harm respond to it, and sometimes, even they do not. So, as you can see, everything I was doing was nothing more than trial and error.

I finished by using the wand to draw a large circle around us. I followed this with another circle within that one, and warned everyone to stay tightly inside during the time that we were calling night. I decided that it would be best to turn off all the lights, but one, and that one would be one of the lights inside our circle. It was powered by the same battery that gave us our heater, and it was on a six foot stand and could be swiveled about with a lever that projected from the back of the light's base.

After I completed my protections—or so I hoped they would be—Frank produced an automatic pistol, said, "And in case the mumbo jumbo fails to work, I've got this. Nine rounds."

"If the mumbo jumbo fails to work," Nora said, "then you might want to hope that a certain part of your anatomy is well greased, because that may be where this thing inserts that pistol."

"Still," Frank said, "it makes me feel better to have it. I mean, really, does any of this stuff work?"

"You asked me here because you know me, and you know what I do. It's worked in the past. Mostly."

"Mostly?" he said.

"There are no absolutes," I said.

Frank nodded. "Fair enough. I suppose being down here, feeling as if there is something out there... Knowing there has been. Thinking back on those photos and those footprints, somehow I find it difficult to put my faith in a few candles and circles and bottles with paper in them."

"For this world, they are pointless, and will have no effect. But for the other worlds, which are the ones we're dealing with, they may prove our salvation."

"And what if it turns out to be of this world?" Frank asked.

"Then," Gary said, "maybe it'll be a good thing you have your pistol."

Frank sat for a moment considering. "I apologize for pulling you into this Dana, you too Nora, Gary."

"Nonsense," I said. "It's what we do. And besides, whatever is down here, it should be stopped. Nothing says it will consign itself to this area forever. It might decide to come topside."

"So, what do we do now?" Frank asked.

"We roll out our sleeping bags and wait," I said.

"And exactly why are we doing that?" he asked.

"Because it feeds on people," I said. "We are people."

"We're bait?" Frank said.

"That's about the size of it," Nora said, nodding as she did, tossing her hair.

"Is that a good thing?" Frank asked.

"Not if it breaks through the protection," I said. "Listen, Frank. You brought me here to figure this out, but you don't have to stay."

"No...That's all right. I can't leave you here. I don't want to be here. I won't kid you. But I'm staying."

I nodded. "Very well, then." I glanced at my watch. "My suggestion is that we take shifts sleeping, and that we keep guard two at a time. That way if one of the two gets sleepy, the other is there to rouse them. Say four hours per pair."

"And if both of the guard team get sleepy?" Frank said.

"Then we just may have a problem," I said, and I got up to light the candles in front of the mouse hole door.

I'm going to pause here to state that I have often been frightened in my work. It comes with the territory. But when it came my time with Nora, the second shift, I felt a sensation that went more deeply than fright. It was a kind of haunting in my bones. Frank and Gary had endured their shift without incident, or comment, but within fifteen minutes of Nora and I taking a sitting position on our sleeping bags under the light, I began to feel almost nauseous with discomfort. I looked at Nora. I didn't have to say a thing. She just said, "Yeah. Me too."

Within moments, the air became colder and the stench we had smelled down that long tunnel to nowhere, became evident and so thick you could almost saw it into blocks. The flames from the candles at the door fluttered.

There was a shuffling, like an old man dragging a bum leg. It moved along the path that led to our hut, and the nearer it came, the dimmer the light above us seemed and the more the candle flames guttered. For a moment I considered turning it off altogether, so as not to attract whatever was outside, but I knew that would be a pointless endeavor. Whatever was out there, if it was of the nature I suspected, would find us anyway, and it wouldn't need a light, and a light wouldn't deter it.

I reached in my bag and took out one of the vials of powder I had. It was harmless to living humans, but as sharp as acid to most things from beyond. But therein was the problem. Most things. I had no idea what it was I was dealing with. I only hoped it shared certain characteristics with past supernormal denizens, things some called demons or spirits or haints.

The shuffling became louder, and soon it was obvious that whatever was out there was right next to our location. I glanced toward the open mouse hole door, trembling, waiting.

"Shall we wake the others," Nora said.

"Gently."

Nora touched them and whispered them awake, warned them to silence. Now all four of us were sitting up on our sleeping bags, watching the mouse hole.

I couldn't see anything, but I was overcome with a feeling of dread, and an awareness of something being at that opening. Then, in the candlelight, I saw the dust just outside the door form into one of those unique footprints, and without meaning to, I let out my breath, causing all of us to jump a little. I hadn't even been aware that I had been holding it.

Then the footprint was overtaken by a smudge. It took me a moment to figure it, but I came to the conclusion that our invisible stalker had bent down and put what might be a knee in the smudge of its print. The dirt there shifted and the candles were knocked aside, some of their flames going out. I knew then, as I was sure the rest of them knew, that whatever invisible horror was there, it was crawling inside.

Frank lifted his revolver. I said, "Save it."

The power of the candles was no power at all. The invisible thing came into the room. Its footprints in the dim light proved that. There was a roar. So loud and so awful it shook my brain inside my skull. The air crackled with electricity. The light in our circle blinked. The monster was charging the circle, breaking through all of the exterior spells like a determined bull crashing through an electrified fence.

"Jesus," I heard Frank yell, and he fired a shot. He couldn't help himself. In fact, he fired twice. The air crackled. There was a blue and green and red burst of fulmination that formed around whatever it was, gave it a kind of outline, a shape. I can't really describe that shape accurately. If I could, it wouldn't be a shape readily recognizable. All I can say is that I couldn't see the whole of it, but the colorful, electric-like outline of it alone was enough to wither my hopes. It was over ten feet tall and there were arms tipped with claws. There were even a couple of flashes that revealed its prominent, wide, toothy mouth.

It was a momentary display, almost subliminal, but it was enough to chill the blood. It moved through the magic defenses until it came to the first invisible wall, meaning the outline of the circle. It hit that wall with a sound like an eighteen wheeler going off a cliff.

The circle was powerful enough that it knocked the thing back. I could tell that by the flames and electrical shocks, the shifting of the invisible creature's footprints in the dirt just outside the barrier.

It came again. Another clash, and this time I saw the circle give a little. Dirt shifted, the shape wobbled.

I thought, Oh hell. This is it. It's going to break the circle and tear us apart.

Obviously, I am here, so I was not torn apart. But it did break the circle. It took three more rushes, and on the third one the circle folded in on itself and broke. The air filled with smoke and crackling light, and then we could see it. See it well. It was only for a moment, but longer than before. It was even more strange and horrible than I had originally thought. It carried its stink with it, like a battering ram, and that came inside the second circle, but the creature did not.

The second circle, the smaller one, held.

I stood up then. The vial of powder in my hand. I had already twisted off the lid. I yelled out a short spell, and tossed the powder.

The powder went outside the circle and hit the beast. There was a bellow so loud it knocked me down. The thing clawed at the air, leaving fiery marks that hung in space for long moments. I struggled to my feet, tossed another handful of the powder. Another bellow. But a lesser one this time, because the thing was moving away, and swiftly.

It was no longer visible. There were no more sparks. Just a shuffling sound as it dropped to its knees, or rather what passed for them. It wormed its way so violently through the mouse hole that a chunk of the wall broke loose, widening the path.

Then there was silence and the stink floated away and the air was still.

"It's gone," I said.

"Are you sure?" Frank said.

"Yeah," I said. "It's gone."

"How can you be sure?"

"Guess I can't absolutely," I said. "But from experience… It's gone. Feel how the air has warmed, relaxed. The smell is gone. I know, that's not a very good explanation, relaxed air, but it's the best I know how to describe it."

"No," Frank said. "I feel it. But what was it?"

"It's a spirit of sorts," I said. "The hot astral remains of something dead."

"Hot astral remains?" Frank asked.

Nora said, "Yeah. It's what we call a malignant entity. It's what remains of something that once lived, and it's not happy, and it is out to make us unhappy."

"Will it come back?" Frank asked.

"They usually do," Gary said.

"When will it come back?" he asked.

"I don't know," I said. "It took a good hit, but so did my protections."

"Can you reinstate them?" Frank asked.

"She can," Gary said. "But my suggestion is we grab a few things and run like bastards. At least for now. We need some consider time. This thing is powerful."

"Agreed," I said. "Thing is, whatever that was, it was just probing the protection. It might decide it can bull its way through. And it might be right. If it is... Well, not good."

It seemed like a long trip to the surface. We went past a number of homeless people, shuffling about in the near dark. I thought of our equipment down below, and I thought of that thing. These people were at it's mercy if it chose to ascend. Or, if they went below.

I considered trying to warn them, but it occurred to me they might think we were merely trying to hide or protect something they could use to survive. It could only lead to curiosity, and them exploring below, perhaps bothering our equipment, which we had abandoned. So I chose not to. I hoped they thought we were the same as them, survivors in the wilds of the city.

When we came to the surface, it was surprising to find that it was mid-day. We ended up trudging our way to Frank's office, stretching out on the couches there, and on pallets on the floor. Each of us slept, the combination of the intense drain of adrenaline, the effects of fear.

Hours later, I awoke and found Frank was in the examination room with Nora. This was where Frank dissected rats and the like. They were sitting at his long work table, and Nora was talking excitedly.

Nora saw me, said, "Well, sleepy head. How you feeling?"

"Not as good as you," I said. "I must be getting old."

"No. It's just that I've discovered something," she said. "It's the excitement giving me energy."

"Something good?" I asked.

"Interesting. Come over and look."

She had a small digital camera. It was one of the cameras from below.

"You were quick getting that," I said.

"I went back and got all the cameras when I woke up," she said. "I slipped off while you three slept. I was afraid you wouldn't let me go otherwise."

"I might not have," I said. "It's probably safe right now, but I couldn't say it's safe for sure."

"Look here," Nora said, and leaned over and gave me the digital camera. "It's ready to go. Just touch the button."

I held the camera and propped my elbows against the table, watched as the invisible force entered the hut and began to tear at our protections, move the circle, then retreat when I threw the powder from my container. I noted how some of the powder hung in the air, clinging to the invisible thing. That immediately gave me an idea, but it was one I tucked away for later.

"I have more," Nora said, taking the camera, placing it aside.

I pulled a stool up between Frank and Nora and saw that what she had was a run of printed photographs and a chart she had made with a swathe of butcher paper and a ballpoint pen.

The photographs were of the wall markings.

"I looked at these more closely," Nora said. "They actually are familiar. At the time I didn't think so, and that's because there's a different flavor to them than I expected."

"What kind of flavor?" I asked.

"They are reminiscent of Mayan writings, as well as a number of South American markings. But my guess is they are the forerunners of their writing, so it looks a little different. It would be like the difference between print and cursive. Not literally, but that's the idea. Slightly different emphasis here and there. But I've started doping it out. It's pretty fantastic."

"Why am I not surprised," I said.

"Because an invisible monster tried to kill us?" Frank said.

"Okay," I said to Nora. "Tell us what you have."

Nora's face was flushed with excitement. "I can't say it's entirely accurate. My translation, I mean."

"But you think it is?" I said.

"Yes. I think it is. Simply put, what's down there is the spirit of an extraterrestrial."

I gave Nora a look. "Even for us, that's kind of…out there."

"Out there is right," Frank said.

"I know how that sounds," she said, "but is it really any more fantastic than other things we've experienced?"

"Yes," I said. "I think it is."

Right then Gary came into the room rubbing the back of his neck. He said, "What did I miss?"

"Nothing yet," I said. "Nora has discovered she can read the markings below, and that she thinks our problematic monster is the spectral remains of an alien. The outer space kind."

"You're yanking my leg," Gary said.

"No," Frank said. "She's not."

Gary took a stool at the worktable.

"Here's what I got," Nora said.

Nora's chart was a breakdown of the markings. Once she showed me how it was similar to Mayan writings, and also how it differed, it began to fall in place.

From what Nora made out, the story in the markings was that once in the long ago, a space ship (yeah, actually, a space ship), came here from dark beyond. It may have been an intentional landing, or an accidental landing, but it came. Nora showed us the markings, which looked like a shooting star to me, and I said so.

"Yes," Nora said, "and my first thought was that it was referring to a meteor or comet. But the rest of the story is about how beings came out of the star."

"It could be symbolic," Gary said.

"It could," Nora said. "But it fits the rest of the story. It seems that beings, human-like from the drawings, came from somewhere, out there, and landed here when it was little more than a prehistoric tribal gathering. They interacted with man...And see this."

Nora was pointing to one of the photos taken of a marking on a wall below. It was a crude marking that didn't really look like anything to me. "Okay," I said. "What about it?"

"Really look at it," she said.

I really looked at it. Nothing.

"Oh," Frank said. "I see it."

"See what?" I said.

Gary said. "I'm with Dana. Out in the wilderness here. It doesn't mean squat to me."

"It's one of the tracks," Frank said. "One of the tracks we saw down below."

I leaned over and looked again.

"I see it now," I said.

"Thing is," Nora said. "This was a marking that has been rubbed out. Not by time, but intentionally. And it's not the only one."

Nora bent down and pulled a satchel from under the table. She opened it and took out the rubbings we had made of the wall markings.

"I started studying these things, and realized the markings were picking up shapes that had been sanded down, but some of the impression remained. You have to look at this in a strong light. Frank, can you push that light over."

Frank slid the desk lamp closer. Nora shuffled through the rubbings, picked out one, pushed it under the light.

"I've outlined this one a little, to make it more visible."

I studied it carefully. A chill moved along my spine and I felt the hair on the back of my neck rise. It was a shape that I can only describe as being insect-like. If an ant had two legs and strange feet, it might look something like that. Something like it, not exactly like it. It had bulging eyes and long arms with claws on the tips. Parts of it I had seen during the attack on the circle.

"There are a lot of these in the rubbings," Nora said. "All of them had been scrubbed out with something, but not all the impressions were gone. They just got the surface, muddled them a bit, but the rubbings brought them out.

"And there's a history here. Once I caught on to the writing, it all started to fall together. Actually, it's easier to read, more sophisticated in a way than Mayan or Aztec writing. I think these prehistoric ancestors were advanced. Perhaps the star visitors had something to do with it. I don't know. But, in time, the humans wanted any memory of these things removed. The aliens, and I don't know any better name to call them, seem to have been here for some time. The markings go back a long ways. It's odd, but the earliest are the sharpest and the most advanced. They became considerably more crude as time went on. I think it's because of those things."

"The aliens," Frank said.

"Yes, and no," Nora said.

"That's a safe answer," Gary said.

"From what I understand, and there are gaps, and things I can't decipher, but it seems a race of beings came here from the stars, and among them were a race of other beings. Workers. Drones."

"Like bees or ants," I said.

"Like that," Nora said. "Thing is, these things revolted."

"Good for them," Gary said.

"Going to have to say yes and no again on that one," Nora said. "Seems the aliens, and the indigenous peoples, now most likely the same people, as I'm sure they had by this time intermixed—"

"Meaning we're all from Mars?" Frank said.

"I don't know about Mars," Nora said. "But if this is right, it's likely that our DNA, or a lot of DNA, is mixed with the star travelers. I call them that because I like to say star travelers. It has a nice ring to it."

"The rest of it," I said.

"The rest as I understand it," Nora said. "And there are a few guesses here. But the human/alien mix lost out in a battle to these drones."

"Oh, come on," Frank said.

"I know how it sounds," Nora said. "But that's what it says here."

"Maybe these were our first science fiction writers?" Gary said, nodding at the photos of the wall markings.

"Except that we've met one of these critters," I said. "So they're not fiction."

"The population came to worship the drones, but the drones started dying out. My guess is they couldn't reproduce. Maybe they were all of the same sex, or had been neutered, or, well, I don't know. But they died out. The last one long ago. Somewhere around then the whole civilization, such as it was, fell apart. Or at least their records did. They could have left. Disease. I don't know for sure."

"But how could that drone still be alive," Frank asked. "It would be ancient."

"It's not alive," I said, because right then I got it. "It's no different from other situations we've been in. This is the spiritual residue of one of those things. For some reason that spirit has survived. My guess is it's trapped in that area, tied to the place because that's what it knew in life. Just like so-called ghosts in houses."

"We've encountered a few of those," Nora said.

"It's a ghost?" Frank said.

"In a manner of speaking," I said. "It's a residue."

"An awfully spry residue," Frank said.

"Correct," I said. "Not everything that dies leaves a spirit. It's not about heaven and your soul, or any of that. It's about circumstance. Sometimes, for whatever reason, a residue of something living remains. It can be benign, unable to actually interact with us on this dimensional plane. I think our spectral visitor is from another dimensional plane and we call it a ghost because it slips back and forth. Or sometimes it's trapped in between. The worst ones are the ones trapped here completely as a spirit. Their spirits have substance. And if they're angry—"

"They can hurt you?" Frank said.

"Exactly," I said. "And the spirit of this ant drone from the stars—"

"Star traveler," Nora said.

"Very well," I said, "Star Traveler, is as angry and powerful as they get."

"So we get more potions and light the candles again?" Frank asked.

"We may have to do that," I said. "Probably will. But I think this thing is stronger than the spells I have. Maybe it's because it's from… Out there. I don't know. I had a feeling that if it had pushed harder, it would have come through all my defenses, and we wouldn't be here now looking at wall rubbings and photos. What we have to do is find out why it's still here."

"You're sure it will come back?" Frank asked. "It won't just fade out."

"Not as long as it can kill," I said. "It feeds off fear, death, anger, passion, that sort of thing. It may have lain dormant for centuries. When that old village was discovered, and people began to go down there, it sensed it, gained strength. And with the killings, it's stronger than ever. It saps up a life force like a kid sucking chocolate malt through a straw."

"And it'll come back at the same time of day?" Frank asked.

"Usually does," I said. "It's possible it has other times it can break loose, but we know for sure the time we met it. We'll use that as our guide."

"Then we have more than one chance to get at it?" Frank said.

"Probably," I said. "But it has more than once chance to get at us. And I think it may be able to take the wear and tear a lot better than our human flesh can."

Two days later we started back down.

I had prepared new protections, and Frank hired the two burly men again, as guards and helpers. They wore side arms this time, though I knew the guns would most likely be useless. I could also tell they were both still reluctant to go down there, but too proud to let on they were having feelings of insecurity. Truth is, I would rather they have stayed behind. Their method of dealing with this thing would be of the natural order, and that wasn't going to cut it. I tried to explain to them just what to expect, but they looked at me in a way that said: Talk on, lady. We know you're crazy, but we're getting paid, so talk on.

Frank's assistant, Raymond, came as well. He carried down for me two large cans of bright red paint and a flame thrower; one of those things with a tank and arm straps. After delivery of those items, he quickly went topside. He wasn't having any part of what was down there. It was all instinct on his part, and it was a good instinct.

We camped in the roofed hut again, and I was pleased to find that everything was as we had left it, except for the cameras that Nora had brought up, and now brought down again. Word had most likely gotten out among the homeless that the farthest place down below was not a good place to be; that there was someone, or something, down there.

This time I drew the circle bigger, and thicker, and filled the drawn line with some of my powders. I had been able to find most of the ingredients without too much work. Nearly every city, if you have the right contacts, and know who to ask (and I do) have people who carry and use and sell those kinds of things. Often out of their houses, frequently out of the back of herb and novelty shops. Anyway, I pulled out the protections I needed and set about making the hut as secure as I could manage. We set up four infrared cameras, two in the back corners of the hut. Two in the front corners. Nora used the stands we had left down there, fastened the cameras to them, pushed them tight against the hut wall and taped them securely to the adobe with good ole Duck Tape to protect them from falling over.

Secretly I had brought buttons of peyote with me to chew. Too much of it and I would have been useless, but a bit of it, under stressful, and supernormal circumstances, would heighten my connection to whatever was visiting us from the border between dimensions.

I also had a handful of flares inside my safari pants pocket, a lighter, and matches. I wanted to be well armed with fire and light, two of the stronger nemeses of the supernormal.

We had timed our arrival to coincide with our previous adventure, and I had timed it so that our protections would be in place and we would be within the circle several hours before the thing showed up. These sort of "hauntings," if you will, nearly always take place at the same time. It is rare that the pattern is broken. The only thing that might disturb the pattern is us. Once we were discovered, our dimensional monster was much freer to work outside the box. In fact, our meddling, if we failed, could make matters worse. It could give the thing such a rush of energy, it might be able to completely move into our realm, no longer be confined to its spot down below.

Inside the smaller of the two circles I drew, I had everyone find a spot and insisted they stay there. I had Frank explain to the two guards that they were being paid to do as I said, not as they wanted. I felt this was necessary after my preliminary conversation with them. I had him tell them that the spot I assigned them in the circle was their spot until further notice. If they thought I was crazy, they might at least respond to Frank who was supplying them with payment. The guards were, by the way, named Jake and Fritz, and both looked to have come from the same mold. Burly, with a shaved head. The biggest difference in them was Jake wore a mustache and small beard, while Fritz was clean shaven. Both had faces that looked to have been chiseled out of stone. Still, tough or not, I could detect their nervousness, and I noticed that their hands never strayed far from their holstered weapons.

Once we all had our positions, the light turned on inside our main circle, our head beams strapped to our foreheads, I carefully slipped the peyote buttons into my mouth and began to chew slowly. Gary and Nora glanced at me and knew. We had on one other occasion needed such an aid. I thought it best Frank and the other two not know, lest they think I was drug-crazed, or was putting myself into a condition where I would be useless. I was Frank's anchor, the one who knew the other worlds, someone with experience. He had enough worries without fearing I wouldn't be able to hold up my end.

The peyote was bitter. I picked a stick of beef jerky from our supplies and nibbled on it, giving excuse to my constant chewing. I drank from a bottle of water, then checked my watch numerous times, sometimes within seconds of the previous checking. I wanted to have the peyote in my system before IT arrived.

I said, "It has a certain time period in which to do mischief. If we can hold it off during that time, when that time passes, then we have a chance to find its source. It will leave a kind of residue that I think I can follow."

"But how?" Frank asked.

"Leave that to me," I said.

I glanced at Fritz and Jake. They were both looking at me in a way that made it clear they thought I was an idiot, and that Frank was a bigger idiot for believing in me.

"When it starts," I said to them. "It will be unlike anything you have ever experienced. My assistants and myself have been witness to this. We know it's real. I understand you doubt me. But when it happens, when it starts, stay inside the circle. If you step out of it, even into the outer circle, I can't promise you protection. And while I'm at it, I can't promise you complete protection even inside this circle. So, if you want to go, now is the time to go."

Jake looked at Fritz. Fritz nodded. Jake looked at me, said, "We'll stick. But if you don't think guns will do anything, why the flame thrower?"

"Fire," I said. "For whatever reason, fire seems to work against all manner of evil. Dimensional, spectral, you name it. If it has bad intentions, and it's in our dimensional frame, it can taste fire. That doesn't mean fire always stops it, but it usually works."

"Usually?" Jake said.

I managed to grin. "There are no absolutes, as I always say."

"What about the cans of paint?" Fritz asked.

"I'm hoping that will become evident," I said, pulled my clasp knife from a pocket in my safari pants. I flicked out the blade and slid it under the tops on the paint cans. With a flick, I removed the lids.

I looked at my watch. It was almost time.

It was much as before. The air turned stale and stank to high heaven, and this was soon followed by a kind of electricity in the air, as if we had suddenly sat down near a power plant. We could hear it coming, and it seemed to be moving faster than before, with anticipation. As I have said, the spirit—and I use that term for lack of a better one—had a time block in which it worked best. Why that is, is hard to determine. Sometimes it has to do with its previous life, when the host of the spirit was most active. Or when certain events happened that led to its demise. But though there was a normal time frame, and the thing had a kind of pattern to follow, it also could deviate somewhat within that pattern. It could gain greater strength. It could become so strong that the rules that governed it could suddenly no longer apply. It could begin setting its own rules. Bottom line was we needed to destroy it.

So it came, and we sat, and we fidgeted. I heard Jake let out his breath loudly, realized he had been holding it. I realized then that I was holding mine as well, and was in fact becoming a little light headed. I let my breath out, softly. The noise outside the hut grew, and then it slowed, and I knew that it was at the doorway. That it was most likely bending down, looking inside, seeing us sitting here. I wondered if it understood what our intent was? I wondered if it feared us? Perhaps it had no real thoughts outside of finding us, destroying us, and feasting on our life force.

I felt sick to my stomach. I felt my eyes water. My body was trembling. This was not only due to fear, but to the peyote. And then I saw that footprint in front of the doorway, clearly outlined in the dirt, in the light of the candles I had lit. As before, I saw the footprint smudge over with the print of its knee as it knelt. The candles were knocked over. If their magic had any effect at holding the creature at bay, it was negligible.

"Oh, hell," Gary said, without even realizing he was speaking.

I unscrewed the cap on my powders, put them in front of me. I glanced at the flame thrower and gently eased the tank onto my back by sliding my arms through the straps. I made sure the cans of paint were well within reach. Everything seemed too close, and too far away at the same time.

As the thing stood we saw its footprints in the dust again. We saw this because the light in the middle of the circle was bright enough to reveal it. That was when I realized I could see a wavy line image of the thing. It was the peyote. I had entered the realm that is thought of as the spirit world, but is in fact either dimensional, or inter-dimensional, which seems to be some place in between where you can shift either way instantly.

Everything was bright and the stink was stronger than ever now. Spinning around the thing I could see all manner of vibrating lights. There were images that fled past it, and over it, and through it. Images of men in simple outfits made of cloth and skins; there were others, alien forms that looked almost human, and alien forms that looked like our intruder beast; they were present, and they were not. Those images were its memories, a clutter of this and that. The beast itself was of both worlds, and was invisible to the others in the hut, but solid and dangerous, nonetheless.

It moved closer and closer, but due to the peyote, it all seemed to be happening in super slow motion. This thing, this poor thing. I could feel its hate and anger, confusion and pain. It made my stomach churn and filled my head with images.

It had come out of the blackness between the stars, come out of it riding in a space craft controlled by its masters. It had come down from that deep blackness and crashed into our planet. Trapped here, it continued to be a slave, along with those like it. In time the drones rose up and the drones became the masters. Then the drones died out, one by one. They were long-lived, but like mules, sterile; the offspring of two kinds of creatures on a far away world, bred for work, brought here to our world by space craft and default. They had taken over as the masters, but long-lived as they were, without a way of procreating, they ceased to be. Finally, there was just the one. This one. Perhaps a child when it first came to our world.

The people who were now a mix of human and alien life forms similar to our own, the drone's former masters, and finally its servants, rose up against the last drone, and it fled. Fled back down that tunnel and—

Then the images, the sensations stopped. I was adrift in a murky sea of thought and fear. Time came unstuck. It was moving. It was working its way through our protections. I could see those protections, bright walls of power—yellow and green, red and blue, like colorful strands of wire. But this thing was ripping through them. The circle pushed back, like a snake writhing away from heat. I stood with my container of powder, and flung it. It was like acid hitting the wavy shape of the creature. It recoiled. Then it lunged forward. I tossed the powder again. It recoiled once more, regrouped.

I grabbed up one of the paint cans, sloshed the paint in the thing's direction. The paint splattered on the monster, splashed on the adobe floor. Now our attacker was visible in splotches. I grabbed up the other can and tossed it low down. It hit in such a way that part of the creature's peculiar legs and feet could now be seen. I did this thinking that making it somewhat visible might supply the others with a modicum of confidence. This may have been a mistake, because Fritz stood up and started firing his revolver. Paint flicked up from the thing but it didn't go away.

"Forget the gun," I said. I pulled the nozzle of the flame thrower free of its clip on my back, and pointed it. Before I could cut loose, Fritz and Jake were both firing. And now Fritz panicked, made a break for it, trying to make an end run around the thing, darting his way toward the exit.

IT moved fast. IT grabbed Fritz. There was a flurry of red paint and then red blood as Fritz was torn asunder and his insides hit the wall of the hut and blew apart in bursts of intestines and gore. In my peyote filmed eyes the blood and the paint were much alike. They formed into small balls of red and dropped like a broken strand of ruby beads. They fell slowly, and then suddenly, they fell fast. The paint and blood drops striking the ground were loud as tom-tom beats.

The destruction of Fritz happened so fast, there was no time for him to even let out a yell. And Jake, now he was outside of the protection, maybe attempting to go to Fritz's aid, maybe attempting to find a path to escape. He fired his hand gun in rapid succession, until it was empty. It was like tossing peas at the paint-blotched behemoth. It froze in its spot, as if trying to determine if those pistol pops meant anything. Jake started backpeddling, trying to get back inside the circle.

It was too late.

As he turned to run the thing swept low and grabbed his ankle and whipped him over his head as easily as if he had been a wet rag, and then snapped him like a towel, slammed him into the roof of the hut, then into the wall. Blood sprayed like a spring rain, drenched us.

I know this sounds as if it took a while, but I can only tell this as fast as I can tell it. Fritz and Jake were both dead before you could blink your eyes twice. I had the flame thrower at the ready, but it had all gone down so quickly, and with Fritz and Jake in the way, I had hesitated to use it. Now I squeezed the trigger, cut loose.

In my peyote-rich state the flames appeared to reach out like a fiery finger, then the tip of the finger plunged apart, and the fire was not red, but all the variations of red—pink and rose, orange and rust. The flame curled and licked and tasted. There was a noise that sounded like something between a dinosaur scream and an eighteen wheeler locking its breaks.

Flames crawled all over it, as if trying to find a proper place to lie down. Our monster, wearing a coat of fire, lunged forward, completely through the first circle. The circle at the edge of my feet wavered a little. Nora dropped down, and using the blessed wand, drew a stronger line to replace it. But the line didn't hold. The thing grabbed her by the wrist.

She yelped. Gary grabbed her arm, tried pulling her back. Frank was on his feet. He picked up the empty powder bottle and threw it in the direction of the flames. It was like tossing spit on a house fire. Useless.

I gave the flame thrower another burst. The flames formed the shape of our attacker, crawled over its body until it was a writhing torch.

The monster weakened. Nora broke free. Gary yanked her back. She clutched her wrist. It was bleeding. It was a bad wound.

The inner circle wobbled.

"Oh, hell no," Frank said, seeing it collapse.

"Stand firm," I said, and cut loose with another burst of fire.

This time the screech was even more powerful than before. I could see it in the flames, see its tongue slashing in its wide-toothed mouth, hear the paint crackle like someone wadding up dried leaves.

Then I could see its memories buzzing around it like spectral bees, flowing in and out of its narrow eyes, images and shapes and impressions too strange to describe, the actual manifestations of hurt and betrayal. Even in that moment, knowing if I failed that it would tear us apart, I felt sorry for it. The peyote not only allowed me to see into its spirit world, its past, its thought imagery, I could actually feel all that it was, and all that it had been, and there wasn't a moment of satisfaction there.

In that instant, its will broke. Our circle had held. The creature leaped backwards, still looking at us with those narrow eyes. It wheeled, jumped, flailed, and clawed, bouncing off the wall and clamoring up it like an electric spider. It clung to the roof like a bat, smoking from the flames. An instant later it dropped to the ground near the mouse hole, slammed its huge fists against the wall, knocking it apart. It shoved itself through the gap it made, and it was gone, leaving behind the smell of burnt flesh and paint, and a whiff of gray smoke.

Immediately, the air warmed. The stench moved away from us. Much of our fear departed with it.

I stopped, looked at Nora.

"You okay?" I said.

"Forget it," she said. "For heaven's sake. Stop it. Stop it."

I nodded. "Frank," I said. "Get Nora topside. And Gary, you go with her."

"I wouldn't do it any other way," he said.

I stepped out of the circle. Frank grabbed my arm. "Is it safe?" he said.

"Right now. Yes. But it won't be later. I have to finish this."

"I should stay," Frank said, and he tried to look at me like he meant it.

"You should do as I say," I said. "And you should call the police."

"What do I tell them?" he said.

"Whatever it is," I said, "they won't believe you."

Gary grabbed Frank's arm. "Come on. Now."

They went out of the hut and headed for above ground. I turned toward the tunnel we had investigated earlier. I could see a trail of smoke drifting out of it, the equivalent of Gretel's crumbs, and I could follow it. Besides, I had some idea to where it was going.

The tunnel was full of its stink and the air was as chill as an ice tray. Tendrils of smoke drifted past me as I went. The peyote was still doing its trick. The smoke appeared heavy, like strips of cotton suspended in amber.

I had turned on my headlamp, using it to light my way. I was holding the flame thrower before me, wondering how much fuel was left in the tank.

The smell diminished and so did the smoke. The air warmed slightly. This meant either the spectral alien had gotten far ahead of me, or its time had run out and it had been whisked back to the dimension from which it came. If that was the case, it would be more difficult to track it. A part of me was glad for that thought. Finding it with no real protections outside of the flame thrower might be disastrous.

It was all I could do to keep going. It was all I could do not to think about the size of that thing, what its claws had done to poor Fritz and Jake.

Finally the tunnel narrowed and I came to the pit. I could smell smoke rising up from below, but it was faint. I got down on my knees, leaned over into the darkness, moved my head around to get a better look at the drop-off with my head light. I pulled a flare from my pocket, broke it against the edge of the pit, and tossed it. It went flickering downward, like a falling star. In that momentary glow, I saw something I had not noticed before. About six feet down, there was a kind of trail that wound off to the right and moved around the pit in a circle, around and around. A crude circular staircase where the stair steps were little more than bumps of rock. It was slick looking, as if someone had wiped it down with buckets of snot. I discovered there was a fragment of a step where I was kneeling, but the rest of it, and any steps that might have gone with it and matched up with those below, were gone. It made sense that our astral visitor was somewhere at the end of all this, down deep in that pit.

I gathered my nerve, swung a leg over the edge of the pit. My foot dangled into nothingness. The flame thrower suddenly seemed very heavy and awkward. I clung to the step fragment with aching hands, lowering myself as low as I could before I dropped, hoping to hit those slick looking steps and not go sliding off into a bottomless dark.

I took a deep breath and let go. I fell and hit close to the pit wall. My feet went out from under me, but I landed on my knees and didn't slide very far. I stayed on solid rock. The nozzle on the flame thrower came loose, and clattered backwards, but of course it was on its hose, so I didn't lose it. My knees ached as bad as if I had been hit there with an iron bar.

I got my feet under me and looked over the edge where I could have gone. My headlight didn't show me much down there, the dark was too thick to penetrate.

I gathered up the flame thrower nozzle and slipped it in its place, and kept descending. The steps were very slick, and there were squirts of water coming out of the walls. It stood to reason that all of this had been sealed off by shifting rock and time, but that recent water activity had changed things. Had opened up what had been closed, and perhaps that connection to the outside world had caused this thing's spirit to stir.

I kept going down. I paused once and looked up. There was darkness up there, but it seemed lighter than below. Finally the steps ceased, and the ground became flat. I could see something shiny in my head beams, but it was impossible to make it out. I pulled one of the flares from my pocket, struck it against the rock wall. It hissed awake, brightened. I tossed it.

In the light of the flare I saw an amazing thing.

Rock and metal twisted together. The metal was bright and the rock was dark. Slowly I realized what I was looking at in those flickers of light. The remains of a huge spacecraft. It had come down from the heavens long ago, collided and slid and ended up here as part of the earth. A civilization of sorts had built up around it. Time had covered it up. I stood there looking at it for a long time. In spite of everything, it was awe inspiring. It was crumpled in spots, like wadded aluminum foil. The rock jutted into part of it, and it seemed to be all of one, a mighty and magnificent sculpture made by an insane artist.

The flare went out.

I walked toward the craft, following my head beam. I went along until I found a gap in the ship's wall, a rip from collision. I eased inside, turned my head to move the light about. There was all manner of dirt piled along the sides of the gap and inside of it there were ridges of it, piled there by collision and time. I went deeper in, saw bones of all manner strewn about, big ones, little ones; the remains of humans and drones, and beasts that no longer existed.

There was writing on the metal walls. The kind of writing I had seen on the upper dirt walls. It was dark and crusty looking. My stomach lurched and the air began to move and it had color. It was a color beyond the spectrum of the rainbow. It was a color out of space and time that could be seen as well as felt. Hell, I could taste it. In the waves of color there were memories, the monster's memories, and they hit me like a fist.

In the waves I saw the ship. I saw the drones, down below in the lower hatch. They all wore a strand of shimmering metal around their necks. And I knew that it was some sort of advanced form of containment. In those necklaces of shiny metal there was what we of lesser knowledge would think of as magic. But it was technology that confined the drones so they could be used as the star travelers wished. And I saw those humanoid aliens too. They swirled around me like clouds. I grew weak. I had to squat to breathe the better air close to the floor.

Gathering myself, I stood up and moved along. The presence of the thing was stronger. I unhooked the flame thrower. The ship became narrow. I was in a hall. I trudged down it, the flame thrower before me. The hall turned right and I turned with it. I stepped out into a vast room full of decks of controls, dull and dusty in the glow of my head beam.

Above it all, against what had once been the view shield, now busted out and replaced by rock, was the monster.

I had been wrong about its long dead spirit. This wasn't just its corpse. It was alive. It was pinned, crucifixion style to the rock. It was pinned there by great bolts through its neck and arms and legs and torso. Bolts that should have killed it, but hadn't. It writhed there and made a noise like a lost pup. Its long beak of a head was dipped, and its body was trembling. It looked like a bundle of withered sticks in a series of bags. It had long bird-like claws for feet and hands. It appeared to be partially petrified. It wore one of those control necklaces I had seen in my vision. And it lived.

It turned its head so slowly at first I was not sure it was moving at all. I saw its eyes, sunken and dark, a brittle spark flashed there, hatred and anger.

I caught movement out of the corner of my eye. I turned, and there was the paint splotched specter. It flowed out of the shadows toward me, moving rapidly.

I lifted the flame thrower, but it sailed by me, toward the thing pinned to the rock. It moved there quick and smashed up against it and was absorbed. The peyote's magic wiggled inside my head, flooded me with understanding. I knew then that the last of its kind had not been killed. It had been punished. It had been pinned here centuries ago, its control necklace freezing it in place.

It had hung there all that time, like Prometheus on his rock, somewhere between living, somewhere between dead. A drone designed to work with little food or water, a beast of burden that could live for centuries on little more than air. It had dangled there in pain as the civilization it had been forced to build died out, or moved on. The last of its kind, displayed like an ornament. Now it was ragged and angry, so angry that over the centuries that anger had turned into a wraith, an astral projection reaching out in blind revenge.

But now, its astral self had returned to its source. Had given up the ghost, so to speak. At least for the moment. Perhaps to recharge its anger, its ability to project.

I stepped closer, looked up at it. Never have I seen such sadness. It wasn't a kind of face I recognized. Inhuman, strange, but a tired and defeated thought projected from it, heavy as an anvil. It clumped around inside my head, like a fat workman moving furniture.

I knew what it wanted.

It wanted it all to end.

It wanted to be past pain and anger.

It didn't want to live another century or more before it finally came completely apart, or the earth moved and tore it asunder. It didn't want to live another day, another hour, another minute, another second.

I lifted the flame thrower, and just before I pulled the trigger to make the fire jump, the feeling of anger and hate went out of the air, and it nodded its head as if in anticipation.

There's not a whole lot to tell now. I did what I sensed it wanted. I burned it until there was nothing left but blackened bones. I knew that would end whatever astral projection it had created inside its tortured brain. All it really wanted was peace.

As for the rest, well, the peyote wore off. I climbed up and out. The cops came down. I had to go back down there with them. They had safety harnesses and all manner of gear this time. It was an easier go. They saw everything, including the space ship and the charred remains of the angry traveler. They were startled, of course.

We had more evidence. Our cameras had caught the paint-splotched thing at work, tearing Fritz and Jake apart. No one in a position of authority wanted to digest that.

It was decided by the law that it just wouldn't be talked about. Story they told was Fritz and Jake died in an accident while helping us explore. That was the official line. Although there may be a true file stored somewhere. Our cameras were confiscated. There was talk of prosecuting us, but they couldn't decide what for. They let us go.

A final note. They sealed off the old ruins with explosives.

That's all right. I know what happened. So do Frank and Nora and Gary. It's fresh in our memories. It's only been three weeks.

By the way, Frank retired the day after it all came down. Rumor is he's moved somewhere warm and he no longer exterminates. I got stiffed. Frank never paid me for my work. I haven't heard from him since.

Finished, Dana stood up from the storyteller chair, went to find a drink. Several members tried to talk to her about her story, but she wasn't talking back. She said simply that she had told it, and now she was through. They could believe it or not.

She concluded her visit with a bit of small talk, finished her drink, and went outside. I went out with her. There was a big black car waiting for her. A man and a woman were outside of it, leaning on it. They were a good looking pair. The woman's arm was in a sling and her hand was in a cast. The man opened the back door for Dana, and she slipped inside.

Before he could close the door, I said, "Will you come back? Will you tell us more of your adventures?"

"It could happen," she said, and the man closed the door. He opened the door for the woman whose arm was in a sling. She worked herself into the front passenger's seat. He went around to the driver's side, got in, and drove them away.

Introduction

“Blue Amber”

“Click-Clack the Rattlebag”

“Cavity Creeps”

“The Glitter of the Crowns”

“Doll’s Eyes”

“Bloaters”

“Detritus”

“Monster”

“Orange Lake”

“Nathan”

“Blood Moccasins”

“The Case of the Angry Traveler”